MOMENTITIOUSNESS

MOMENTITIOUSNESS

AN ADVENTURE IN SEMIOTIC ARBITRAGE

Jason Leclerc

Archway Publishing books may be ordered through booksellers or by contacting:

Archway Publishing
1663 Liberty Drive
Bloomington, IN 47403
www.archwaypublishing.com
1-(888)-242-5904

ISBN: 978-1-4808-0350-3 (e)
ISBN: 978-1-4808-0349-7 (sc)
ISBN: 978-1-4808-0351-0 (hc)

Library of Congress Control Number: 2013920724

Printed in the United States of America

Archway Publishing rev. date: 12/20/2013

LIMITS

(Author Introduction)

From, for, and to a generation where acronyms have become words—replacing pronouns with the lazy anonymity of vagueness and mystery—the author has emerged to write about it, using it: from it; for it; and to it.

This should suffice:

ADD. OCD. POT.
WSJ. NYT. FOX. MSNBC. FB. CSM. WWW. FB. COM.
PS3. NFL. NCAA. NBA.
WMD. USA. NSA. GOP.
TLH. DAB. MCO. LGA. TPA. ORD. DCA. MIA. BOS.
TJ. AL. FDR. JFK. RR. BO.
SCHS, IB. FSU, UG. BU, UCF, MA, MS. UCF, TNT, ABD, PHD.
WW. RWE. HDT. JLB.

LEAST SQUARES LINE

PRIMER

Semiotics: A branch of linguistics concerned with the study of signs for which words stand as both metaphor and example. Classic Semiotics posits a relationship between the:

Signified—the object for which the metaphor is necessary

Signifier—the thing that represents the actual thing

Sign—the thing that represents the relationship between the Signifier and Signified.

Arbitrage: The tripartite exchange in a free and unfettered marketplace that yields a profit in the absence of added value. Because of information gaps—or wrinkles—that occur through time, one thing denominated in one equivalent unit may be denominated differently in another equivalent unit yielding a surplus when the second and third equivalent units are traded.

Semiotic Arbitrage: A critical method that overlays the tripartite imperfections exposed during a semiotic methodology with the metaphor of trade-based arbitrage. As a system for approaching the truth, it bares the inconsistencies in traditional narrative— history and literature—by positing that those inconsistencies

yield a richer understanding of multiple truths in trade. In the time-space continuum, Semiotic Arbitrage deposits cultural profits, derived from the error coefficients along the least-squares line, into vast and fluid—universal—banks.

DA DO DEW DO

Leaves of grass,
Morning dew'd
With a promise from
Almighty, and a challenge:
I Do.

ONE CENT IN MANHATTAN

DESIGNED—I'M NOT SURE WHY OR HOW OR EVEN WHEN—AS A complimentary badge, you leave a single shiny penny face up on the table after you've received excellent restaurant service. In Chelsea, good service is hard to come by, so seeing this penny left on the table next to yours made me grin in the promise of the experience you were about to have. I was a server for a while in college and would have preferred a twenty-five-percent gratuity over the symbolism. I have a feeling that this server, probably an aspiring actor, would have preferred the same. The checks here are big: the penny could easily have been thirty-five bucks for the three people who had just left as we were being "sat." Maybe they left it on the credit card receipt. You can do that nowadays, have it both ways: symbol and substance.

"I am such a B-list celebrity…" he trailed off into a huff and a sigh, *"So B list."*

You smiled, "B plus."

Y'all sighed in a raspy C major.

Every detail derives its musical sense from the concrete totality of the piece which, in turn, consists of the life relationship of the

details and never of a mere enforcement of a musical scheme—
Adorno, On Popular Music

Sitting outside on the patio of a Chelsea café across from a friend whose up-and-coming presence in - the New York acting scene has not yet peaked nor approached plateau, you preferred guiding the topic to the feta crumb sitting on his cheek. You had met each other through a mutual acquaintance (and this specific fact rather escapes you) sometime longer ago than thirty-six hours and shorter ago than two years. As you started to reach across the table to flick the crumb, a neighboring table of loud and preppy thirty-something pretty boys simultaneously leaned inward as if to build a teepee—perhaps a steeple—with their heads. "Don't anybody dare look," you imagined them saying as one coyly caught your eye and looked away self-consciously. "Oh my God, it's him," you actually heard, not imagined. You grinned, recapturing the glance of the same boy who could not bear the thought of not seeing what he was dared to not look at. The teepee—steeple—-was dismantled as each of the four boys leaned back and reached for something: a glass of merlot, an ultra-light beer, an ultra-light cigarette, the waiter's ass. They school-girlishly giggled.

One one-hundredth of a dollar. Almost useless, it doesn't even buy a gumball anymore. I usually throw pennies away when I receive them, something for the bums outside 7-11 to pick up instead of begging me to ignore them. I usually don't even keep quarters. Change jingling in my pocket only weighs me down.

You were, after all, with a B-list celebrity. You were intrigued. From a supporting role on Broadway to a series of dandruff-shampoo commercials

the relations between the evil and the cure, between dirt and a given product, are very different in each case—Barthes, Mythologies, "Soap-Powders and Detergents."

in which his head was immortalized into two hemispheres (one of which was tingling while the other was poorly lathered and tingle-less), he was certainly best known for his recurring role on a trendy situation dramedy set in the City. He also had a bit role in a play-come-movie from which he said he still received royalties. The boys at the adjacent table cooed. Your acquaintance ate his feta-and-spinach focaccia. You paid the check and suggested a walk to the park. Central Park would be "fine," he interrupted, "but it's sixty blocks away." He rolled his eyes as you walked out to catch a cab.

Do you want to walk along? Or walk ahead? Or walk by yourself? One must know what one wants and that one wants —Nietzsche, Twilight of the Idols, "Fourth Question of Conscience."

You smiled at the boys who smiled back. The one who had previously reached for the waiter's ass made a move toward yours which you hands-freely blocked by unsmiling at him.

Lincoln's head adorns the penny, the front of it, since 1909. Maybe that's what good service means: he freed the slaves and saved the Union afterall. Plus he was a Republican.

You know many famous people. You know many wealthy people. You know many beautiful, intelligent, and political people. You see them on TV, hear them on the radio, read their words in newspapers and magazines. You can call them when you feel like chatting, you can stop by their homes when you want face time.

The face of Garbo is an Idea, that of Hepburn, an Event— Barthes, Mythologies, "The Face of Garbo."

You have long since been unimpressed by celebrity and even more unimpressed by people who are impressed by celebrity. This aversion to the idea of celebrity is probably not very different from a native New Yorker being unimpressed by what is to you—whose personal transportation is as much a badge of freedom as the only way to get around—the gritty and foreign idea of sewer-routed mass transit.

I examined the back of a penny I found on the ground because I'd never really looked at one so closely; it says "E Pluribus Unum," which means, "Out of many, one." What a fantastic idea, rife with symbolism, that one penny becomes a badge of a whole people. Intrinsically, not so valuable, but the richness of meaning is overwhelming.

The image that is read, I mean the image at the moment of recognition, bears to the highest degree the stamp of the critical, dangerous impulse that lies at the source of all reading—Benjamin, <u>The Arcades Project</u>, "Theoretics of Knowledge, Theory of Progress."

So, you walked through the park, past the softball fields, under the carved stone archways, through the well-trodden pathways. You talked about the impending Broadway actors' strike which, though he wasn't actually working at the time, he supported. You discussed a political albatross which was strangling the new mayor: the homeless. You talked about the fourth of July in Manhattan, his new SoHo apartment, the Brooklyn Bridge, and his new shoes. You talked about everything except Fossy, Chicago, Sex and the City, and dandruff. Finally ducking into an Upper East Side bar as the sky turned yellow with dusk, you noticed that people were looking at you as much as they were staring at him.

I met a seer,/Passing the hues and objects of the World,/The fields of art and learning, pleasure, sense,/To glean eidolons.—Whitman, "Eidolons."

Though you didn't have B-list celebrity in which to bask, you did have the mystery of anonymity on your side. Your celebrity by association was far richer. Indeed, you caught more glances, smiles, and embarrassed looks than it seemed he did. "Oh there's that guy from," you imagined them trailing off. "Who's he with? A writer? His agent? A model?"

His first glance found him—Mann, <u>Death in Venice</u>.

Lincoln died for the Union, martyred forever as the second father of our nation.

O powerful western fallen star!/ O shades of night—O moody, tearful night!/O great star disappear'd—O the black murk that hides the star!/ O cruel hands that hold me powerless—O helpless soul of me!/ O harsh surrounding cloud that will not free my soul.—Whitman, "When Lilacs Last in the Dooryard Bloom'd."

You ended your tour of the Upper East Side. You returned to your hotel and he to his new apartment. He had to meet the movers and prepare for an audition in the morning. You would see him soon, you knew.

With another friend, you stepped out onto Forty-Second Street in Midtown. You were totally and luxuriously dressed down: shorts, flip flops, a ballcap, and some shades which, in a moment of silliness, you had paid five hundred thirteen dollars for. You were going to a cook-out at one of his buddy's midtown lofts.

Being a bit shy, you insist that you are not presented according to your vocation, but to your avocation. So you were introduced around with the air of usual vagueness that you insist upon ("he is a student" is how this friend introduces you; for other of your friends you are "a poet"). An especially catty member of the group winked at you as if you were in some special two-person fraternity: "You're an actor, aren't you?"

The singularity of 'vocation' is never better displayed than when it is contradicted—but not denied, far from it—by a prosaic incarnation: this is an old trick of all hagiographies—Barthes, Mythologies, "The Writer on Holiday."

"No."

"You look awfully familiar."

"Nope, just a student from Central Florida. I write a little." You could sense tension beginning to build. You flashed your bright white teeth and blinked nervously—almost flutteringly. You breathed in deeply through your nose.

And all he gets is a penny?! Perhaps this is because there are so many of them. The U.S. Mint says that there are billions of pennies in circulation. Technically, the government calls them "cents." They cost more to make than they are worth, about two-point-four cents worth of materials in each one.

As a circle began to form—you sensed an impending steeple—your friend intervened on your behalf: "Who him? Oh, he's nobody!" Such a seeming insult never felt so good. The circle crumbled and one of them whispered something about Abercrombie and Fitch to his friend. A faceless source was definitely heard: "Well, I know he's somebody. I just don't know why these people have to be so bitchy."

Even the youngest child carries a shiny penny. It is not too much to have: one cent. And then, when there are more cents, sense. A sense of history caught up in the future with the hope of raising up a new American to carry on this mantle.

After a few Grey-Goose Cape Codders (don't forget the lime, please), the tension from the previous whispers and nudges was released. The usual questions about your visit were piled high, much more densely than you could answer. "Yes, I was at that party." "No, I wouldn't be going there this time up." You finally excused yourself for a bit as you found a mostly empty couch being held down by an extravagantly handsome and broodingly quiet guy. You sat and basked in each others' awkward snobbiness until your friend came and introduced you. You shook hands. Your friend raised his eyebrows as he turned his back to your sofa mate and mouthed with silent exaggerated words to you that the guy on the couch was the weekend anchor of a local TV news show. In Manhattan, that's really something, you thought, grudgingly wallowing in your unmitigated bitchiness.

Productions of the human brain appear as independent beings endowed with life, and entering into relation both with one another and the human race. So it is in the world of commodities with the products of men's hands.—Marx and Engels, _Capital._

"Great party, lots of nice folks. Can I get you a drink?" It was as if he were reading off the teleprompter.

"No thanks," you answered. "We're just getting ready to go. Nice to meet you though." It is obvious, in retrospect, that your status as co-celebrities (even though yours wasn't actually a celebrity—but that he considered you "somebody" also) warranted the comment and invitation. "Maybe we'll see you out later."

"I hope so." You were the gracious recipient of the anchorman's smile. He loosely and flirtingly bit his lower lip.

On the other side of the penny, opposite the head, on the side with the "E Pluribus Unum," is an engraving of the Lincoln Memorial. So gracious in detail, the statue of Lincoln at the center of the building is visible. Odd that they would stamp a picture of a memorial on a memorial.

Knowing that a system which takes over the signs of another system in order to make them its signifiers is a system of connotation, we may say immediately that the literal image is denoted and the symbolic image is connoted.—Barthes, Image-Music-Text, "Rhetoric of the Image."

You left with your friend after giving thankful nods and hurried handshakes to your host and his other acquaintances who re-encircled you at the exit. The doorman in the lobby tipped his hat to you as you sauntered into electrified Manhattan.

In a city of ten million residents are twenty-million eyes, twenty-million ears, and ten-million each of noses and mouths. There are one-hundred-million fingers with which to feel and touch. There are billions of lights and scents and tastes and sounds swirling from the gut of the island. The Manhattan gaze is hypersensual, and it is not difficult to confuse these sense perceptions. Seeing is not so different from hearing or smelling, or even saying—taste your words.

The Medium is the Massage—Marshall McLuhan, The Medium is the Massage.

Times Square's lights obscured the black sky and the sidewalk bustle obscured the lights. The smells intoxicated you. You turned your ballcap around so the bill faced backwards and put on your happy-to-be-walking face. You became part of the bustle, the not-so-distant lights sparkled .

For a time, during World War II, the penny was made of lead. They weren't actually lead, but a tin alloy that fundamentally changed the coloration of the coin from the familiar copper to a sheen more silver. Something about needing the copper for munitions to fight the Nazis. Lead pennies, they called them. Like the women who gave up nylon stockings by painting lines on the back of their legs, and the rationed butter exchanged for stuff called "oleo" that made all meals stateside taste "a little odd," as my grandmother described it, there was a sense that sacrifice was necessary. We'll save our cents in order to save our way of life. What are pennies, anyhow?

"What's it like?" your friend asked. "Why does everybody stare at you?" Your engorged senses perceived the same. You embarrassedly feigned non-recognition of the source of his inquiry. "I don't know what you're talking about, whoever 'they' are must be staring at you," you deflected.

It is an important mechanism, for it automatizes and disindividualizes power. Power has its principle not so much in a person as in a certain concerted distribution of bodies, surfaces, lights, gazes; in an arrangement whose internal mechanisms produce the relation in which individuals are caught up.—Foucault, Discipline and Punish.

New York is a voyeur's paradise. Scopophilia reigns. People watch New York City and expect New York City to return the glance. Diners and cafes that line busy thoroughfares (every thoroughfare in Manhattan is busy) have huge plate-glass windows through which walkers and eaters alike can and are intended to be seen. Storefronts exclaim that it is as exciting to be a shopper as to be seen shopping, and finally to be shopping and see those that see you shopping. Aspiring actors, writers, scholars, restaurateurs, and clothing designers all make their way to this place in search of the gaze that was so instantaneously and indelicately turned on you. People go to museums and theatres and universities to be seen seeing the arts that the city has to offer. This city with twenty-million eyes looks out in order to be looked upon. This jealous and needy gazing framework pervades the city: power is disseminated not merely by conveying the gaze upon objects, but with the expectation that the gaze will be returned in a mutual sharing of celebrity, power, beauty: sublimity. You disrupted this equilibrium.

So with Lincoln looking on, presumably from every pocket, America defeated the Nazis and the Japanese and the Fascists. The slaves that we might have become to totalitarian hatred remained theory, speculative reason for thanksgiving and an emerging Military-Industrial complex. This driving force of American imperialism has since been augmented by Media and Entertainment. We produce and consume for the entire world: food, software, ideas, Hollywood. Hundreds of trillions of pennies spread across the earth in the name of freedom and in the name of money itself: market, capitalist, economy. Because the Union was saved and our American Christ was slain, there is always hope.

According therefore, as this produce, or what is purchased with it, bears a greater or smaller proportion to the number of those who are to consume it, the nation will be better or worse supplied with all the necessaries and conveniencies for which it has occasion—Smith, Wealth of Nations.

You did not know the protocol. What your admirers wanted in return for their candid on-the-spot interviews and ultra-sensual stares was an acknowledgment that—by virtue of being in your presence—they had value despite their own existences in the mundane. You should have indulged them and empowered them by acknowledging that "Yes, I am somebody." If you could be somebody in a city with twenty-million eyes, then they could be somebody in a city of twenty-million eyes. If you could be an actor or a model or a writer or a politician, then they could be too—even if it was by mistake. By becoming the object of the gaze of this city, you allowed the city—the home of your admirers—to be its own subject, to be empowered.

Society absorbs via the apparatus whatever it needs in order to reproduce itself.—Brecht, The Modern Theatre is the Epic Theatre.

The final day of your visit, you ambled down Fifth Avenue, again on the Upper East Side. Your friends circled and played, lagged behind and caught up. They jeered and cut up with each other. They would look and point in windows, up at the tops of buildings, down at homeless people mumbling to themselves in building entrance ways, at crazy New York City cabbies, and at you.

But flanerie itself had been more complicated, existing as a kind of deadpan parody of the scientific method, a reduction ad absurdum of disinterested observation, practices as an end in itself.— Jean, <u>Surrealist Games</u>.

You continued on intently, going wherever it was that you were going. You carried a Barney's of New York bag, your hair was perfectly spiked, your pale-yellow Lacoste collar was turned up, your jeans sat just where you liked them on your hips. New York people continued to do their thing—to look and watch. You looked back as if to say "Yes, I can be famous if you want me to be." You slapped a smart smile on your face and took off your shades: "I, too, can look."

I don't know which one of the two of us is writing this page.— Borges, "Borges y Yo."

Perhaps, then, a penny isn't just so bad for good service. Without the penny, and without what the penny represents, what would thirty-five dollars be? Would it even matter how good the service was? Without the penny and what the penny represents, what would any of us have? A bunch of Deutschmarks, I guess.

Manhattan blushed.

Manhattan blushed.— You, <u>One Cent in Manhattan</u>.

Manhattan blushed.

TANGENCY ONE:

STILL

The grass is still wet,
    The blades upstretched
    And glistening…
And, now, so too
    Are my shorts
    And now my back.
The sun is still low
    In the sky
    And cirrus splatter
Wispy paint across
    Mellow blue'd and
    Hazy morning.
The breeze is still soft,
    Supple as it dances
    Around my arms
And hints at tickling…
    The as yet undaunted
    Promise of today.

MOMENT ONE

WALDEN

CAREFULLY, WITH THE LIGHT TOUCH THAT MY GRANDMOTHER'S arthritic hands might have softly extended in the last decade before her dementia set in, I grasped the tiny flaccid creature. You don't realize how really small a bird is when it isn't flying, when its wings aren't extended, when it is limp in your palm. I cupped it, marveling at the tiny closed eyes as my own filled with tears. My slightly creased forehead reddened under the pressure of internal flushes and external sun. My neck tingled and my throat lumped. My heart beat slowly and I fought to huff a clean breath. My sorrow seemed bottomless.

When I heard the hollow bell-like timbre of the impact—was it a finch this far south?—against the clear glass of the recently cleaned front double-pane, I was further distracted from my work. My mind was already wandering as the un-light words in arcane mid-nineteenth-century constructions rustled in an airy soup of jumbled thoughts. Oddly situated in my periphery, dust and pollen danced in stark bright beams[1] between the yellowed pages and the elaborately crown-moulded plaster intersections that alternately centered and bounded my comfortable space.

---

1   The camera has no soul. It has no heart or mind. The camera does not judge. It does not determine. The camera cannot love. It cannot reason. The camera does not know. It does not know right or wrong. It does not know right from wrong. The camera is but a means for the reproduction of a time, of a space, of an image, of an idea.

The very portal through which the brightest streams of light filtered in from the eleven o'clock May sunshine reminded me that God's sun is best-suited for reading America's own literary Yahwist. Neither a knock nor a rap, it was a simple sonorous "thud" that echoed through the sparsely furnished solarium—so named for the wall of morning facing glass designed to always properly house me as I read and drank iced tea—in which I sat with the hardbound collection of Emerson essays splayed across my bare knees. Late spring, it was already too warm and humid to have the windows open: a fact for which I instantly cursed my own selfish exile from Walden to the sterile walls of Academe: from Thoreau's simple-life essaying to Emerson's cleanly delineated lofty American poetic criticism. I was walled in.

The second bump was lighter, yet still it carried through the room and sat upon my ear like a far-off tree falling, the memory of which was instantly created. Transcendentally, I pondered His knocking; with some regret I concluded that this was not my day, nor would I ever be worthy of a personal visit from the Almighty. As if I needed one last piece of evidence that the Lord was not waiting for me at the front door, I concluded that He would not knock with such timidity.

I moved Ralph Waldo, face down, to the raw leather couch beside me as I floated toward the source of the sound. Piercing the solemnity between inside and out, I cracked the door and peeked my head through. My body followed as my eyes surveyed the knotty pine-planked porch that wrapped the front corner of the house.

It lay there peacefully just over the edge of the wooden platform, drained of the life-force which had twice driven it into the glass.

Twice, the creature of the outdoors, not knowing the rules of construction or architecture, attempted to pierce the impenetrable. Meant for us men to see safely in from the outside and out from the in, as frames around our own constructions, this mostly invisible solution to the opacity of solid walls—this window—stilled a creature made to dance in the clouds among angels.

The second knell likely broke its already slightly fractured neck, I surmised as my finger lightly smoothed over the tiny spot that connected its solemn head to its dainty body—where its wings tucked neatly and seamlessly into its softer-than-anything-I-ever-remembered-touching's abdomen.

It trembled in my hands, lingering at the indeterminable edge of death. I opened my hands and cradled it, imagining my long-gone grandmother's hands—the hands that had dressed my childhood scrapes, the hands that had rapped the back of my obstinate teenage head, the hands that had made me sweaters when I went off to college, the hands that had painfully gripped my own when she no longer knew who I was, the hands of a healer—as my own cupped this felled, twitching creature.

I looked at my own hands and the tiny spots of blood that I had not previously noticed.[2] These spots merged into ready creases on my palm and I knew that, were it not for my home—for my shelter from nature—this bird would be flying. My focus shifted back and forth between the bird and my hand until finally the bird and my bloody hands were one conjoined form linking life and death, memory and dementia, man and nature, Thoreau and Emerson.

I was traveling thousands of miles away from here when my grandmother finally passed; I didn't fly home for her funeral. Instead I wrote a poem—"Hands and Wings"—and folded it up and carried it with me until my career finally took me back to this town where I could build this home—a loose replica of hers—and lecture at the university just a few miles from where I grew up. Eventually, the folded poem found its way into a cherry-stained maple keepsake box filled with old jewelry—watches, crucifixes, and silver chains as well as my grandfather's dog tags—that I had stopped wearing over the years but with which I could not part.

---

2 Early in the summer of 2001, NASA sent a camera into space. Clearly, it was not the first device pointed toward the sky, following in a long line of spectacles fixed upon the heavens dating back to before Galileo.

The yearning to recapture life and re-breathe it into this bird had, by this time, flown from me.

I gently laid the feathered corpse back on the ground, shaded by the front porch where I had found it. I concentrated on it with my eyes, though my heart had long since abandoned it as anything more than a totem. My bloody hands once again captured my attention. They were not dripping with blood but, given the size of the bird, this may have been all there was in it as it bled out from its tiny pierced carotid.

Thoreau and Emerson argued as I contemplated leaving it for nature to reclaim or burying it in a good Christian way. Thoreau won and I left her—I had determined from the mental archives of seventh grade life science that the females of bird species were less brightly plumaged than the males—on the spongy St. Augustine grass and returned inside.

I sat for only a moment, reaching for Dr. Emerson when I was again bestirred. Bestirred isn't the right word. In my recollection of seventh grade, a memory was jarred loose from my mental archives. This was not the first time this had happened. I was overtaken. I was possessed.

Straightaway I flew to the bedroom and, from under the sturdy mahogany four poster that sat high enough off the floor to stack eight-inch-tall plastic storage containers, I pulled out a bin and began to riffle through it. When I was young, about six or seven years old, the same thing had happened at my grandmother's home. The same exact thing: a bird flew into her—god, she could clean glass so streaklessly and completely that it disappeared—sliding glass door. We found the bird limp and lifeless; we tried to save it, but it had already died, she told me.

"It is flying in heaven now,[3] with your grandpa."

---

3   This camera, affixed to a satellite, launched atop a fiery missile into the heavens themselves, able to reproduce images that no human eye had ever seen, settled into an orbit specifically designated for concentration.

I remember thinking even then, "Isn't that what birds do when they live?"

I was not yet born when her husband, my grandfather, passed away; he was always present in her spirit and he was our constant companion during my two-week visits every summer from 1980 until 1989. He had fought in the Second World War. He had built this home. He had helped raise my mother. He had known the great Walt Disney himself. He had died of a heart attack, suddenly, leaving her a widow at the age of fifty four. He had left her to keep up this home and its acreage. He had left her to be both grandparents to me, her only grandchild.

"You can never leave me," she demanded. I never would, I promised. I lied.

With her hands resting on my head, and sliding down toward my shoulder, I sobbed. We buried it: no box, just straight into the earth. "That's the way to bury critters," she told me.

It was the first dead thing I had ever touched, though it was nothing more than a finger-probe: a poke.

She did all the heavy lifting.

We fashioned a cross out of two sticks that we tied together with some green palm fronds we tore into strips. The mound of black soil into which we carefully placed the body stood starkly against the bright green grass that surrounded it in the corner of the lot near the herb garden where the mint grew that we picked and muddled into our sweet sun tea.

I waited patiently with earnest, pre-adolescent solemnity and, while she took her afternoon nap, I returned to that swollen ground and dug that dead bird up. I was not done with it. I was not ready for it to be dead. I was careful to put the cross right back where it had come from and to be certain that the ground was packed to the same density. My black fingernails might have betrayed me had she checked them, but after a week at her house my fingernails were always dirty. Holding the soil-covered avian corpse in my left hand,

I gently brushed it with the other. I wiped the tears from my cheek with my shoulder.

More than a couple of times, after comfortable meals, as we were putting away leftovers, she would tell me that Walt Disney was not buried when he died but put into a big plastic container, just like Tupperware, so they could bring him back to life one day. If plastic, a fancy new invention that had emerged during her lifetime—she could remember a time before plastic—could preserve a man like Walt Disney, she lectured, it could certainly keep meatloaf good for a couple days: to be resurrected for sandwiches on doughy white bread.

Moving with determined stealth, I quietly swiped the smallest Tupperware container I could find from the cabinet beside the refrigerator. Translucent avocado green, it was the same size as the one she used to store fresh herbs when she would pick them and bring them into the house. With a single hand, I managed to remove the tightly sealed plastic cap; the fresh oily essence of basil mixed with the scent of spearmint and wafted to my nose.

The small black bird body, still dusted with the fresh earth, never left my other hand. "Perfect," I silently decided as if to answer an equally silent query about the appropriateness of the container for the purpose. I dropped the body into the vessel with only slightly more delicacy than I might have a chocolate chip cookie, remembering to "burp" the container twice to expel the excess air.

The petite plastic container found its way to a hiding place among my effects that worked equally well for illicit magazines and marijuana during later stages of my youth. Packing and moving and moving and growing and moving[4] and living and learning and packing and moving and not-burying-my-grandmother and crying and leaving stuff behind, this tiny Tupper (diminutively, as grandmom always called it in the same way someone else's Abuela may have

---

4   By negotiating the centripetal force created by the gravitational pulls in our galactic Milky Way, the WMAP satellite fixed itself in the universe 100 million km above our Earth.

called it "Tupita") came, tucked at the bottom of a box which finally landed—unopened and unreviewed—in this bin fifteen years ago. It landed under the bed ten years ago and was packed in the furthest, unvisited recesses of my memory at what must have been the same time.

Here, now, it sat at the cusp of resurrection.

The smell of new death—two years in the Peace Corps had acquainted me with the scent—swirled with a hint of basil and mint as I removed the still airtight top. The bird was amazingly well-preserved, stiffer than the one on the porch, but as still as the day thirty years ago when I placed it in there.

I had now proven to myself that this was, indeed, the second time this happened to me. I planned a strange marriage of old death with new as I brought the plastic casket with me into the solarium. Emerson remained quietly on the couch, himself reading the memory of my recent touch, while I continued toward the front door. As I opened it, I glanced through the smudged sidelight toward where I had left the dead—what I will still assume was a—finch.

It was gone.[5]

A rush of pungent air whooshed past me toward the only partly cracked portal to the porch, rustling my hair as it did.

I looked down into the open Tupperware container which had now been exposed to twenty-first century air for about four minutes and saw that it was empty.

I looked about my feet, wondering if I had somehow—in a startled state from my discovery of the first bird's absence—dropped this one. It was nowhere to be found.

It was gone.

I stepped outside to see a fully obscured, black sky. The sun sat behind an oncoming dark cloud—amorphously approaching as

---

5   It relayed what its outward-into-the-universe fixed lenses gathered to the scientists in places like California and Hawaii and England and Chile and Japan: concentration.

though shot from Heaven in my direction. I dropped the empty plastic container as I reversed my direction, returning through the portal from the porch and back into the glass-encased solarium. I slammed and locked the door as my gaze transfixed upon the living flock descending on my home.

One by one, the leading edge began to ping the front of the house.[6] I watched in awe as the winged herd stampeded toward, and finally against, my home. Each east-facing window in my graciously re-created 1930s bungalow held under the flying deluge of feathers and blood; noon became midnight. Wings became blindfolds, smashed against every opportunity to see outside. In the sea of black death, even the room in which I stood became deepeningly darker and darker. My eyes struggled to capture the last bits of light until—and I could not tell which—either my eyes stopped working or the sun did. I held what should have been my hands before what should have been my face.

I was gone.

As they fell, one by one, ten by ten, then by the hundreds, the thuds became claps then thunder, and the unknowable voice of God boomed. The attack ended after a lifelong minute, and conspired in a siege of silent conception. My screams went unfulfilled and ended before crossing my lips.

Then, it was over.

They were gone.

And these birds, too, now flew in Heaven.

I dried my eyes with my shoulder as I fought to huff a clean breath.

---

6   Upon exploded white dwarf stars, known as Type 1a Supernovae—
     stars exponentially more massive than our own sun packed into
     volumes sometimes 100 times smaller—one at a time, these ar-
     tisans of science concentrated.

WORDS

THE BOOK, ANCIENT BY HIS STANDARDS, WIGGLED ITS WAY INTO HIS clumsy hands from the bottom of a precarious pile in the back of the dusty shop. Not even bothering to parlay its contents, he was none-theless contented by the cover, by the coarse green cloth bound and tattered, by the silent mildew which climed its spine. "The Book," the spine read and he was on his way. After the requisite bartering that always accompanied such a find, he concluded, "We'll take this one," as he left a crumbled five-dollar bill and a pile of lusterless change upon the counter in its place. The single-lighted door creaked as he opened it, tripping a bell that chimed once and then again behind him as he left with his treasure perched below his damp armpit.

Unfazed by the immediate transition of his environs from dank cool wood and words to the boundless and horizonless street onto which he stepped, his immediate concern was with the trove of yellowed and creped pages that awaited his anticipatory gaze. He was unaware that the sky was blue and that the sun beat down upon his young skin. He was unaware of pedestrians in his midst, of cars whirring by, of others watching him—reading him.[7] He

---

7 Their process was concerned with seeing, not yet ready or will-ing to contemplate. And in that concentration, in that state of suspension in time and space within the universe, while measuring things such as redshifts in the vicinity of these exploding stars and temperatures of photons that exist in den-sities smaller than a few parts per 100,000 within the cosmic microwave background (CMB), they became distracted.

walked, head down, being read and waiting to enter the glory of words which became part of his haplessly zigging and zagging body.

When instantly the shock of his new surroundings approached him in the form of a piece of unleveled sidewalk, he tripped forward without a hint of mitigation. As his face careened unimpeded toward the hot and cracked square of concrete, his book fell from its perch and his hands—at perhaps the last possible minute— decided to take the brunt of gravity's impertinence. His hands, bloodied by the fall, only very partially protected his face from complete devastation. A rosy abrasion welted upon his cheek, his already disheveled hair lashed directionlessly, and a scowl that matched the pain writhed through his entire body. If there could be an end to this moment, he thought, it must come quickly and with numbness.

Searching around for his book, he noticed that it, too, had been victimized by the fall. It lay complicatedly fanned out upon a stretch of grassy verdure which glistened from an earlier sun shower. He noticed the different greens as they juxtaposed themselves in a way that even the most astute modern visualist could not have anticipated. The leaves of grass were of the shade that inspires children's dreams of green: the green of crayons and simplicity, the green untainted by jealousy or greed. The coarse green of the book's cover was dingy and mossy, seeming not even green in comparison, certainly not imbued with the green of life within which it lay. An aged green lay among the painted green of the manicured streetscape. Where the greens contrasted, the book and grass shared their wetness, a wetness that seemed as natural to the former as it did grotesquely unnatural to the latter. The book awaited retrieval, again wiggling in a light breeze that blew the street-scented heat over a prostrate body and through riffled yellowed pages.

With abrazed hands, he pushed himself upwards. His elbows popped inaudibly beneath the weight of a thirteen-year-old frame as he lifted his head toward the vast sky. He paused and lifted his gaze from the ground which had consumed his leisure and pride toward that vast blueness that swirled colorlessly around him.[8] In his suspended movement, he inhaled a breath of consternation, a reverse sigh that filled his lungs with anger and staleness; his nostrils flared with the effort. Now, looking up and down the sidewalk and side to side, his perspective rose with his body as he positioned his feet below his center and continued his upward movement. He saw calves then knees then thighs and, at once, faces of concern washing past him. Appraising his abrasions, he dusted his knees and slapped together his blood-blistered hands and finally exhaled with an exasperation matched only in severity by his anger with a body more prone to gravity than erection. His evolution complete, his hands free of everything but pain, he regained his trajectory and walked on, more determined than before to get to that indeterminate somewhere he sought.

In its place among the grass and dollarweed, the book stayed behind, neither whimpering nor flitting in its newly attained freedom. Mostly unhurt by the fall, it was nonetheless abandoned, a new fixture in a new context against which it would eventually proclaim a new and less dramatic independence. For this and subsequent moments, however, the book remained and proclaimed in its static postulation, a decoration: an intrusion into nature by man's beneficence, a sullying force among an equally contrived paradise. Open to nature, the words physically connected with the leaves of grass that tickled the crunchy pages. Where no human fingers or squinting eyes had interacted with these pages for ages untold, these manicured blades of grass exacted a relationship never intended by authors or publishers or editors. As if to end the dalliance with a single blow, a pink, scraped hand righted the binding and closed the cover around

---

8   Indeed, the concentration upon these objects by individuals through the means provided by the soulless camera became a source for a collective distraction: What do these subtle redshifts mean?

the pages and words as it lifted the book into the air and placed it, again, under a sweaty armpit.

Booked and bookishly, together, they tripped their way back down the sidewalk, across the street, and out of view.

ROCKING CHAIR

THEY FIRST MET WHEN SHE WAS SIXTEEN. HE HAD JUST ENLISTED IN the Navy—thirteen days after the Japanese bombed Pearl Harbor. She was dating his younger brother and, when her deep turquoise eyes first met his, all he could think was how sorry he was for him. He was going to take his girl: not exactly the best Christmas gift he could offer. It was, however, the last selfish thing he ever did in his life.

He had engineered the trip to the high school, ostensibly to gather some paperwork that he needed for the recruiter. The grey stone building, electrified with the excitement of puberty, hormones, and fear about a newly declared war, buzzed. For him, as he walked these halls for the first time since he graduated six months earlier, they glowed. He channeled this electricity and walked upon it as though floating on some newly reckoned atomic power. With some help from the receptionist in the office, he got her class schedule. He could have had any girl in the school that day—including the receptionist whose knees buckled and forearms goose-pimpled as he spoke to her in his baritone which had just recently quit cracking—toweringly brave as he looked in his uniform. The navy blues wrapped around a spotless specimen of man, a recruiting poster made alive, his cobalt blue eyes ripping through everything unfortunate enough to fall into his simple, uncontemplative gaze.

Standing outside her classroom when the bell rang, he made no excuses for his presence by the door. It was not his place to make excuses; the commitment he'd recently accepted precluded him from such trifles as appearances or explanations. With clarity of purpose honed by the bravado of a man who had offered his life for an ideal called America, he held his hat in his hand. He watched her as she walked from her desk and loitered by the window for a moment gazing at the newly white landscape in a way that he would watch her gaze for the next sixty years. He watched her, as she steadied herself on the sturdy casement and as she pushed herself off of it. He watched her as she wandered, dreamlike, to the teacher's desk to discuss—was it last night's homework assignment or something else—a topic that ended with a smile so big that it pushed her shoulders back and her perky bosom forward. It was far too cold for the skirt she was wearing and far too winter for the blouse. He was glad for both, though he imagined himself a hulking overcoat wrapped around her: already warming her in his storied, electric arms.

She passed through the door last of all, the only one from the class who did not acknowledge him. Deliberately coy or uninterested? He was not sophisticated enough to discern the difference. Had he been, it would not have mattered. He watched her pass, a full head below his own. Her ginger hair radiated a clean he'd never smelled. He summoned the electricity from his shivering ankles and forced it up though his veins, up his legs, through his chest, and finally out his mouth. He whimpered her name. He was limp, deflated, now having shot every atom from his being in her direction. He could not see her misty eyes rolling back nor her freckled face contorting with the light-headedness of having not breathed since she left the window, nor that she was biting her lower lip, nor that her ears were flush.

"Yes?" She looked back. The game was, indeed, coyness. An inexperienced coyness, mostly unpracticed, and certainly never used on her current boyfriend whom she liked well enough but had never occasioned to kiss.

The youngish teacher—whose own core was ablaze and sending a scent which would undoubtedly excite her male students into frenzy during the next period—watched on from the corner of her eye as she wrote on the blackboard in feigned anticipation of that next group of innocents. The deliberateness with which she wrote on that board indicated that it was just a cover. She wanted her name to be on his lips. The chalk cracked and skid along the black slate with a startling screech. Abandoning her task, she walked back to her seat and took another preoccupation as she strained to listen. "Yes?" she whispered to a phantasm before her. "Yes," she affirmed. She was melting in her cold wooden chair.

Now re-righted and re-energized by the glance she cast back as she acknowledged him, he spoke her name again, audibly. The next words he spoke were unrehearsed and unplanned, but had echoed in his mind with each step since he'd left—with the same singularity of purpose that he'd mustered earlier in the day to the recruiter's office— his parent's home. Unconsciously, with the same autonomic power that made him breathe, he started the next sentence, "Will you?"

"Yes." She interrupted. "Will I?" she echoed first him, then herself. "Yes."

This was the first time she had even spoken to him. He would love the moments when he heard the sound of her voice a zillion times more. This was the first time she had interrupted him. He would forgive her this habit a zillion times more. She breathed for the first time since walking through the door and her color returned, a pinkish snowy white. This was the first of a zillion times that he would shiver in the presence of her breath. Her heart—once weakened by a year-long affliction with scarlet fever—beat out of her chest. This was the first of a zillion times he would rejoice in that sound. She dropped her books, her lily gaze never leaving his. This was the first of a zillion times he would forgive her weakness.

With that, they were affianced.

They danced in each other's eyes for a moment, he twirling in the pastel turquoise, she dipping in his steely cobalt: in each other's skies—clouds together.

The moment stretched along his calloused hands, a farmer's—now a sailor's—hands along an arch toward her own. With an outstretched finger, he lightly dabbled upon hers. For every bit of rough and work that his hands carried, hers carried an equal degree of supple. The only thing he'd ever felt so soft was the corn silk that he rolled into cigarettes, perhaps a newborn calf. Other than his mother, he had never touched a woman. Truly, he had never touched a woman in the way he was touching this creature.

When asked sixty years later, sitting beside her on their front porch,[9] in their rocking chairs—rocking—to describe the feeling of her skin—that moment—that day, summoning all of the memories he could muster and all of the words he had learned in a lifetime that carried him from Long Island to Missouri to California to the Aleutians, and finally to Central Florida where he built them a home and provided for a family, he nodded deliberately. His creased eyes searching the distance for the perfect words, he smiled a corn-silk, tobacco, and sweet-tea-yellowed smile—a smile bowed slightly leftward—and beamed. Speaking with a resonant yet labored voice, at once as a farmer and a father, as a sailor and a husband, as a grandfather and a hero, he said, "It was very nice."

And so it was: very nice.

---

9   What are the implications for our understanding of the universe? What of time and space and me...and us?

MOMENT TWO

FLAG

THERE WAS NO EQUIVOCATION. HE HAD TO GET TO SCHOOL. COMING from a thrilling VFW ceremony, he was nearly ready to jump out of his skin with anticipation. He held a brand new American flag in his pudgy hands.

His obsession was gripping if not startling. He loved the flag and he loved that he was appointed the student assigned to its care. Not that he had any competition; his responsibility was taken more seriously by him than by any adult in the school. His fascination with the stars and stripes found other odd outlets such as coordinating red-striped tube socks with blue-planed shorts and shirts, drawing flags on his hand in the way that his fellow students wrote the names of paramours, and insisting that his parents allow him to paint his bedroom walls red, white, and blue. His understanding of color, science, and crayons revolved around ways in which he could re-align traditional aesthetic considerations to reflect the sublimity of the color combination. In fact, when drawing rainbows, red, white—in this reality, a color—and blue were the top three bands, while greens, purples, and oranges sat below them. These same pictures often placed stars in the day sky right beside giant smiling yellow suns.

As a twelve year old, his concept of metaphor was yet undeveloped,[10] so the flag did not merely stand for an America that he loved, it was an absolute object of adoration, like his dog, tater tots, and his mother. This is not to say that he didn't also love America or Ronald Reagan in the same way, but they all had the same intrinsic value. One was not merely a symbol of the other; they all stood in a pantheon of things patriotic, not simply representing, but being. Too, his sense of love was nascent yet, and there was no distinction by the type of care or profundity with which he addressed the objects of his seemingly excessive adoration. Thus, he was bound by the same rules and expressions of intemperate love that he rained upon his dog, tater tots, and his mother.

So, this oddly patriotic child was granted access to a special closet, special because it was created to assuage his need for it, in the back of the school cafeteria, where he could access the box in which it was stored at night. Only he, the principal, and the school custodian had keys. He wore that key round his neck on the same piece of twine that he kept the house key he used to get into his backdoor each day after school, because both of his parents were still at work for several hours after classes let out.

One day, after school, he rode his bike to the city library and checked out R.H. Newcomb's *Our Country and Our Flag*, which he read cover to cover. He committed its rules to memory and they became as intrinsic as "Take your shoes off before coming in the house," and, "Be home before dark." His favorite song, while his friends enjoyed Stevie Wonder and David Bowie, was the "Star Spangled Banner." Indeed, when in a public place and the song would be played, on television before a baseball game or on the radio on the fourth of July, he would insist that all around him stand and

---

10   For these gazing cosmologists, such rigid stares set into mo-
      tion the questions that Roland Barthes describes as the issue
      of metaphor and its relation to metonymy in Proust's seven-
      volume tour, In Search of Lost Time. "'What is it? What does it
      mean?'—the real question of any essay.

remove hats. Except for a couple of incidents where alcohol was involved, his parents and all of their friends learned that it was easier to comply than receive a lecture from a twelve-year-old boy on love of country. Of course, his favorite poet was Francis Scott Key and Betsy Ross inhabited the same historical realm of significance as George Washington and Ben Franklin. For the sixth-grade talent show, he performed "You're a Grand Ol' Flag," on the recorder flute. The music teacher, an aging hippy, did not have the patience or stomach to endure the special time allotments required to teach him the much more difficult national anthem.

Not quite understanding the artistic significance or cultural statement that was made by them, he discovered Jasper Johns's iconic representations[11] and became an unflagging fan.

Every morning, he would choose a friend to assist him in his duty. He would purposefully enter the school while all of his classmates played tetherball, basketball, hopscotch, and freeze tag in the yard. He was permitted special entrance to the nearly empty—save for a few early-arriving teachers—corridors of the campus. He would emerge with the triangularly folded bundle and would lead his assistant to the flagpole on the southwest corner of the school's front lawn. Neatly and reverently, they would unfold it, he sometimes adding commentary and other times seeking affirmations of how "cool" this was. He always took the role of clipping the flag to the halyard while his friend held the fly end outstretched and horizontal. He always loved the last moment when the rising flag left his assistant's fingertips to catch the wind as he seriously raised the flag, hand over hand over hand, on the rope. As he wrapped the rope around the cleat, he looked to his companion with an expectant gaze, waiting to see if he knew to cover his chest. With the same assumptions that Catholics make about their Protestant guests' knowledge of when to

---

11 Metonymy, on the contrary, asks another question: 'What can follow what I say? What can be engendered by the episode I am telling?'" (Longtemps 278), as inquirers approach an understanding of their subjects.

kneel and genuflect during Mass, he would immediately launch into the Pledge of Allegiance. With only minimal hesitation, his guest would join him. He beamed. This never became old for him. He, after all, got to say the pledge twice each morning; he was granting his helper the same gift.

Afternoons were equally special. Leaving class five minutes before everyone else—considering his day started before everybody's too—was but a byproduct of the heavy responsibility that weighed upon his young and spritely spirit. While the pool of students who wished to assist in the morning hoisting of the stars and stripes was often shallow, there was almost universal hand-raising when the teacher asked who wanted to help at day's end.

This stern and solemn task was not always approached with the requisite degree of respect that he demanded—especially relative to the morning volunteers. Nonetheless, he used it as an opportunity to indoctrinate classmates in the finer points of flag folding and general knowledge about the flag. He would discuss, for instance, how before Hawaii and Alaska became states, the stars lined up in perfect rows and columns instead of how they are staggered presently. He would talk about the thirteen stripes and the thirteen colonies. He was also insistent upon absolute earnestness and care, explaining that if the flag touched the ground they would have to burn it and bury it in a special ceremony. He especially liked to shock the girls when explaining that the red stripes meant blood. Again, at an age where metaphor is just out of reach, the more squeamish girls would cast the flag from their hands forcing him to scramble and contort his own grip to prevent the blessed flag from touching the ground. Eventually he learned to have the girls grasp the flag on the white stripes before telling them about the blood.

He always got his volunteer to help him fold the flag perfectly, insisting that if the proper planes were not showing at the end that they would have to start over. When complete with this task, his flag friend was dismissed early to get on the school bus, walk to a parent's car, or retrieve a bicycle. This reward usually provided a thirty-second head start over the rest of the school. This prize may well have been an hour of horseplay, for it was coveted among all his peers.

Occasionally, his assistant would walk with him to the closet for the placement of the flag in its nightly resting spot. This was always a moment of pride, as he dug into his shirt collar to retrieve the key which set close to heart all day. He never failed to explain that only he, their principal, and the custodian had such a key.

National holidays and notable deaths broke up what might have otherwise been monotony as they called for the half-masting of the flag. He argued with his teacher on the day President Reagan was shot, insisting that he must immediately lower the flag. His teacher finally reassured and contented him that "if he dies tonight, you may put it at half-staff tomorrow." It turned out that all flags were ordered at half-mast the next day by the governor, thereby quieting all controversy on the matter. He felt vindicated and often reminded his teacher of his vast knowledge and intuition regarding all things flag. Slightly more mature, the teacher acquiesced and allowed him to maintain his expert status, the point of deferral on all such future matters. He was usually right.

When a storm threatened, he watched the window with a stern anticipation. Perhaps he had over interpreted the rules about rain. If he was sure that a sun shower would pass, he would not fret. He would, however, not stand for his beloved flag enduring a thunderstorm. Thus, he became almost as adept in meteorology as in flag esoterics. Not aware that his insistence that the flag come down during storms implied a distrust of its strength and resilience, he coddled it like a grandmother, more concerned with the "old" than the "glory."

Invoking the spirit of revolutionary minutemen protecting it from gunshot and cannon fire, he more than once braved thunder and lightning in order to honor its preservation. On one occasion particularly, when nearby lightning bolts had hit a transformer and knocked out power to the school, he rose from the dark with a proc-lamation. As tornado sirens could be heard in the background and his teacher scrambled to make order out of the chaos in her class-room, he stood and felt his way toward the door. She cross-checked him as she ordered him under his desk. He refused.

Words were calmly exchanged between the two that ultimately ended in a piercing scream from the boy: "I don't care if you don't love our country, but I will not," he pounded his feet on the wooden floor with the weight of a militia as he shouted the words "will not." "I will not," he repeated for emphasis, "stand by and watch our flag desecrated just because you're afraid!" He continued, "Do you think the Russians would leave their flag out in this storm?" His pitch reached fever, about to burst into tears at any moment. Another word would have been inaudible.

She stepped aside, deciding that the safety of the thirty other speechless and horrified students in her class was more important at this moment. Later discussions with the principal about the incident spanned from suspension for insubordinate behavior to nominating him for a medal and commendation from the President. He took off his horn-rimmed glasses and handed them to her. She obligingly took them,[12] stunned. The sounds of rain on the roof, booms of thun-der that came every three seconds, and the far-off sound of tornado sirens, were accompanied by the blazing scurry of his feet down the hallway and toward the front door.

The teacher watched through the window in silent disbelief as the roundish four-foot-eight boy braved the storm. He was soaking wet with his first step out from under the sidewalk awning. The wind and rain were so heavy that she could not see him after he had passed more than ten yards from the door. She continued to watch—the event lit only by lightning bolts—when the flag rapidly descended

---

12 They work from a point of concentration: scientists upon the universe: Proust upon Time (over his life): Barthes upon Proust. They work toward a state of distraction that is inherent in their training: habit.

the pole in fits and starts every two feet until it vanished for a second. Then she could see it floating in what must have been his hands. The sirens stopped in the background and the torrents abated for a moment so she could see him rather clearly with the flag in his hands as he climbed the building's front steps. Another clap of thunder coincided with his slamming of the front doors. He had disappeared out of her view. One of the students dared ask into the darkness from beneath his desk, "Is he okay?"

"He's okay. He got it. Now stay still."

His steps pounded down the hall with a chilling Poe-ness that stood in stark contrast to the frenzy with which they left. The class remained motionless, listening. His teacher said not another word, and remained still and calm in an exemplary effort to encourage her students to do so. The lights came back on, but the teacher insisted that everybody in the class, "Stay just where" they were, and all complied. As he got closer, everybody could tell that he was crying after all and that his steps were infused with grave solemnity rather than pride. Finally, a phantasm appeared at the threshold. He was not crying hard, but rather whimpering. He was dripping wet, as if the rain had fallen so hard upon him that it had filled him up and that it was now flowing back out of him like a pricked water balloon. His thin straight hair hung down over his eyes and his clothes clung to him making his absurdly shaped pre-pubescent body all the more absurd. In his arms he held the flag. It, too, was dripping. He stood in a puddle that threatened to become a lake that threatened to overtake its banks.

"Alright, everybody." The rain continued in torrents, but the thunder, lightning and sirens had moved past. "You may, with no talking, come out from under your desks. I want everybody to sit, silently, and put your heads down until I tell you to get up." Again, the class followed directions and the sound of scooting desks and chairs, some rustling papers, and hushed whispers combined with the sound of rain falling on the roof.

The teacher, knowing that her next action would set the tone for the rest of the year and would probably have a profound effect on more than one of these children, walked slowly over to the drenched boy and grabbed two corners of the flag. Paralyzed, he began to cry more loudly as a few heads peeked up around the class. "Heads down!"[13]

"It touched the ground," he said as his heart sank and his red eyes burst forth a round of tears that made the storm outside seem a misting. "I let it touch the ground. I am so sorry!" He wished for the earth to swallow him, for invisibility, for anything other than the pain in his heart at that moment. He still had all of his grandparents, aunts and uncles. His puppy was in good health and his parents had never done anything but shower him with affection. He never wanted for anything and his mother supplied tater tots from a seemingly bottomless fry-daddy well.

In his short life, this was his first moment of despair. It was, indeed, the first time his soul had truly hurt. Perhaps, he would find out shortly thereafter, this was the moment that made metaphor a graspable concept for him. Perhaps, he might later understand that, with the destruction of this flag, he was truly born again.

"I'm sorry." Gripping the soaked mound of red, white, and blue close to his chest, he allowed himself to be embraced by his now sobbing teacher.

"It's okay, honey."

"I'm just so sorry. So sorry"

"Shh." She touched her index finger to his lips. She took off her cardigan and wrapped him in it. She brushed his hair out of his eyes with her other finger. She squatted down and carefully slid his glasses

---

13 Enabled by their technologies and understanding, they take the shutter clicks of the camera as the visual representation of their views. Eschewing myopia, the tools used by the scientist and artist, those that seek the obtuse in the specific are not dissimilar.

onto his face. She smiled at him as she shook her head with an at-titude that only a sixth-grade teacher can affect.

Together they walked into the hall as she cautioned the remaining thirty once again, "Keep your heads down."

Nobody stirred.

CROCHET

I NEVER UNDERSTOOD HOW IT WORKED OR WHY SHE DID IT, BUT I do know that the symmetry and tightness of the knots became less perfect as she aged. I'm not even sure how crocheting differs from knitting, or if they're just two sides of the same coin, but I do know that they both involve yarn and needles and lots of time. When I was young and she was less old, she had a seemingly unending supply of all three.

The contents of my childhood closet attest to her prolific yarning.[14] Mittens and caps, afghans and sweaters, slippers and scarves—most of which were never worn or used except on the Christmas morning they were received—fill teeming boxes of keepsakes that have been moved countless times, unopened, over the past twenty years. Curiously, the boxes have found their way back to her cellar, like some crafted boomerang or the gag gift that always emerges at office holiday parties.

And now I'm taking stock of these boxes, carefully preserved and stinking of mothballs and mold, and wondering how to save them. As I riffle through the piles, I am reminded of my youth and my encroaching agedness. As I pick through the unworn labors of her

---

14 Solutions, explanations, meanings are not solved "by optical means, that is, by contemplation, alone. They are mastered gradually by habit, under the guidance of tactile appropriation." For they are, Benjamin continues, "a matter of habit" (Mechanical Reproduction 16).

zesty summers and the later arthritic toils of her autumns, I can only imagine the pride and vicissitude with which she completed one item after another: Done! Done! Done! And I never wore a one, one, one.

I find a black-and-grey-checked blanket that was always too itchy-scratchy to cuddle in and I wrap myself in it, hoping that somehow it would be less itchy-scratchy now, and that I could resurrect it for my wife—whom I don't have—or my kids—whom I never will. I consider giving it to the dog, but am uncertain that this would be appropriate. I ultimately decide that disuse trumps misuse and that the dog will have to survive with a store-bought snuggle blanket. Deep down, I fear— but would never admit— that the dog, too, would put on a show of feigned appreciation only to push it to the corner of her own bed.

My wife died three years ago today. I am grateful for the time I had with her and that she never knitted or crocheted. I shared her with a career. She was born into the family business which she, with a gift for business and a savvy poker face, turned into the largest landholding company in the southeastern United States.

We were the most dapper couple, clearly more enamored of each other than any of our hosts, on the holiday party circuit. We could finish each other's sentences,[15] finish each other's martinis, and finish each other's plates. She knew how I was put together, and I knew how to dress her like the Chanel model she might have been had she not the love for her business. She was flawless.

Every year, on our anniversary, she gave me something that I really wanted, a gift that seemed to matter. For our first anniversary, she bought me a car. Not just any car, but the car that I had wanted all through college, expecting never to have. Who, other than her, might have imagined that a twenty-two-year-old high-school teacher should have a 5 series. Brand new, still smelling of showroom and leather, she

---

15 Beyond mere contemplation, the distractedness of habit confirms the assertion that the question of art—specifically our methods within language—like that of science, is metonymic, one of "what follows?"

CROCHET

placed the keys in a square sea-foam-green box on a monogrammed Tiffany keychain. She cheated on her career with me and spoiled me out of guilt. She enjoyed my company and lavished me with gifts.

She was older than me by a decade and knew that I was gay, although I never actually told her. Every year on our anniversary I would slip her the bone. I didn't hate it.

Don't misunderstand, I loved her. The gifts were incidental though substantial. In addition to cars and vacation homes, I had jewelry, every conceivable fad gadget, and a speedboat. One year, she even bought me a horse so I could better understand the culture of the high-stakes owners we schmoozed as we sipped juleps every spring at the Kentucky Derby. My reciprocation was hardly out of obligation. Though I didn't much love the idea of having sex with her, when the moment came—sixteen times all told—I rose to the occasion like a champion (which my horse, by the way, never became). I did make love to her in a tender way and she appreciated it. She never sought love—or even companionship— from anybody else, nor longed for more from me. Samantha Stevens, making the mid-series change from gay Darren to gay Derwood, had nothing on us.[16]

Her freakish death was sudden and disarmingly tragic. In a quest for thrills that I could not achieve in the bedroom, I decided that I wanted an extreme weekend. I mentioned it in passing over western omelets one morning and she surprised me days later by driving me - to the airport where she garaged her company jet. She had chartered a plane to take me skydiving. Funny, I had never done this before, so we had to bring along a tandem coach. She had no desire to participate, but came up nonetheless. She wanted to kiss my cheek as I shoved out and then meet me safely on the ground.

I jumped. The plane crashed. She and the pilot were killed in a

---

16 The camera enables this. In fact, the camera demands it and has since it turned the course of history. "At the origins of photography," writes Robert Ray, "an intersection of related problems: the legibility of the surrounding world, the status of the detail, the relationship between image and language" (Ray 33).

fireball after both engines simultaneously failed and the plane careened into an unoccupied house in a gated community in the suburbs. It could have been much worse. I landed safely and saw only the plume of smoke far in the distance, not knowing for nearly an hour that my darling had been stolen from me in a horrific disaster. All I had left of her was a bright red smudged lipstick remnant on my cheek. The tandem jump coach provided a solid shoulder to cry on and remains a close friend to this day.

I continued teaching for three full years after I lost her—today was my last day—although my net worth was well in excess of thirty million dollars after I divested myself of the controlling interest of the company with an amicable equity sale to the board of directors. I'd give it all if I could have her back.

Instead, I'm giving it away. Who the hell needs thirty million dollars? Any of her relatives I could find received enough to keep them happy and worry free for the rest of their lives. The Bill and Melinda Gates Foundation received a huge endowment, and I've built a new auditorium at the high school where I teach—taught. I've also granted to the Fund for Renewable Energy and preserved five-thousand square miles of sensitive wetlands in the lower Mississippi Valley.

I've become quite the daredevil and extreme skydiver.

Perhaps I will endow a program in crafting at the University,[17] for knitters—for crochet. Perhaps I should name it after my dear grandmother, whose arthritic hands could not even two-hand a glass of lemonade near the end of her life. Perhaps, I should take up the art myself, and carry on the sturdy tradition that generations of women before me mastered and passed on as part of an itchy-scratchy tradition of love-wrapped disappointment.

After all, if I can love a woman, I can love a scarf. If I can lose one, perhaps I can fill the void with the other.

---

17 What disparate paths of understanding do our distractions lead us along from that image upon which we concentrate to the words that we use to approximate it?

CROCHET

BAIT

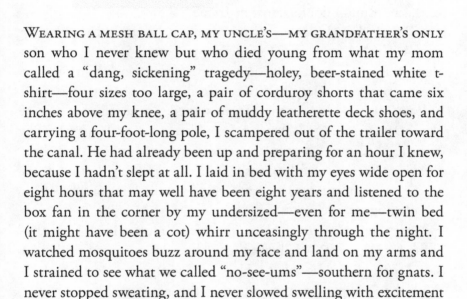

Wearing a mesh ball cap, my uncle's—my grandfather's only son who I never knew but who died young from what my mom called a "dang, sickening" tragedy—holey, beer-stained white t-shirt—four sizes too large, a pair of corduroy shorts that came six inches above my knee, a pair of muddy leatherette deck shoes, and carrying a four-foot-long pole, I scampered out of the trailer toward the canal. He had already been up and preparing for an hour I knew, because I hadn't slept at all. I laid in bed with my eyes wide open for eight hours that may well have been eight years and listened to the box fan in the corner by my undersized—even for me—twin bed (it might have been a cot) whirr unceasingly through the night. I watched mosquitoes buzz around my face and land on my arms and I strained to see what we called "no-see-ums"—southern for gnats. I never stopped sweating, and I never slowed swelling with excitement for the morning.

I watched as he rolled quietly out of bed, careful not to rouse me, and pulled on his fishing gear. Still, with my eyes clenching shut each time he looked my way to assure himself of my uninterrupted slumber, I watched him in the weak combinations of moonlight and the red clock numbers. I watched in awe at both his ninja-like silence and of the towering shadow that he cast in the already dark room.[18] I watched him make sandwiches in the faint light of the refrigerator that he used instead of turning on the overhead incandescents. The familiar sound of tearing aluminum foil was followed quickly by the sound of its folding around gooey white-breaded works of gastronomic art slathered with mayonnaise and stacked high with pink, fatty, boiled ham. I watched him crack five trays of ice into our cooler along with a half gallon of sweet iced tea we had brewed together the previous day. I listened to him pee—a force that I could only aspire to—and then heard the smack of the aluminum door against its frame.

The red digital numbers across the room, on the kitchen counter read 4-4-1-A. I knew that I needed to wait until 5-3-0-A, the time that we agreed I could get up. I had never seen a clock read either of those times before; sleeping as was customary for a boy my age, until at least 7-0-0-A when Looney Toons started. I watched every tick of the minutes until 5-1-9-A when I could stand it no longer. I burst from the bed with an unbridled exuberance and in less than three fluid movements was fully dressed for a day of fishing. I raced down to the banks of the canal where I could see the faint outline of his looming figure, back toward me.

"Hey hey, slow down there, little fella. Now, did you eat anything for breakfast?" He looked up at me with a creased smile that sliced through the moonlight. He knew the answer before he asked. With that, he spun around and cast a shrimping net off the end of the dock in a motion reminiscent of a dance move. With a "whoosh," the spinning net caught the wind like a crinoline before landing in a perfect circle on the brackish water. The white net reflected off the same fading moonlight and slowly sunk out of sight.

"No," I sheepishly admitted.

---

18 This answer is Legion as are the paths. Most of all, the chaos that ensues in the wake of this distraction is founded in the simple fact that "even the most perfect reproduction of a work of art is lacking in one element: its presence in time and space, its unique existence at the place where it happens to be" (Mechanical Reproduction 3).

He told me the night before that eating was to be part of my morning tasks, that I'd need the energy for all the fishing we'd be doing today. I skulked back into the trailer as I heard him shout behind me, not hen-peckishly—he couldn't summon a bit of the femininity required for such a tone—but stern nonetheless, "And make sure you drink all the milk you pour over that cereal. Remember, a mama cow could've given that milk to her calf, but gave it up for you. Don't waste it."[19]

"Yes sir," I answered half discomfited, half beaming. I knew that once I had finished my cereal and drank that nasty old milk from the bowl, that I would be that many moments closer to being out on the open water with him.

Carefully, with two hands gripping the yellow box that was easily as big as my upper torso, I poured the Cheerios into the stainless steel bowl. It was deeper and had a smaller diameter than the ceramic bowls at home. Additionally, it had no lip, which I knew would facilitate—at home, I inevitably spilled milk down my front because of the wide lip on the bowls—the milk subtask, therefore speeding the entire clean-up-free process. Unfamiliar with this bowl, I could not gauge how much I was pouring for myself, concerned not with being able to finish—though mindful of his admonition—but with how long it would take to eat. I filled the bowl halfway up with cereal and sprinkled just enough milk overtop to make the mound rise. Milking cereal was an art that I had just about mastered. Too little milk and the cereal was too crunchy and dry. Too much and it sogged before I could finish eating it. My goal was always to minimize the amount of milk left once the cereal was gone. Despite my insatiable quest for sweets, I hated the sugary milk—which it was my civic and human responsibility to not waste—that was always left behind. From beginning to end,

---

19 For our cosmologists, this metonymic quandary is doubly intensified as the outward gaze into the universe traverses time as it traverses space.

breakfast took eight minutes, ideally coinciding with the bright red 5-3-0-A on the digital clock. I did not mind that there was more leftover milk than I wanted. I gulped it down without hesitation, for the appointed time had arrived.

When I bolted back down the path from the trailer to the dock, I saw him shaking the net which now sat by his feet and reaching down to pick out the shrimp. Carefully culling, he threw some small fish, rocks, shells, and glass bottle pieces back into the canal and loaded the shrimp into a red-and-white cylinder that dangled over the side of the boat, bobbing in the water. "That oughtta be enough, about thirty."

"What are those for?"

"That's bait."

"Ohhhh." My wonderment was unambiguous, but still sprinkled with confusion about what "bait" was. It was not the first time he had excited such a feeling of inescapable newness in the previous few days I'd spent with him, nor would it be the last time over the next thirty years. He may as well have been showing me how he could make the moon disappear behind the horizon, which he apparently had. The sun was peaking up and the golden night was transforming to an orange morning before my astonished eyes.

He picked up a faded carrot-colored life vest and slipped it over my head. He playfully tightened it, tugging exaggeratedly on the black nylon straps. He donned one of his own. I beamed, exposing every one of my teeth, save the two that I had traded with my pillow for a quarter each earlier in the week. He mussed my hair. I looked up, thoroughly immersed in the marvel of the moment.

"What do we do with those shrimps?"

He reached into the bucket and pulled one out. Its long antennas glistened as they flopped and flittered in his hand. Grasping the tiny creature between his thumb and forefinger, we watched it gyrate for a moment. "Bring that pole over here," he motioned with his head toward the fishing pole I was holding over my shoulder. I complied.

"Now, very carefully, unlatch the hook and bring it and hand it to me. Be very careful, it's sharp and…" Again, I complied as his raspy, morning voice trailed off.

I handed him the shiny silver hook as it dangled on the gossamer floss from my rod. "Like that?"

"Yes, that's just fine." He grabbed the hook. "Now, you wanna get that hook in there, right above the tail, but not in it. Too high, near the head, and you'll kill it. Too low, on the tail and the hook will rip right out when you cast."

The crunch with which the hook pierced the shell of the tiny creature reverberated with a striking pain through my body: concussive. I watched the shrimp continue to gyrate on the end of the line as he released it. The astonished wonderment in which I was reveling just instants before was immediately transmogrified into a piercing immitigable horror.

His eyes glistened proudly, reflecting the nascent morning sun as it rose behind my head. His bicep, painted with an ancient green anchor and some words I did not yet know how to read, flexed from just below his white shirt sleeve. His mostly straight, slightly gapped, and beige-ish teeth appeared behind his tan and sun-freckled lips as he half-smiled in my direction. "Got it, kiddo?"

I dropped the pole onto the ground. Rather, I allowed the force of gravity to steal the pole from my suddenly flaccid body. The shrimp continued to flop on the ground, the end of the hook with it, as both shined against the emerging day. I was struck motionless and dumb, my fingers powerless to grasp anything and my mind equally powerless for the words to describe my terror.[20]

"Whoops." He spoke for me, not accurately translating. "Are you alright, fella?"

---

20 A distance measured in light years burns the retina with the residue of a Big Bang that occurred hundreds of billions of years ago. The cosmologists' search, then, is very literally answered, at least in part, by their own presence as a metonymic response to the universe's call.

I could not respond, but he understood quite instinctively—after only a couple seconds—that we would not be fishing that day. Silently, with the same ninja-like dexterity he exhibited earlier, he removed items from the boat: poles, tackle boxes, extra life preservers that we were going to use as seat cushions. His demeanor did not change a bit. Although raspy, his breathing had not a hint of frustration in it. He pulled the bobbing bait caddy out of the water and smiled as he dumped all of the shrimp back into the canal, watching to make sure I was watching him. He nodded as if to seek assurance, wordlessly asking, "How's that?"

He motioned for me to come over as he pulled the remaining item, the blue plastic cooler, out of the boat. I hopped over my fishing pole as I ran the rest of the distance to the dock where he sat with his feet dangling just above the water's surface. I sat down beside him. I could feel a wave of color reacquaint itself with my skin. I looked up at him, thankful without saying so, and struggled to make out the writing on his arm which was just above my eye level. With the other arm, he reached into the cooler and pulled out a sandwich wrapped in aluminum foil. In a flash, both hands were engaged in the tinny un-tombing of our lunch. The sun had now gained supremacy of the morning sky and a pesky mosquito buzzed loudly in my ear as I swatted blind and unsuccessfully toward it. He handed me half of the diagonally sliced white-bread masterpiece in his hand and we enjoyed the coldest, soggiest, slimiest, most disgustingly mayonnaise-slathered—best—ham sandwich of my life up to that point, and since.

MOMENT THREE

MOMENT THREE

EQUILATERAL

Nowadays, the rules are just plain different. Courtship, sexuality, matrimony, parenthood: rituals with rules written for other people in other times. Nowadays, the only rule that seems to matter is love. We had been best friends since the fifth grade and, now, with nearly sixteen years standing in the interim between our meeting and this moment, she stood ready, flaunting rules as she had her entire life, to take a husband. Though friends and beaus had entered and left her orbit over the years, and though our affection had taken more than a couple of momentary breaks for things like jealousy and college—I tested the gravity of our relationship for eight agonizing months away from her while she remained home attending junior college—two constants remained: she was my best friend and I was hers. We were as tethered as the earth and the moon, and my tides rose and set as routinely as her menstrual cycle. We finished sentences that the other needn't even start, we were of one mind, regaled in the co-dependency of each others' oft solar-flaring drama.[21] We loved each other.

By the time we were budding, I had seen every square millimeter of her body and she mine. We both had chocolate-morsel-sized flat brown moles in the same relative position of our warm

---

21 In pondering what follows what they see, the answer is "me." The distraction leads back to a self-indulgent subjectivity that returns by means of habit and training.

pelvic realities. We discovered these at the age of fourteen, when we were dressing out at my house for gymnastics practice. I lived a few blocks' walk between our school and our training gym and it was always easier to stop by there, grab a snack, and throw on our sweats instead of using the locker room at the gym. I noticed hers because of the way she shaved her strip of black bush, perhaps to mask to the world that she was not naturally platinum blonde, and left it starkly—proudly—exposed. Upon seeing it, eagle-eyed like spotting a single lost tuna among a million spawning salmon from ten-thousand feet in a cold Northwestern river, I could not help but instantly drop my shorts to show her mine, pushing back the thoroughly unkempt tuft of auburn hair that had begun growing around my fledgling penis during the previous summer. Linked forever by our corresponding birthmarks, we came to call them— without abash— "love chips." They became our omnipresent inside joke and icons to our inseparability.

Unable to assuage insatiable adolescent needs to coordinate, we adopted our chips as the central theme to our high school years. Not a single holiday, large or small, ranging from Rosh Hashanah to St. Patrick's Day, could pass without a knowing nod to our link. Chocolate chip cookies, salt and vinegar potato chips, and poker chips, as well as common phrases such as "chip off the old block," and phrases which we coined such as "rip the chip" became part and parcel of our commingled existence. Most famously, she dyed her hair black and slicked it back as we both fashioned form-fitting khaki jumpsuits topped off with mirrored silver wire-rimmed glasses as Ponch and Jon one Halloween.

When finally she lost her virginity (she ripped the chip long before I did) during the summer after sophomore year on a family vacation to the Bahamas, she immediately called me. The older boy, a lifeguard at the hotel where they stayed who had clearly made this a habit and whose lines were as well-rehearsed as his hard dick was smooth, laid quietly beside her on the beach as she described every bit of it to me in the post-coital afterglow. I should have been there but I was laid up at home with the chicken pox from which she had recovered two weeks earlier, and thus was forced to endure the conspicuous absence through snapshots, text messages, and a bevy of ill-fitting cotton-poly t-shirts when she returned. I endured sex vicariously through her accounts until finally my own chip was ripped during spring break two years later. What was for her a physical act devoid of much more than the swapping of fluid was, for me, a ridiculously intimate culmination of what I believed was princely courtship and romantic connections. Before meeting my own first prince, she racked up the better share of a baker's dozen. Of course, her heart was never broken while mine was under perpetual repair. I served as needy recipient to her natural propensity toward dispenser of maternal affection.

And so, those rules, the ones that require a "maid of honor," seem as antiquated as the concept of marriage itself. Even settling as we did upon the title "Chip of Honor," in light of how events and time intervened, seems as old fashioned as jean shorts and mullets. Ordained years before the man who taught her to love was named, I was to stand beside her and hold her bouquet as she dove headlong into eternity with another. He was to be but a transient comet pulled into our solar system, the third chip in our low-stakes game. We committed to each other—she and I—on the sixteenth of July, two weeks before I was to leave for the state university three-hundred miles away, as we sipped on cheap warm champagne pilfered from her parent's liquor cabinet while they were out of town experiencing their own "second honeymoon." Once I finally found the suitable husband for her, I was to be in charge of dress-picking, bridesmaid management, reception planning, and honeymoon reservations. I would be the one making and enforcing the rules.

I survived one and a half semesters before I returned, with a one-point-eight grade-point average and a strapping blonde hunk on my arm.

He dove with me on the school team. Junior year of high school, I had discovered that the same skills that made me a good tumbler made me a spectacular diver. Weighed down, not by the neck full of high-school gold medals I brought with me, my future as a competitive college diver was cut short by the unfortunate combination of dismal grades, sexual distraction, and cheap beer. I had brought him home for myself,[22] but quickly realized that I was not anything more than an experiment for him. I provided oral and he provided the tool upon which I could practice performing oral. We each derived our own type of pleasure, although mine necessitated a male while his didn't.

I knew when their eyes met that I had given him my last open-mouthed kiss. He was not gay. He was, however, exceedingly fun to hang out with. In short time we became inseparable, shining upon each other with similarly sunny outlooks for each other and together. His frothy personality inebriated everybody he came in contact with and provided more lasting effects than the uncounted pints of beer continually emptied in his presence. Best of all, his grades were worse than mine, so I was always the "smart one." Blessed with connections, lineage, and well-filled genes, his place in the class was never in jeopardy. He was guaranteed a place in his family's business upon graduation. All he had to do was fulfill the legacy of the n'th generation at the University, not get kicked out for behavior, and find a suitable bride. He was liked by everybody who came near enough to hear his voice. I was lucky enough to be pulled into his closest orbit.

Even if he was gay, the best any guy might ever have hoped for was being kept by him in some hidden city apartment where he might visit from the country a few times a month when "on business." As far-fetched as that might have been, I decided to end it before it ever

---

22 The subject of every snapshot, of every pondering, of every study, of every gazing into space becomes the gazer: soul, heart, mind; judgment, determination; love, reason; knowing time, knowing space, knowing images and ideas; making meaning.

got started. He never knew that I ended anything, having never recognized anything's genesis. This speculation became quickly moot in
light of the warp speed of their courtship and connection.

So, we became best buddies, inseparable, and it only made sense
that I would bring him home to meet her. Of course, he could never
approach the tight orbit that contained her and me; in our previously closed galaxy he became a comet whose trajectory was increasingly inward-spiraling. To be sure, I treasured him, but not in that
"I secretly hope that one day he will realize that he loves me," or the
"if I get him drunk enough one night maybe we will swap spit or
semen…and he will realize that he loves me." Our friendship—once
I committed upon our "breakup"— was completely platonic and
never tinged by anything more than faux and contrived gay over-
tones. Indeed, it was a near mirror image of the sheer and unalter-
able nonsexual relationship I had with the other chip. I believe, and
have no reason to suspect otherwise, that his feelings for me were
unswervingly identical.

Though she never enrolled as a student, she undertook all of the
rules of fanaticism that made her otherwise undifferentiated from
the most buoyant and effervescent sorority girl. We maintained the
charade by fabricating a forged diploma and an obscurely timed
summer graduation for her in order to convince his parents of her
worthiness. So true was her commitment to the University and so
rabid her adherence to the art of tailgate etiquette, that she always
carried a small vile of glitter just in case, in the unfortunate event
that she should cut herself while hosting a party—in her living room,
or outside the grand stadium—she could sprinkle the wound with
it proving that she did, indeed, bleed garnet and gold. Her chance
presented itself once, while she was cutting limes for Corona Lights.
True to her plan, she aroused the astonishment of all her guests as
they gathered round to provide bandages and advice regarding her
wound. He beamed and dutifully tended, even as she became lighter-
headed than she should have—the cut was deep—in order to keep

replenishing the gold flakes. He loved her. She was, to every observer, the absolute complement to him. I loved them.

As though written on some ancient tableau—Hamurabi's lost rock—in which love was originally defined, we grew together from three twos to one three; we completed each other in ways that fulfilled our galaxy as though it was the only galaxy that mattered in the universe. While their affection for each other came to manifest itself sexually, I gained strength from both their individual loves for each other and for me.

We took a three-bedroom apartment near campus and moved in while he finished his degree. Though she slept in his bed each night, we each had our own bedroom. As much as we loved each other and as willing as we were to share everything and anything, from underwear to cookie dough, we each needed our own bathroom and closet. I needn't belabor this prima facie reality beyond pointing out the demographics of our lair: gay boy, diva, and uber-prep.

She and I were not made for schooling, subsisting instead in the lessons that life taught and basking in new knowledge garnered from around us and filtered through each other. We had all we needed in the world and were able to carry our small portions of the bills from the modest stipends we received from our own parents for whom our educational statuses were fully invented. I took a job as a bartender at the Capital Bar, where state legislators tipped sufficiently to fill my wallet enough to keep up with my roommates' lifestyles. This remunerative pastime also provided introductions to a few passing romances and more than a few one-nighters. Already positioned within a perfectly lovely universe, I never found anybody worth the gift of our gravity.

She did some local modeling, becoming the perfect face and boobs to adorn a few—actually thirteen in two and a half years—game programs for basketball and baseball games. She could also be found on six of the billboards, scattered along I-10 and I-75 for "the bookstore" on campus where every alumnus and fan was expected to buy team gear and enthusiast's apparel. She was gorgeous and they were gorgeous together.

We wholly expected that, upon his graduation, we would all move back to his hometown—which we did—onto the family estate. The three of us took up residence in a three-thousand-square-foot Victorian that looked over the groves toward his parent's home. When we ran out of orange juice or wanted a full-fledged breakfast—biscuits, gravy, chicken fried steak, cheese grits—we would hop on our three ATVs and race along the main trail through the rows of citrus trees to the "big house," where Momma would drop whatever she was doing to fill our bellies. For a "good Southern" family, generations deep in the ways and customs of gentility and American castes, Momma and Poppa accepted our small family with as little caprice or misunderstanding as a hound dog puts into licking its own balls or panting on a muggy August afternoon. They loved us unconditionally and we accepted their love without equivocation, happily returning it with the full bounty of a limitless universe.[23]

Alas, beyond site, where light is not just a beam but also a shot from a thoroughly unknowable past, the universe is fraught with darkness.

We had to make the choice: slowly watch the fast-growing tumor overtake his frontal lobe and cause him to slip into dementia then eventually starve his organs of their autonomic functions or remove it and the piece of medulla oblongata to which it had already spliced through the cerebrum and anchored itself. After considering fourth and fifth opinions and stripped of scientific possibilities and mathematical odds, we knew that our options were equally unbearable: either rob him of his mind now with the hope that the amazing power of the human body to heal itself would rebuild the synaptic tissue

---

23 Ultimately, the question of "what follows" implies a beginning at which the metaphoric value of language resides in self. The making of meaning in the arts and in the sciences has long assumed an essence of "thingness," an essence that Benjamin calls an "aura."

over time and return him to us or wait it out in the hope that a sixth or seventh opinion would emerge alongside some new technological answer to the problem.

As rapidly as the tumor—first detected during a cat scan for what we thought were quick-onset migraines—was expanding, the difference between an unsuccessful Option One and a miraculously protracted Option Two was a matter of months. We decided to hold onto the sure thing and ease him and ourselves into a slow and torturous descent toward the abyss of brain death rather than risk losing him all at once should the surgeon's scalpel prove useless or unsteady. Within weeks, his speech was slurring and his thoughts jumbled in his mouth to pour out incoherently among strings of spittle and tears. She and I took turns with him—fourteen hours at a stretch with two overlapping hours in which we all sat in a room—staring at each other, loving our togetherness.

Three times over the next six weeks, as he slid further and further from us, she managed him into arousal and slid onto him until he came inside her. I was there each time, watching his face. Each successive time, his bliss was more distant, evanescently present in the twitch of his cheek and the dilation of his pupils. Shortly after the third time, in about the seventh week, he stopped breathing on his own and we moved all of the accoutrement that would have filled a hospital room to our home. Round-the-clock medical surveillance was employed to ease his pain—our pain. At this point, we sought our seventh and eighth opinions; all conclusions were that this exponentially metastasizing errant-cell stampede could not be corralled.

Nine weeks after the first asteroid impact to our lives when we learned about the imminence of his departure from our life-realm, I finally accepted that there would be no brides-maids nor dresses nor honeymoons to plan. I accepted that he would be in a coma for only a short time before we lost him altogether. I wanted to transplant my breath where his was now mechanized. I wanted to lie upon him and give him the beats of my heart. I could not bear the thought of being without him. As much as I loved her, I now loved him. As much as I loved her and as much as I loved him, I loved us above all and could not fathom what imperfect line would remain where once a circle was. Momma and Poppa, suffering as deeply as any parents can suffer, from across the groves, gazed upon our fading constellation with guttural and inconsolable grief first for us and then only second for themselves. They were losing their only beloved son; they knew that we were losing our life force: our perfect third.

The first five years of their relationship was an endless honeymoon, fulfilling implicit vows, taken on that Spring afternoon when they first met, consummated countless times in countless ways from cheek pecks to full and tender penetrations. The first five years of our relationship was a continuation of a cosmic symphony that began with chocolate chips falling upon young bodies then slowly and tenderly ripping open to cleave wholly with a new spirit: reaching back to the beginning of time and forward toward its end. Honeymoon completed, procreation interrupted, we needed to join the boundaries of our orbit before he broke free from the yoke of our gravity.

Because the rules nowadays are different, nobody dared question our plans for matrimony. Before God and before Momma and Poppa and before all the stars in the universe and before the cicadas buzzing loudly in the groves at dusk, we were married:

"I do."

"I do."

"I do," he silently whispered as his ghost escaped the body which his brain finally ceased to manage. We kissed; we kissed him, each on a cheek. I squeezed her hand and his—weak and withered—with identical passion. She squeezed back; he did not. Luxuriantly, we breathed in his passing aura. Intoxicated by escaping life, for a moment I saw clearly the conception of the universe.[24] She too saw it

---

24 "The authenticity of a thing," according to Benjamin, "is the essence of all that is transmissible from its beginning, ranging from its substantive duration to its testimony to the history which it has experienced" (Mechanical Reproduction 4).

and, releasing our hands, grasped it and held it in hers—interwoven—over her ambitious womb.

In a mostly mechanical activity aimed at consummation and achieving conception, she and I honeymooned in his omnipresence, creating the living memory and fulfilling the promise of our perfectibility.

Blonde and beautiful, writhing with enough life for two creatures, enough to hold us bravely at the cusp of event horizon for nine quickened months, we gave birth to the perfect child.

Oscillating between grief and ecstasy, we lived concurrently in memory and hope, in the wonder of our loins. Our son sustained us and we raised him: the garnet-and-gold-bleeding heir to the bountiful sweet-scented groves. Our lively child bowed our line into a circle once again. At night, he would lay upon my chest and our hearts would beat together, urging each other's on. During the day, he would effervesce with the wonder of discovery as he wandered the groves sniffing blossoms and ripping open fruit to expose sweet flesh and boisterous juice. I would stare into her eyes and she would rub my hands as we marveled at our chip, our unblemished, tethered-yet-independent son, chipped off the old block.

And we were perfect together.

FOOTBALL

AFTER CRISS-CROSSING THE ROAD FOUR TIMES AND HITTING EVERY convenience store within a mile, we finally found rolling papers. Of course, neither of us had a lighter so I had to go back in again. In addition to being mildly intoxicated from the Budweisers we drank en route, we were both unmanageably edgy. We needed to smoke to settle our nerves and our anxieties. In the name of bravado, neither of us would voice our apprehension. We knew that we would be inextricably changed. He rolled the joint like a pro; I chugged another beer. The searing February morning sun beat down on us from a crisp blue sky painted with wisps of whimsical cirrus as we sat in the parking lot at the intramural fields. We smoked. I finally relaxed. He finally relaxed.

A sudden pounding on the hood of his pickup announced the arrival of one of his brothers. They were all brothers and all the brothers brought their girlfriends, most of whom were sisters. This was their Sunday ritual. It predated me. "We" were not yet a ritual, and I never expected that we would become one. Nonetheless, that he took me along meant something. He was making a statement that I didn't ask him to make. He, who usually just came to play with his brothers, who usually never brought anybody along, wanted me to come. He wanted me, who was neither brother nor sister, to watch him interact in his world. I, who was out of school and decidedly not Greek, talked the talk even if I didn't strut the strut. Before the echo from the hood-slapping ended, we were opening our respective doors. A rush of smoke filled the vicinity as he passed the joint to the noisemaker. They laughed and shook hands—it was actually more of an elaborate handoff—as I cracked a beer for our joiner. I introduced myself to whatever his name was; we shook hands—handed off and back—and they walked ahead of me. I grabbed the cooler from the bed of the truck as we moved through the clearing toward the football fields. They extinguished the roach and disposed of it. It became part of the scenery.

Within minutes, the worn brown and lightly greening expanse of fields teemed with shirtless, glistening frat boys and uncountable dainty blonde Barbie girls whose pink lipstick matched their pink flip flops which matched their pink bathing suit tops. The football was flying all around and then to me. Instinctively, I threw one deep to another of the boys whose name was, I believe, Matty or maybe Matt E. For each pink-and-tan girl there was a chair, and for every fourth girl there was a dog. There were dogs on leashes, dogs off leashes chasing Frisbees, dogs running after the football, and dogs slurping up water out of stainless steel bowls.

The girls spread out their blankets; some even brought umbrellas. They had chairs. I had my backpack and a cooler. He didn't think to tell me I'd need something to sit on. By now, he was on the field in scrimmage mode. The four fields were being marked off as other people's brothers continued to arrive in droves. Today's games would determine the intramural champion. We had a three- to four-hour afternoon ahead of us, assuming his team continued to win. It would really, I posited, come down to the team least stoned and most sober. They fidgeted with their flags and he showed his teammates how to tear the sleeves off of their shirts in such a way that they could get maximum muscle effect. They donned their uniforms and began to play. Knowing that it was my duty to take off my shirt, I conformed and—at least in appearance—fit in with the tanned and tight bare-chested boys that I resembled. The winter sun was hot on my shoulders. I squinted.

In this morass of people, suddenly and frighteningly I was all alone. The ball was no longer being thrown toward me. The games had begun. I was a mere spectator, after all.

I was alone; I had no friends there. These were all his friends and his friends' girlfriends. They were all sisters and brothers intermingled from a social bloodline that spewed forth perfection like the ash from Vesuvius;[25] they were all Greek to me and I was from an equally far-off place to them. I imagined myself a Cretian. I sat off by myself on the other side of our Mediterranean isle for a while, self-consciously wondering how I could break into the sea of pink and tan fifteen yards down field. I wondered if I should. I brooded and I watched. I pounded another beer and was feeling full.

My liquid courage arrived as I picked up the cooler, picked up my backpack, and slowly moved toward the spectator's area. I caught the unsunglassed eye of one of the girls who smiled at me. Her eyes wandered down my tan and pinking body, then back up with a pause at my shorts and the muscular V that sprouted upward into my stomach, toward my chest. She asked me if I was his friend. I confirmed that I was. Barbie and I chatted a little. She introduced me to a few other girls who also politely smiled, flashing whitened white teeth surrounded by that same pepto pink lip gloss I'd noted was the unofficial uniform. Lots of brown roots showed through yellow hair while lots of bikini bottoms peaked out through unzipped bottoms-fraying jean shorts. The first girl offered some pink mixed-drink concoction she had prepared before coming and which she had poured into one of several emptied out pink-labeled jugs. I declined in favor of my Red, White, and Blue. I should have taken the drink.

Exposing the only completely bare chest in a sea of pink unnerved me. I self-consciously—in an attempt to move the gaze of my

---

25 The experience of the cosmologist becomes part and parcel of the knowledge created during the process of concentration. When combined with the myriad experience of the scientists' own subjective queries, the distraction leads to convergent praxes.

new acquaintances from my body to my face—put my shirt back on as we all chatted mindlessly a little more before the question about how I knew him came up. I froze—the fear paralyzed me in a way that I hadn't felt since the time my mother caught me reading her red-covered romance novels when I was ten. Not even the unobstructed Florida sun could warm the chill that seized my body. I goose-pimpled, I could feel my nipples harden against the cotton of my t-shirt. I blinked, attempting to think of just how this should be answered.

I certainly couldn't tell her that he and I met through a friend at *that* place where we'd met. I couldn't tell her that he'd spent the last fourteen nights in my bed. I couldn't tell her that, after playing one-on-one basketball twenty-two days before, we had taken a not-so-innocent shower together, mutually agreeing to our mastery of the art of soap dropping. I couldn't tell her about the planned tennis matches that never made it to the courts. I couldn't tell her that we had made a habit of taking long lunches together that did not include lunch. I couldn't tell her that he was the topic of thirty-three sappy poems that I'd written in thirty days.[26] I couldn't tell her that he was the reason that I smile and sweat and—still in that smitten stage—breathe. Between blinks, all I could think of was what I couldn't tell her.

With a whistle came the thaw and he was beside me. They had won their first game. He asked if I had gone to the library yet and, in the process, provided the out that I needed. "I'm gonna go now." I reached deep into the cooler, grabbed a water, and handed it to him. I smiled at my new girlfriends as I pulled on both straps of my backpack and started off. I'm still not sure if my non-answer was implicating or vindicating, but at least it was liberating. I waved myself off as I set off on my quest for the library.

---

26 Hoping for authenticity, the reproduction of the practice of peering into the unknown results in a withering of the aura of the work of art (Mechanical Reproduction 4).

As I reached the scrub-pine shrubbery that marked the beginning of the path out of the football-field area, I paused. I looked back and saw, running back and forth and around in a chaotic frenzy, the boys and girls of my consternation. I could make out pectorals and belly buttons, shoulders and sweaty tufts of dark underarm hair. Briefly, they were all the same: perfect in form, mere bodies. In varying states of undress and almost uniformly Davidian and Hellenic, the interplay between these distant and now faceless moving statues reminded me of the civilization that I had escaped. Long ago I had walked away from the footballs and the blankets, knowing that I could—at best—visit each in short spurts; my real place was between them or watching from fifteen feet away. The fact that I was ripping him from this civilization, this carefree existence of sweat and play, chilled me anew. The fifteen feet became a football field's length and then I was on the pine-needled path with a new and unpopulated clearing ahead of me.

I watched my feet for a bit. I thought about walking: not so much the theory of walking or its metaphysical implications as the process of walking. I watched one foot go before the other and just as quickly be overtaken. I thought about how gravity is both fought and used with each step. Perhaps it did grow into the metaphysical.

Suddenly deciding to eschew the library for a clearing by a retention pond called—in this manicured and planned nature—a lake, I plopped down on the ground. Once again, I removed my shirt and embraced the earth, bare-bellied. I reached into the backpack and found my solace, my journal. I caught the moment with a thirty-fourth sappy poem. I channeled Longfellow channeling Hart Crane channeling Walt Whitman. It was all clouds and sunsets and bodies and hope.[27]

I yawned and felt the swirl of alcohol and marijuana acting upon

---

27 More plainly, the oscillation between the individual and the social and between concentration and distraction provide divergent narratives of "what follows" the image toward language.

my now inactive body. The flying oblongata, the pinks and Greeks, the penalty yardage, the anxieties that had less to do with winning or losing than with being accepted into the game all faded away. I superextended my toes and fingers and flexed my calves and then balled into one giant fist and released. The journal sat by my head as I rolled onto my back and felt no chill. I felt no heat. The promise of today was being realized in this moment as I closed my eyes and I could see the pink of the sun in my eyelids. Critters—microscopic and some a little larger—danced on my legs, chest, underarms, and head in a rhythm that both tickled and soothed. The morning sun crept higher in the sky and only his presence could complete this moment.

Not knowing how long he had been there nor how long I'd slumbered, I leaned up on my elbows and saw him: chin on fist, elbows on knees, sitting on the cooler and holding a beer.

"We lost."

Summing up our mutual love for sport, and the acknowledgment that we, in the face of our anxieties, were consciously forming a new team—for our own game—I responded: "I love…football."

PRINCESS

"I can't believe she's gone!"

"Huh?"

"Oh, you're awake?"

"Well, of course I am now."

"I still can't believe she is gone. I just can't believe it." His eyes were glistening while mine rolled. He had been watching TV coverage for the five hours since we got home. It was now six in the morning and the CNN coverage showed no signs of abating. Neither did his apparent ability to consume every endless minute of that coverage.

At this point, craving little more than a water and some hang-over-reducing Advil, I decided upon the least-resistant course, which meant not indulging in the million ways to say "Shut the fuck up and go to sleep, you crazy fuck!" and instead feigning emotional complicity. "I can't believe it either," I mumbled almost barfing on my lie. I did believe it; he had awakened me every thirty minutes since I tried to pass out to give me an update. I knew unequivocally that it was fact. CNN, NBC, CBS, and ABC had all confirmed it; what was there to not believe? What I wanted to say was that "I don't care. Now come over here and blow me."

"It really is a loss."

"Such a loss." For some reason, I felt increasingly compelled to comfort him in this, the darkest moment of his life up until the day his Nanny died. I turned my attention in the direction of his gaze, toward the television. The looping video of red flashing lights abounded and filled the room. I imagined I was still at the concert from the night before, listening to the "The artist formerly known as..." sing his signature tunes. I hummed a riff of "Nineteen ninety nine" in my head as I flashed forward to the present and watched him hugging himself, rocking forward and backward on the edge of the bed. He started crying again. I wished for doves to appear and relieve me of my melodramatic misery.

"She was the 'People's Princess'," he repeated Wolf Blitzer's corny commentary.

"It's true," I agreed. I did agree with this.

"And those poor boys...orphans."

"Technically, they are not orphans," I couldn't resist the opportunity to tamp down on the spiraling drama. "They still have a father who, independent of this, happens to be the next King of England."

The response landed with the thud I expected, but I was self-satisfied for a moment.[28]

"He is a horrible ugly monster." He won that round. "They might as well be orphans."

By this point I knew that I was up for the long haul and that slumber would elude me for the near future, at least until the coverage paused.

I rolled out of bed, made a horrifyingly unappreciated big deal of arranging the unattended morning wood in my boxers—was gorgeously invisible—and slogged into the kitchen where I grabbed a Michelob Light and some pain reliever. I would need both of these to make it through what promised to be an excruciatingly long morning.

We had been boyfriends for over a year and had already moved on from the monotony of monogamy to drinking buddies. He was

---

28 We are all cosmologists concurrently seeking the universe in ourselves through the reproduction of this training in the post-hermeneutic scientific arts. We concentrate upon our initial point of inquiry, the subjected Type 1A Supernova, and become subject doubled as we are distracted by the life around us.

adorable, if not a handful. I found that ignoring the fact that I knew he had hooked up with other guys wasn't difficult. I expected that, at some point soon, he would be forced to overlook the same improprieties on my end. I had no reason to expect that we wouldn't be together forever; we dwelt nicely together on each others' arms. When we had sex it was fun. When we didn't, it was ok too.

The currently recounted hysteria notwithstanding, I loved him. When I looked in his brown eyes and when I touched his curly auburn hair, I was reminded. When we sat side by side slamming Jaeger or lied side by side in my bed, spooning, it was confirmed as unmitigated truth.

Just the day before, a mutual friend intimated that he had hooked up with him. I had no reason to disbelieve, but was generally unfazed. I allowed our friend to suck me off as penitence. That's how it worked. That's how we worked.

I returned to the bedroom with two beers. I decided to make the best of the situation. I dove into his soul and forced a compassionate tear as I untopped a bottle for him and handed it in his direction. He took it and looked at me with deeply emotional, silent thanks. I played silent connect the dots with the freckles on his cheeks.

I kissed him on the cheek. "You OK?"

For the first time, and certainly not the last, he explained to me his desire to be a princess. He told me about the way his parents loved each other. He told me that he wanted that. I wanted that for him. He had been watching the relationship of Diana and Charles since "The Wedding." I was not sure if he was regurgitating trivia he had heard over the last several hours or if he had genuinely watched them with the intensity that he seemed to exude.

Though we had never actually discussed this topic, it made perfect sense that he would be so engrossed. He wanted a fairy tale. Though I wasn't sure I could provide it, or that I was worthy of such fantasy, I knew he should have it. I knew that he would.

He went on to tell me about her work with AIDS victims, her friendship with Mother Theresa and Sister Elton. He talked about landmines and the children whose obliterated limbs attested to the need for a Princess who'd champion such a worthy and overlooked cause. He talked about Will and Harry. He told me about Lady Parker Bolles with the unabated disdain and personal torture of a woman scorned. He elaborated on glass slippers and lacy, sequined trains.

On into the morning, he persisted. I tarried.

A six pack past dawn, and as a weatherman finally broke into the story with the first Doppler radar reading of the cycle, we knew that thunderstorms would keep us in the house all day.

I ordered a pizza, threw "Purple Rain" into the CD player, and laid beside him for the long haul. We killed a twelve pack and a large pepperoni. We recounted the high points of the previous evening's concert, our mutual love for royalty, and agreed that storybooks needn't be fiction. We had sex. We did not disclose our mutual knowledge of each others' failings. I told him I loved him back.

By noon he was asleep in my arms as I cried by myself for a Princess that I would never know. I kissed his head as he snored.

Twenty years later, when his name remained a green cursive tattoo on my chest,[29] when I was little more than the "boyfriend formerly known as..." he called me when my grandmother passed away, "You okay?"

I cried by myself for a Princess who I would never be.

---

29 Concurrently, we are distracted from the life around us in our concentration upon the dense celestial forms we see in our past: "A man who concentrates before a work of art is absorbed by it...the distracted mass absorbs the work of art" (Mechanical Reproduction 16).

TANGENCY TWO:
ARACHNE

Silken sac unfilled
   -unleashed—upon my heart.
Arachne's gift—or curse—
   Web-spinning: useless art.
Eighty-eight-thousand
   Legs scamper through my veins,
Clog my gut, unbarren
   Tiny, unmused pangs.
Subdermal critters feast,
   Eating from inside out.
Flesh threatening to burst,
   Unnatural, unholy bout.

If only they could speak,
   These, rampant, soulless things.
Instead, I'm but their host—
   Their meal,
That only self-same pyre
   Might heal—
     Arachne stings.

MOMENTITIOUS ONE

BLOOM[30]

JUST A FEW MILES PAST NW 13ᵀᴴ AVE, OFF OF HIGHWAY 441, OUT IN the muddy groves, alive with bumblebee dancing, mosquito buzzing, and the pungent sweetness of orange blossoms spilling their pollen on the moist ground, only the sun knows the tools and antics of carefree adolescence: tepid canned beer, skunky marijuana, big-tired pickup trucks with springy bench seats and rusty beds, and Alan Jackson classics. While each of these might fill particular boyish needs within a vacuum-packed universe of fledgling masculinity, their amalgamation beneath the red-hot knowing sky makes an indefatigable alloy which even the strongest common decencies does not pierce.

And so it was, this first day after graduation, when the most decent thing he knew other than his blessed Nana wandered into his sight. As if she had fused with the sun that sat upon her saturated blonde locks, he marveled at her gait, more steadfast than the sturdiest steed. More sure than the Bible, and more upright than Ms. Apple—his second grade teacher and first real crush—she approached with a certitude of a thousand trumpeting hosts. Shoulders back, hips perfectly square, and seeming to hover over the ground even as her feet sank sole-deep into the living black mud, she was

---

30 *Due to publisher's guidelines related to sexual content, this story has been altered from its original version. To access the original, visit www.Momentitiousness.com.*

glorious—angelic. She walked with a gracefulness that betrayed her eighteen years.

He hid his smile in his pocket behind a warm can of Pabst Blue Ribbon and pretended not to see her, his squinting eyes betraying him all the time. He flicked his roach into the trees to his left and exhaled a cloud of wheezing smoke in the opposite direction. His eyes adjusted to the apparition walking his way, she carrying the weight of every cirrus cloud in the cornflower sky upon her shoulders like a lacy shawl. He coughed hello as the fleeting cannabis vapor sputtered and dissipated.

He had been here hundreds of times in his life, always accompanied by his buddies. Her appearance shattered boundaries, threw off trajectories, usurped orbits. Like an asteroid colliding with his home planet, this creature from the heavens threatened to break off a piece of him, to splinter off a moon for which his rising tide was not ready to swell beneath. She did not belong here. Nevermind, here was her birthright as the only child heir to the family business.

Hers was the realm of confined space: high school classes where they gazed at each other from across the room, church pews where they held hands in grace, Sunday evening dining room tables where their feet touched while her parents and his Nana passed the cornbread and gravy. She was to remain behind the safety of doors, where walls contained her purity and where windows occasioned passing opportunities to glance into the wild. Hers was the realm of the indoors and she had no rightful calling to the groves—his groves—his outdoors.

The rumble of a distant gas-guzzling pickup truck mixed with the sloshing of its knobby tires on the wet ground. This mixed with the cacophony of soprano to bass—seventeen- and eighteen-year-old voices changing and unchanging in an instant—hollers and rambunctious hoots.

Tossing aside his beer and steeling his pinking complexion back from the sun, he said hello and walked toward her. He removed and replaced his ballcap, straightened his hair in between, caught a whiff of his own sweaty musk, and was fleetingly embarrassed. This was a man's scent, he convinced himself, forcing off the uncertainty with bravado. She came into focus. He perspired as she glistened. The rows of trees provided walls that held her in and pushed her forward, though no doors, windows, or ceiling even contained her. She was corralled and striding forward unimpeded as he stumbled in her direction. She was as alive and vivacious in his space as he was clumsy and disoriented in her presence.[31] The rebel yells and sloshing mud continued. The smell of 85 octane gasoline filled the air.

He wanted to reach out and grab her in that way which he—in the fourteen months of their innocent courtship—still hadn't. He wanted to take her hand in his, like his Nana had done for him when he was still all peach fuzz and knees. He wanted to shed his alloy armor and hold her with all his might, to forsake his beer and marijuana and Chattahoochee and pickup truck. He wanted to hold her like a man holds a woman. He wanted to be in her walls, in her bosom, in her eyes, passing collection baskets, and singing hymns, and glancing out through bay windows as the leaves on oaks turned from baby green to emerald then yellow then brown. He wanted to be in her world, not her in his and he wanted to shout it out to her and whisper it in her ear from the most intimate place in his soul.

But he tripped, ungracefully falling to his knees. Then prostrate, he remained, as she continued to float toward him. He worked to right himself as she bent over and stretched toward him. "Hello," he managed again. "Hey," she rejoined.

He scooted onto his butt and wiped his muddy hands on his already muddy, stretched out t-shirt; he fixed his hat again as he gazed

---

31 Stephen Boughn and Robert Crittenden reported in the January, 2004 issue of Nature, that, "observations of distant supernovae and the fluctuations in the CMB indicate that the expansion of the universe may be accelerating under the action of a 'cosmological constant' or some other form of 'dark energy'."

upon her porcelain face. Her voice never faltered. "I figured you'd be out here."

"Ya."

"I'm sorry."

"I know."

He sensed—he knew damn well— they were not alone. "Go on," he shouted into the sticky air. His probably unheeded order to the dwellers in the adjacent rows was not aimed at any specific person but could just as easily have applied to all the demons on earth. Only the trees and crickets responded with a rustle and a chorus. The sky was pitching toward lavender and the sun was calling the moon. A beer can flew overhead, leaving a comet-like trail of stale beer in its wake. Pickup trucks rumbled off into a faint hum.

Without notice, she began to quit her clothes. With the ferocity of an uncaged animal, he repeated. "I'm sorry." Her eyes dampened and her breathing labored.

"Not like this," he whimpered. "Not like this, please."

She would not relent. The glint of her eyes turned to fire, ignited by that strange combination of liberty and guilt. Her clothes in a pile beside her, the last rays of sun crowning her, and in the midst of a million unripe oranges in the groves that her great grandparents first planted, she pushed the powerless man-boy to the ground as she parted his lips with her tongue.

At first fighting to remain upright and seated, then allowing himself to be pushed onto his back—his torso tense, he succumbed to her insatiable ambition as he reciprocated the passionate kisses. She entwined her fingers in his as she forced them over his head, knocked off his hat with her own forehead, and continued to flatten herself against him. Her breasts to his chest, her hips to his, breathing the same air, and rubbing her thighs against his still-buttoned jeans, she reached under his muddy shirt with one hand, then the other. With a deftness that betrayed her innocence, his shirt was off and his back was bare against the cool ground. His now free hands wrapped around her bare back, just below her shoulder blades

"OK." He surrendered.

Just the night before, he was at a wake for his Nana.

This same girl was with him, cold and distant, jealous and unsure of herself in the face of his sorrow.

He wept for the only woman—person—he had ever loved. His no-good mother left him with his grandmother before he could remember. His father left before that. The crown of glory sat upon his Nana's head alone, and he was barren without her. The suddenness of his loss was matched only by the calamitous emptiness in his being.

He only wanted a cinnamon-scented hug and all this girl could give was her unscented insecurity.

Now, it appeared, the ice had melted into a boiling sensual rage.[32] Her body continued to writhe against him as her kisses became deeper and her breathing shallow.

He felt no passion, just fear. He wriggled beneath her, adjusting himself as she ground on top of him. With muddy fingers, she pushed herself into chataranga, then straddled him as she traced a line from between his downy pecs, to his stomach, and into his loose fitting jeans.

He sighed what might have seemed his last as his eyes rolled back beneath his closed eyelids. He couldn't resist, nor could he prove—or even feign—disinterest as the physical betrayal of his battered soul grew even larger and firmer in her tiny hands. She forced off his jeans and boxers without unbuttoning them and wrapped both hands around the mass of his throbbing, blooming youthfulness. Unsheathed, she climbed upon it and screamed as it entered her. A woman of forty would have screamed. Instinctively, he tensed, forcing himself in. He could not stop, she would not let him. They settled into a rhythm that lasted only seconds. He opened his eyes as he reached climax, pouring light into her undulant, windowless

---

32 This "dark energy" accounts for some two-thirds of our universe.

space. Orange blossoms quivered around them as the smell of blood and bleach and musk pooled in damp topsoil mixed with the faint memories of flat beer, skunky pot, and unrecoverable cinnamon and saline tears.

She collapsed on top of him as he continued rocking, digging her fingers into his bare shoulders. When finally he exhaled again, they both lay limp, covered in mud and crying. She rolled off of him and remained on her back beside him. Now, only their fingers touched and that faintly, almost obligatorily.

Insatiate, he rolled back on top of her, still throbbing grandly. The tears which had not rolled behind his ears dried on his cheeks. Wordlessly, he grabbed both of her hands and pinned them beneath his. From above, his body was considerably larger than hers. He kissed her neck as he slowly penetrated her, still wet from his first foray.

The second and third times—uninterrupted by rest or contemplation—were bliss as his empty sorrow became sanctified beneath the fruit of the fertile groves, in the cool mud of the summer, and in the body of an angel. The cosmos was reborn and the boundaries between inside and outside seemed much smaller than the moon upon the tides.

When finally the sun set and the sounds of the groves changed from critter buzzing to a light rain, they moved up to the rusty bed of his pickup truck. Neither dared speak. Where romantics might have expected a shooting star as they gazed through the broken yet still-misting clouds, a hailstorm of empty beer cans instead flew overhead, one landing beside their feet. As they lay naked there, using their muddy clothes as sheets, nearby footsteps rushed into the distance, punctuated by audible teenaged-boys' whispers, then hoots, then a stampede of other, more puckish, steps into the night.

A loud truck engine boomed to life in what must have been the next row over and sped off toward what was quite likely another beer run.

MERRY GO ROUND

ADORED BY HIS ELDERS FOR HIS BUOYANTLY TOOTHY SMILE AND HIS effervescent laughter, his dark brown eyes were always alight with a playfulness that glimmered through any darkness. His tan skin drooped around his soft limbs in a way that made shopping for stylish clothes especially difficult. He was the unwitting butt of silly jokes delivered by his more athletic peers about his attention to fashion: jokes that always thudded around his awkward huskiness and thick-lensed horn-rimmed glasses. Despite the derisive attention from some classmates which he interpreted with naïve pride as popularity, he carried himself with a sense of assuredness that most slightly effeminate young boys never enjoy.

Dough-faced and always attended by girls, he spent most recesses cheering on others in fifth-grade pursuits such as monkey-barring, basket-balling, and soccer-playing. Neither was he averse to nor incapable of drawing smiley faces on the math papers he handed in. His favorite doodle decoration was the caterpillar which he drew with intricate attention to detail, often placing high-top sneakers on each of the many feet he gave it. His disposition was aloofly and goofily bright, certainly brighter than it should have been.

He connected with the girls in a way that no other boys did. Although he bordered on being epicene and was thoroughly unathletic, his male classmates were ever cognizant of his charisma which stoked their ire; their crush-objects were always more charmed by passing lunch and recess with him than with them.

In the pantheon of pre-adolescent events, when scents and hairs appear unexpectedly and in the most inconvenient places, one of the few joys is the first kiss. Of all the boys in his class, he was the first to receive one. It came from a blushing strawberry blonde and he had no reason to know that she had done so on a dare from a group of his male detractors. Oblivious to the setup, he allowed that he could be kissed, when another group of boys in cahoots with the first similarly incited *his* participation in the act. Both were convinced by their respective pranksters that the other was hopelessly head over heels. She liked it much more than he did. She allowed his soft touch of her virgin lips to stir the earliest sensations of smittenness that a girl can experience.

He, rather coldly, wore the experience as little more than a badge of accomplishment: a mechanical act not much different from drinking strawberry Quik milk or eating a peanut-butter-and-grape-jelly sandwich. Fully aware of the significance of the act,[33] he knew the requisite outward social responsibilities of being the first boy in the class to spoil a girl. On his heart, where it could have mattered, the event was neither tender nor touching; he had merely kissed a girl. Her budding femininity bestirred, her takeaway was intrinsically different. Behind the tallest oak tree in the farthest, shade-speckled corner of the playground, she had fallen in fifth-grade love.

Before he knew it and before he could deny it, they were "going out."

When, three days later, he decided that he was too independently cool to be tied to one girl, he let her know that the romance had soured in the easiest way that an eleven-year-old knows: by

---

33 While we have long known that there is much we do not know about the time/space/matter ingredients that comprise the night beyond night, the concentration of the WMAP lenses along with other ongoing and presaging studies confirm that there is something which we do not know but that we can name.

kissing her best friend on the merry-go-round before school. In this simple pair of acts, he was self-elevated in the projected esteem of his class to a level that would find no equal, and practically no duration. Equally unmoved by the second lip-to-lip peck as he was by the first, he once again scrambled to solidify opinions and to create the stir that a two-timer demands among a group of eleven- and twelve-year-old classmates. He knew that this should make up for his patent inability to cross the monkey bars without falling, to make more than one in ten undefended basketball shots, or to never beat anybody other than his little brother at tetherball. All of that schoolyard hopscotching in which none of his male peers ever partook had paid off and was justified by these two pairs of parted lips. None of the other boys in the class had one girlfriend and he had already amassed two. In his perception, his oddly errant mas-culinity had, out of nowhere, been affirmed. He stood as a pudgy totem to the failures of his peers.

In forsaking all other topics, and turning each interaction to-ward his self-aggrandizing dilemma, he sought the advice of his school brothers. As boys of this age are infinitely better at teas-ing or ignoring than communicating or respecting, they decided to display chilled apathy sprinkled with passing cruelty about his drama. These responses found their manifestations in descriptions of each girl's respective shortcomings: she's fat; she's freckly; she's short; she has—in the most disgustingly mean way—red hair. "I'd rather be dead than kiss red on the head," claimed one fledgling poet. Another, in attempting to steal the moment, claimed that he had, in fact, kissed one of them two weeks ago. He veiled the un-corroborated claim in mystery, not detailing which one of the girls he had kissed.

He took all comments in with much more earnestness than the multiple "who cares" that peppered the short-lived conversations. Early in the day, his male classmates' opinions oscillated between feigned awe and complete disinterest. By the end of the day, the boys had wholly forsaken his quandary and abandoned him in his need for male advice on the matter. They had baseball practice, slumber parties, and fort-building to plan for the weekend. As usual, he was not included in any of these plans and was forced to retreat to the girls around him for guidance.

He didn't "love" either of the girls. He knew that. He explained this quite matter-of-factly to the female tribes that formed. He lacked the words and capacity for introspection to capture the nuances of his feelings. He "liked them both okay," he continued to any girl who would listen, but just didn't "love either of them." In his heart, a heart that was certainly of the age capable of puppy-loving, even "like" was an overstatement. That statement—repeated at least twenty times between lunch and the final bell— was the best he could do to capture the words that he felt should have been on his heart.

There were no particular stirrings within him from either kiss, though he did prefer the flavor of the strawberry balm that the ginger had planted on his lips to the vanilla of the second. As he cackled with the girls whose abundance of opinions outweighed the paucity of that received from the less fair sex, his eyes wandered their young faces. He wondered if there was a chocolate option (such a pair of lips could make him a one-girl man). He was being torn in two sub-ideal directions by the throw-away sections of a Neapolitan candy.

There was no dearth of sentiments on the matter among the girls. Most of these opinions were guided, of course, by the jealousies that swirl among clans of this age. He was strangely attractive, in an inarticulately carnal way, to every girl whose counsel he sought. They wanted to taste him, to know his sweet kiss. Some, whose small breasts hid behind training bras, wanted something even more from him. In groups, they chided his callousness. When cornered one-on-one, they reveled in the opportunity to whisper in his ear and smell his awkward musk.

"You must follow your heart,"[34] profoundly—with the earnestness of purpose learned from Oprah Winfrey, or was it Dora?—nodding heads would agree when he stood in the center of girl groups.

"But I like you," was the advice he heard privately from no less than three of his insidiously unhelpful female advisors. These nearly blossomingly sensual girls loitered in his aura longer than he could stand, and none smelled even remotely of chocolate. One surreptitiously pecked his cheek as she lit away. "Three," he thought to himself. He passively sighed as she floated away in the immediate memory of their fleshy tangency.

He found that the theater which surrounded the entire episode suited his disposition well. As he handed in that day's spelling test, he took extra time to pencil two plump hearts on either side of his name. Of course he made a point of holding it up high so that both girls (and anybody else who happened to be watching him) could see it as he submitted it to the stone-faced and quietly oblivious teacher. She smiled when she saw the hearts, feigning indignity at what she interpreted as a sweet, awkward, unrequited crush upon her. Her eyes perused his young, lumpy figure as he walked back to his desk, lingering at the lower hem of the high-cut corduroy shorts he wore. Without grading the test, she knew that he had—as always—scored one hundred percent. No caterpillars today, she noticed. Even with imperfect information, she knew that no girl would ever distract him from his academic excellence.

After a day-long flurry of note-passing, mediation, posturing, and conniving, the young player was finally lured, in the afterschool playground, back to the scene of the second smooch to do the "right thing." He was, guided by some unarticulated ideology, profoundly interested in doing just that: the "right thing." Lurking around, but

---

34 We do not know what it is, but it has a form and it has properties and it has much that follows. Dark energy, it is posited by some cosmologists, is the contra-gravitational force that has sped up the expansion of the universe since it unhinged time and space at the moment of the Big Bang.

not at the round sand pit, clusters of children loitered in the after-school glow of a scorching-hot, clear Thursday. The faint smell of diesel fuel from the parade of school buses hung in the air. Whistles and hydraulic brakes and children's carefree voices were an appropriate backdrop for the serious moment.

He saw the girls walking up together, hand in hand, and knew that the heart-wrenching reckoning was upon him. He did not see that the girls had emerged from a hooting tribe of boys and girls. He only saw them appear before him, as though they had materialized from the far-off, viscous gases of the bright sun. Stern-faced, they neared. He watched his feet as he kicked around the white sand, alternately building piles and smoothing them.

"Hi," he started, as he forced a smile that usually worked well on his elders. He squinted as he took his glasses off to reduce the glare from the sun.

In a flash, both girls had scooped up a handful of sand and thrown it at him from three feet away. Sand in his eyes and mouth, and caught too off guard to speak, he watched in awe as the pale and freckled fist of the redhead hurled toward his face. One punch thrown and one punch landed, he experienced the sound of tiny bones cracking, immediately followed by the shrillest scream he had ever heard. Ginger stood there, suddenly crying. Her best friend bolted back toward the sun, and he reached for his numb now throbbing cheek.

"Huh?" was all he could muster as his attempts to make sense of the scene through the sandy sheen was distracted by the tears and deafening sobs of his short-termed former paramour. He rubbed his face as she held her fisted hand with the other in obvious pain.

Her broken finger took weeks longer to heal than his black eye. The small slit on his lip faded in just a few days. The friendship between the girls, the one that pre-dated the incident and that was re-kindled just long enough to exact the horrifying schoolyard revenge, never recovered. Their final unified moment was that day and, even as they would eventually go on to different junior highs and high schools, they continued in their mutual enmity for each other long into the same college where they were in the same sorority vying for drunken fraternity boys to humiliate.

In the wake of the awful path blazed by this incident, many young boyfriends were affirmed by young girlfriends' kisses. While he may not have been the best at it, he was the first among his peers to make contact with the lips of a girl. He was also the first, as the fading purple bruise below his right eye and the related horizontal scab above it attested—the very first—to wear the wounds of love's battles.

ARBITRAGE

ARISING FROM A MIST OF AFTERNOON COITUS, HE ROLLED OUT OF the bed and acknowledged that she did not. Neither of them was naked from the waist up. Neither of them was clothed from the waist down. Still in her day blouse, her hair tussled with itself for order. Lying on her back, her chest heaved with labored breath and her bare pelvis clenched around an only slight black strip. Her arms lay outstretched over her resting head and hands disappeared beneath the pillow. She wanted to speak, clearly had much to say, but muted herself instead.[35] She had learned, through years of similar scenes—the faces change and the drapes are always different—that no good can ever come from speaking at this moment.

Instead, she remained still, save her undulating chest and fidgety toes, and watched him dress. His task was simple. He never even removed his tie, nor loosened it. As he bent over in the space wide enough for a small single-drawer nightstand between the side of the bed and the shade-drawn window to grab his pants, she admired his peach-fuzzy butt. She admired the tuft of light blonde hair that radiated softly from the top of his sweaty intergluteal cleft and disappeared behind his shirttail. She followed the hair downward across his cheeks and watched it clump more thickly as it wandered down

---

35 Expanding at an ever-increasing rate, the universe races flatly
    outward, threatening to explode our extant conceptions: mate-
    rial and otherwise.

his muscular legs, disappearing behind the blue argyle socks he'd already pulled up. To occupy her mouth in this moment, she exchanged her unspoken words for a grin and contented herself with that. Her eyes traced over every bit of his flesh she could see. She wanted him again right now. His back still to her, he pulled up his trousers, leaving his spottily wet boxer shorts—he had used them to clean up—on the ground. Fundamentally hurried, he had to get back to an important meeting with the Partner.

Finally, he turned back toward her as he worked to tuck in his shirt and then fidgeted with his tie. He smiled, unsure of what to say or how to say it. Certainly, he did not love her. Even if he did, he knew this was not the time to say such things. He enjoyed the sex and would likely have obliged her again had he not needed to return to his office. This was not the first afternoon "meeting" they had scheduled together. Their association through work made the complexity of the situation all the more poignant. For him, it was carnally complicated. For her it was dramatically so. In either case, they both brought their own suppositions to the bed where they dropped them off in a pile with their underwear. In both cases, they dragged those complications back toward their business district commonplace with them.

The first time they hooked up was in a water closet at the hotel where the company holiday party was held. Alcohol was involved and the activity grew more out of a dare than out of actual attraction. They endured beyond the festivity's bitter end when most of their co-party attendees had deserted the hall. They found their way into the hotel lounge where they kept their party going.

"I bet you won't do another shot."

Shot. "Two more, buddy."

"I bet you won't kiss my ass."

Smirk. He dropped beside the barstool on which she sat and planted one, loud and playful, upon her black-velvet-covered derriere. He couldn't help but notice how high her dress was hiked, and how much of her thigh was exposed. Nice legs, he thought, for an older girl.

"I bet you won't kiss *my* ass."

Slam down shot glass. Pushing a dangling clump—the time for attention to her appearance had long passed—of hair out of her eyes, she slid off her stool and playfully slunk down beside him. She steadied herself by wrapping her hand over his high inner thigh as she exaggeratedly puckered her pink lips to kiss his black-wooled outer thigh. He watched her fingers lurch toward his crotch as her face bubbled toward his ass.

"I bet you won't do another shot."

They were already queued up. He did his as she climbed back on her seat. Hers remained untouched. He decided that he would not let her drink anymore. He wanted her conscious.

He leaned toward her and whispered in her ear. "I bet," he paused and looked around and lowered his voice a little more before continuing in a whisper. "I bet you won't suck my dick."

She fell toward him, not out of shock, but in a not-so-smooth attempt to return her hand to its previous location on his crotch. Wordlessly, she led him, stumbling, into the unisex stall in the back of the bar where she proceeded with much acuity to answer his challenge.

She left immediately from there, not returning to the bar. She was far too disheveled, she surmised, to face anybody else other than her driver. In actuality, she had reached that point at least an hour earlier. He, on the other hand, was required by man-right, to make a victory lap around the bar and achieve some acknowledgment from some male—any male—of what he had just achieved. Because the lounge was completely empty save the bartender, the implied obligatory fist bump came from him. They did a shot together and he paid the tab with a decent tip. He was near enough to walk home and he took the opportunity to smoke a cigarette on the way.

He walked to the foot of the bed and gave her a winning smile, the same one he had used on countless girls in college and high school. The same one he'd used on two professors and his uncle's girlfriend once. He was young and dashing and oozed sexuality. His short-cropped blonde hair and ultra-clean-shaven face only magnified his Puck-like demeanor. He was the office darling and the rising star. Everybody under forty nine wanted him. Everybody over fifty wanted him to be their son in law. For all of the sex he oozed, he played it cool. He never let on that he was a sex machine and always feigned embarrassment at even slightly off-color conversation. He could blush on demand and always made an obvious scene when such topics drove him from a room or an office.

She smiled back.

She rolled onto her side and reached down to pull the goose-down comforter over her legs. Her white thigh, dimpled, was still exposed. Her breathing had returned to normal and her coffee-brown eyes had returned to their standard size around her irises.[36] She watched him and maintained her silence, subscribing to the age-old sales technique, "Whoever speaks first, loses." She knew she had it on him. He was far too gregarious—and young—to outlast her. His smile, she knew, was a defensive technique. He was using his perfect teeth to cage his words. She lightly slid her maroon-painted fingernails up and down her exposed torso, searching for an imaginary itch, though not scratching at anything in particular. She closed her eyes as she rolled her head back-long over the pillow, smoothing out the tiny creases that age had been carefully painting on her neck. She dozed off.

She opened her eyes with a start and he was gone.

Each of them had sex with somebody else the day before: she, her husband; he, her husband—neither of them knowing of the others'

---

36 And yet, we see it as we gaze into the past, shutter-clicking our way back from image to language. At least we have named it. We are represented in our own subjective place within the universe

actions and only missing each other by minutes. Although she had only slept with these two men in the past two years, he had three additional other partners just this week—all women.

He had a knack for falling into situations in which women wanted him and he was, given there was a handy location for it, never ever unwilling to oblige. Living alone in the heart of the city, a studio though it was, provided the most reasonable and convenient place for sex. If necessary, however, he would and had shared himself in bathroom stalls (both men's and women's), building rooftops, stairwells, subway stops, dorm rooms, church baptismal fonts, hotels, motels, mortuary parlors, back seats, front seats, vans, benches, showers, tubs, convertibles, sedans, roadsters, pickup truck beds—well, every style and configuration of automobile, including motorcycles, subway cars, art galleries, an orange grove, elevators, beds, couches, tree houses, sectionals, ottomans, dining room tables, breakfast nooks, gardens, theme parks, Ferris wheels, front yards, backyards, pools, hot tubs, saunas, lakes, rivers, oceans, boats, mountain tops, stadium stands, football fields, a television news studio, an office (once—just the day before) and, in the middle of a crowded restaurant, he once allowed his date to jerk him off under the table while the waiter prepared bananas foster right by them.

In his most brazen act, he had full-on sex on the floor of the Chicago Mercantile Exchange during trading hours. Absorbed in their own activities, nobody else said a word, nor batted an eye. Though he'd never taken stock, nor even recognized some of the more obscure ones, he had done it on every single holiday, Christian and Jewish and, of course, on his birthday every year since he was sixteen.

His first experience was in the mud, the day after his grandmother died. His most memorable was with his Information Systems professor during office hours which she always held in the classroom immediately following lecture. He stayed behind when everybody else had left. It was a night class and there was nothing scheduled afterward. They shut the door and within minutes were going at it. He thought her loud, frenzied, and wild contortions were fits of orgasmic ecstasy. After he had come three times in rapid succession, he realized that she was having a seizure. When she came to, he wiped the drool off of her shoulder and allowed her to ride him to one more dribbling fit.

He loved sex and was really fucking good.

His one hard and fast rule, however, was "not a co-worker." Certainly, he reasoned, the boss was not a co-worker, but a boss. Neither was the boss's wife a co-worker. Thus, he had no rules against either bosses or their spouses, although—except for two incidents in college which together represented less than one percent of his total sexual experiences—he generally didn't consider sex with guys his thing. When one makes rules for themselves, however personally arbitrary they may be, they should be respected for following them. His commitment to these boundaries was inspirational. He was not beyond self-congratulation for his idealistic fortitude and was excessively judgmental about people who did not adhere to his standards. Knowing of several office romances, he would not even deign casual acquaintanceship with their perpetrators.

He arrived back at the office with about twenty minutes to spare before his planned meeting. Straight to his desk, he checked emails and portfolio updates. The office was mostly empty, the majority of his co-workers telecommuted on Fridays. Because he lived nearby and was prone to distraction when working from home, he always made it a point to come in five days a week. Quickly, he popped onto CNN for headlines and onto ESPN to check the Cubs score.

At the appointed time, he walked over to the Partner's office, lightly rapped on the closed door, and poked in his head first when he heard the invitation. He pulled the door fully shut and discovered that there was, in fact, a floor-to-ceiling window that faced out behind him. He had never noticed it from the other side, apparently—hopefully—one-sided. He watched the Chicago sky-line, completely still at this altitude save a few passing cumulus clouds, behind his boss's profile. The blunt blue of the sky outlined the head of the attractive older executive who sat on the other side of the heavy, slate-topped desk. Sitting down, he became suddenly conscious that he had no underwear on. He wiggled to adjust himself. He quickly dispelled the distraction and made himself comfortable,[37] stoically facing his boss.

"Listen, I've been working on this report. We are going to put your name on it."

Still still.

"I need you to study this frontwards and backwards and know it inside and out. I need you to really make it yours. When they ask, you'll need to own it, to be able to breathe it."

At twenty-six years old, still unwise about many things—politics especially—he could only respond with a silent beguilement. He mustered a nod and a grin as he reached to accept the neatly bound stack. He was still silent.

The man continued, putting on a smile for show. "I have worked too hard for this business to throw it all away. I cannot afford to lose all of this and my marriage also."

The shadow of a grin turned down and a flush washed over him.

"I'm making you manager."

The rapid oscillation between joy and consternation were tearing up his intestines. His head was swimming with responses, but his mouth was paralyzed. He continued to sit in unabated horror, as his eyes remained transfixed on the Partner.

"I let you fuck me once and, as God is my witness, you will never fuck me again."

---

37 We are threatened, every moment, with a force that tears our thoughts from our minds as the force of negative gravity works to tear our own planet apart and strew it like Uranus' rings about itself: each shutter click of our distraction a deafening bang.

He took a deep breath and stared directly into his Chillingworthian foe's eyes, transfixed.

And with that, the tension of the room was uncoiled, poignantly, almost climactically. For every bit of terror that filled the room just seconds earlier, they were both awash in the afterglow of release.

He looked down and fidgeted with "his" report, leafing through it, though not actually reading any of its words. He smiled his engaging smile as he felt the color return to his face and the feeling return to his fingertips. His adversary, the salt-and-peppered grey-eyed figure across the room stood and walked toward him with an outstretched congratulatory hand. He bore a genuine smile and exuded the acquitted confidence of a practicing and devout Catholic who had just completed a thousand Hail Marys and a million Our Fathers. He stood beside the still-seated newly promoted manager and put his hand on the broad shoulder which threatened to burst from the starched white shirt that covered it.

Together they looked out the window, again at the now-swaying skyline.

"Now, get to work, Son. This will all be yours one day."

Sexual energy charged through them both, one of longing, one more reciprocally empathic. Still, for another moment, they both smiled, one's eyes rolling up to see the slightly stubbled jaw of the other standing over him.

"And, I don't mind if you keep fucking my wife but I'm going to have to insist that, when she asks you, you tell her that you have crabs," his eyes remained transfixed on some distant point on the other side of the giant window behind his desk, "which you do."

MOMENTITIOUS TWO

SALE

I WAS A DEAL-SEEKING WARRIOR, SEARCHING ALWAYS FOR TREASURE on muggy Friday mornings in neighborhoods near and far. What began seven years ago as a quest for a cheap and disposable dining room set to adorn the breakfast nook in my new apartment morphed into an obsessive-compulsive activity, dominating my weekdays, crushing my weekends, and cluttering nearly every room in my home. From this description, you might think that I was somehow unhappy or dissatisfied with how I spent my life. In fact, the only real frustration that I derived from any of this lied in the insurmountable reality that there was only one Friday per week, and that there was only one first stop per Friday.

When, a few years ago (I remember the date April 19th, because it was exactly three years after the Oklahoma City bombing when my sister was killed), I told the proprietor of the restaurant where I worked—I was a manager at the busiest Outback Steakhouse in the state— that I wanted to cut back my hours, she looked at me with a quizzical expression that I wish to this day I had photographed. "You're well on your way to owning your own restaurant. You're willing to throw that away just to..."

I stopped her before she could complete her thought. A visible passion in my eyes stopped her before she could completely reduce my reality to the realm of the inane. I could tell she regretted saying "just" as soon as she uttered it.

Like the accountant who quits his job to hike the Appalachian Trail, like the magazine editor who quits her job to write a novel, like the pawnshop owner who closes his doors to undertake a retirement devoted to perfecting his fly-cast fishing technique, like the librarian who decides that his inner calling is performing Whitney Houston drag numbers, like the Gap manager who wants to go to culinary school, I wanted nothing more than to fish out items from others' trash heaps in hopes of finding a priceless gem.[38] She watched this obsession emerge and knew that I would not be happy without its fulfillment. She understood. She, too, had a similar moment years ago when she abandoned her vacuous twenties as an airline stewardess.

She also understood because she was with me, by my side, the day I first discovered this avocation. In fact, I was with her, at her unrelenting urging, when I visited my first yard sale. "Why do you want to go to a store and buy a brand new one when you can get a perfectly good one for pennies on the dollar?" she challenged me. "C'mon, it'll be fun."

She had recently divorced and was looking for ways to fill the camaraderie gap that had emerged. At the time, she managed and I bartended. We climbed slowly up the ranks, however close those ranks may have been, together. While she clearly earned her position of leadership by putting in long hours for paltry pay, doing a rotation in each department, and sleeping with the district manager, I gained my status through mere staying power. I was a good server and bartender, enjoyed the flexible hours, and genuinely liked people. I sat down once and figured out that my average hourly salary was thirty five dollars an hour. Granted, I only worked thirty hours per week, but that gave me more than enough to live on comfortably.

And so it was that combination of decent cash and lots of free time that made garage sale-ing possible. But it was that very first

---

38 Willemen and Ray (and others) fear "delirium" (Ray 35). Delirium ensues when distraction and concentration produce too many possibilities without anchors.

experience in the quest for the dining room set that made it magical. As it turns out, I never bought a set for my breakfast nook that day. I did, however, purchase—on a whim of sheer fancy—a baseball card collection at an estate sale of a family who had prematurely lost its only son to cancer.

Despite his bereavement, the father had apparently picked through the binders to confiscate the obviously valuable units. In his quest to cleanse himself of the memorial clutter, he did not pick carefully or deeply. I paid $65 for three 3-inch binders full of cards. This worked out to approximately eight cents per card. Though I never collected them myself, I had buddies who did when I was growing up. They were always talking about this and that card that they wished they had, or this or that card that they had just acquired. One of the names they discussed frequently was Barry Bonds. Not a baseball fan and certainly not a baseball card collector, the name didn't mean much to me except for its alliterative value. When I opened the first binder and flipped through to the middle, there he was: Barry Bonds. I decided that if he was there, certainly others were too. In a collection of nearly 1000 cards, I could at worst break even.

I slid headfirst into the research of these rectangular mementos. In short time, I came to think of the cards as nothing more than commodities in and of themselves; for me they were not a totem of some great ball player with a name like "Barry Bonds," but rather a piece of valuable cardboard, the "Bonds card." I mentally stripped the totem of any humanity.

I sold the Bonds card for $250, and I was told later that I could have sold it for more if I had gone to a baseball card convention or had acquired an agent. I had no interest in diluting my profits and opted instead for complete control of my new pastime. I split up the collection, finishing the task that the father had incompletely and hastily started. At the end of the decimation of the collection, I had turned my sixty-five-dollar whimsical and uneducated investment into nearly $4300. I became quite the baseball scholar, pouring through statistic books and traveling from pawn shop to pawn shop. Granted, the full divestiture took several months and consumed nearly every moment of my free time, but the return was intoxicating and addictive. I anticipated that I could retire in short order if I continued hitting such homeruns.

Before I sold the final remnants of the cancer victim's assemblage, I began hunting for other such collections.[39] I hunted out garage and estate sales week after week, looking only for card collections. None yielded anything close to the margin that my first foray brought. Nonetheless, as a starter, I turned about $600 into $6000 in my four months as a novice. In that time, I also found a marble-topped café table and two wrought iron chairs for my breakfast nook. Of course, I since sold the set, turning a profit of $200.

Over the ensuing several years, while still working at the restaurant, I developed a strategy for optimal sale-ing. Never one for current events, I began reading the paper each day.

On Sundays, I would scour the personal interest sections for each day in the previous week for weddings, deaths, promotions, divorces, and other such life-affirming or ending events. I would also check the legal notices for businesses closing, bankruptcies, foreclosures and building demolitions. I would then cross reference these names against addresses in the white pages.

On Mondays, I would map each of the addresses in their relative proximity to my home and chart a driving course through the city.

On Tuesdays, as I drove through these neighborhoods, I would look for dim lights in the target homes, inordinately large trash heaps, moving vans, and signs for upcoming sales. If, as I drove by, I saw a bustle in the yard or driveway that even remotely hinted at an unplanned asset liquidation, I would stop by. My car was always clean and I was always well groomed. Using the interpersonal skills that I had garnered and mastered through my years in the service

---

39 Delirium is the dark energy that threatens knowledge. Delirium is Milton's chaos recaptured, unleashed.

industry as a bartender and waiter, I built immediate rapport with the aggrieved or celebratory or sexually frustrated or down-on-their luck people I met. I got the story and the inside scoop on anything they might be getting rid of.

"Gosh," I would always start each sentence— I've discovered over the years that the Andy Taylor "Gosh," was much more disarming than the Gomer Pyle "Golly!" They would always divulge what they expected to be the gem of the treasure chest right off. I would continue by filling in the blank with a respectfully belittling description of what they had just told me about:

"Gosh, a 1977 280 ZX? That's old!" or

"Gosh, an old signed Madonna poster? When's the last time *she* put out an album?" or

"Gosh, a stack of vintage Playboys? You'd probably have to burn those." Or

"Gosh, a 1963 Spider Man comic book? Too bad they would never make a Spider Man movie like they did for Superman and Batman."

Followed by a "but," I would always have some relative or friend who might think it was cool or interesting or fun to have or a neat project to undertake:

"I have an uncle who's into fixing old cars."

"My niece really likes that Cyndi Lauper; I bet she'd like Madonna too."

"My neighbor would get a real kick out of those as a bachelor present."

"I think I just heard my wife mention that her little brother was into comic books."

I'm not even married.

Often, within ten or fifteen minutes of small talk and just seconds of negotiating, I would make the deal right then and there, offering condolences or congratulations as was appropriate. Folks didn't want to deal with the hassle. They were not thinking rationally—whether out of sadness, anger, or elation—and thus wrote away their potential windfalls in exchange for low frustration and pocket cash. Sometimes, in order to soften the blow and put the whole situation behind them, I would pick up the entire lot.

"Now, go enjoy your Saturday now that you don't have to do that stupid yard sale!"

In many cases, I made most of my purchases on Mondays and Tuesdays as I just described. I would round the cities and neighborhoods and mark the locales that I would return to on Friday morning. As it turned out, my fictitious friends and relatives were actually people that I had met at other sites and, through conversations, had given me a glimpse into their own wants and desires. On some days, I would leave one home and arrive at the next—sometimes just streets apart—and sell at an exorbitant profit what I had just loaded into my trunk. By displacing the traditional market, I reached buyers and sellers in a location where their defenses were down and their approach to transactions was as with neighbors rather than adversaries.

On Wednesdays, I would check the garage sale listings from the paper and use this opportunity to reach the sellers that I did not meet on Monday or Tuesday. I would cull the list based on marquee items and neighborhood. I learned quickly to avoid neighborhoods near schools or police stations. If a phone number was listed, I would make an appointment to visit before the sale started. I always carried cash, but always less than I needed. This strategy always saved me at least twenty dollars, lest the seller lose the deal because I had to leave to get cash out of the bank.

Thursdays were inventory and re-sale days. I always took Thursdays off from the restaurant because my Thursday activities were the most time intensive. In addition to the retail customers I could create on the fly during my sojourns, I developed a list of regular wholesale clients and re-sellers who I'd visit with my treasures. Knowing that they needed to turn a profit, I always allowed them to buy my goods at a slightly lower price than I knew they were worth. This strategy helped keep my inventory and overhead low, my cash flowing, and my market ready. I knew that if I allowed my customers to hit an occasional homerun that they would be somewhat more disarmed by my margins and do me the occasional "favor" of taking something off my hands.

I would also list individual "liner" ads for some of my marquee items. Rather than clump everything together, indicating a garage sale approach that solicited junk-seeking bargain shoppers, the one-line ads, strategically placed in specific "For Sale" sections of the classifieds sought specific buyers with specific desires. I would field these calls throughout the week and invite buyers to my home which was becoming, increasingly, a showroom. If I could entice someone to my home, I could sell them something.

Fridays were easy days. I was usually done with the garage sales by midmorning. I would rest up before I went into work at the restaurant on what was usually the busiest night of the week and I would always be behind the bar. Of course, I took the opportunity to broker deals between four-dollar margaritas and cold Budweisers. The best deal I ever entered into at the Outback was the one in which I bought my home.

A real-estate big shot got drunk fast on the double shots I was pouring him one Friday night about four years ago. I had filled my breakfast nook, extra bedroom, and all but about one third of my living room with my goods. I needed space. He needed to sell his house before his future ex-wife got it. "I'd rather give it away than let that bitch keep it," he snorted into his beer mug. We shook on it that night and I went with him to his office, which he opened up at 11 p.m, after my shift, to accept the cash-down deposit of $20,000.

I paid more than half the price of the house in cash and my bank financed the balance which represented less than twenty percent of the appraised value of the forty-two-hundred-square- foot, four-bedroom, four-bath lake home in the heart of the city. The three-car garage was clutch. All of the furnishings came with the house. After ransacking the attic and stripping the walls of their mundane,[40] yet moderately valuable wall art that included some original Thomas Kincaid and Ansell Adams prints, the house practically paid for itself.

Having a built-in warehouse also helped, and the spare space filled up, but not so ridiculously fast as to outstrip my ability to sell it. I still had the equivalent of a two-bedroom four-bath home with a garage bay for my BMW. Although three thousand square feet were showroom, it did not overwhelm my living space.

Saturdays were relatively leisurely days. I would usually work a short shift at the restaurant on Saturday evenings and entertain visitors and potential customers at my home. During my downtime, I would sit by my pool or fish off of my dock. On rainy or especially chilly days, I rented tapes from the video store or caught up on the latest grunge music.

Thus, my weeks were completely full of work. Between my increasing levels of responsibility at the restaurant and my buying-and-selling business, I discovered that I had very little time for goofing off. Fortunately, my job at the restaurant afforded high levels of social interaction. Between customers and co-workers, I ensured a constant source of camaraderie and friendship. I also had a steady stream of customers and suppliers. As my co-workers discovered my extracurricular success, I became targeted as a bank. I quickly stymied any chance that I might become a savings and loan by instead serving as an in-house pawnbroker. I always collateralized the debt of my friends and ensured no hard feelings by splitting profits on the sales of any collateralized debts.

---

40 Fully, sixty-seven percent of our distraction is dark energy—now named; a systemic signifier of an unknown—overcome, through, and enabled by habit. In following the frayed edges of our myriad "what follow," our metonymic bent builds pressure in our individual and collective minds.

I found that the best way to turn a big profit was to dismantle goods and collections into their constituent parts. As I had with the baseball cards, I bought by the lot and sold by the unit. This commanded extra work, but eventually my customers knew to call me for rare or eclectic items: a hood ornament from a 1977 Buick, a fish-eye lens attachment for an old Hasselblad camera, a working motor for a Crosley turntable, iconic National Geographic issues. Slowly, I would pick these wholes apart and sell them off in parts.

My world became cluttered with the detritus of a thousand treasures and the towers of this junk began to overwhelm me. When, at last, I discovered that my avocation had become a vocation, it lost its luster. I realized that I had two jobs and no fun. Having emerged from one career to chase an obsession, the obsession had metamorphosed into a consumption. Though not exactly crumbling upon me, it was nonetheless filling in around me and the sustaining thrill had long ago worn off.

I once was whole, but now I too had sold myself off in units. I was, myself, becoming a single Barry Bonds card.

I was only working one day a week at the restaurant and was beginning to miss it. I certainly didn't need to work there anymore, but it was the only source of interaction that I had with real people. A haplessly social creature, I began to crave relationships. An increasingly shrinking personal space threatened to crush me, and all I could do was close doors and pretend that entire rooms didn't exist.

To add to the disheveled angst, a new website called EBay was gaining steam and it threatened to dehumanize the last bit of localized fun that existed in my selling game. I could either move online or move out. I could either turn my showroom into a warehouse, or turn my home into a junkyard. I placed a hard moratorium on purchases. I counted my money, much of which I had stashed in cash throughout the home. I removed money from the hiding places throughout the house and deposited it in the local credit union only as necessary. I only kept enough money in the bank to pay my monthly bills, which were few: utilities mostly.

As I took stock, I noticed that there were themes within my collection of junk. Certain types of goods surfaced over and again. Apparently, I had some inarticulate attraction to cameras. Never had I considered myself a photographer, although I did garner a pretty healthy knowledge of how cameras worked. I also had a tower of books about cameras that I had purchased in order to study how they worked. I had dismantled hundreds of cameras and had an entire corner of (what should have been) the den dedicated to parts of cameras. There was one which, for some reason, I had neither taken apart nor sold. In a slightly tarnished silver case, with a slew of custom, well-maintained lenses and accoutrement, I had for some reason stowed a 1930s Alpa Reflex 35-mm camera. Despite many requests to break up the set, a series of sales which would doubtlessly have yielded about $20,000, I kept the piece completely intact.

I picked up the hefty case and heaved the camera out, inspecting it for flaws. I found none, nary a scratch nor scrape. Something that I had never noticed before was that there was still a roll of film in it. Carefully, I returned the camera to its case. On an exciting new mission, feeling the same tinge of anticipation that compelled me for the first several years of my sale-ing, I rushed out to my car and found myself quickly swerving through traffic.

I arrived at the camera shop, this time not as a merchant, but as a customer. More and more people were bringing in digitized pictures, so the proprietor had less and less reason to inhabit his black room. The few camera shops that still existed in town had made the decision to send out film for developing. This shop owner, though, clung to the romance of the room, choosing to develop film on premises and to maintain a certain level of intimacy and privacy that such a private studio provides. In our conversations, he had hinted with that sense of discretion—the same required and expected of pharmacists, gynecologists, and madams—that he had seen some "very interesting things." Of course names and details were in short supply.

I explained the discovery, and asked him to develop the pictures.[41] I had acquired the camera from the niece of a long-deceased amateur who, as I was told, "took pretty pictures of the birds in the mountains." Indeed, the shop owner and I quickly discovered, lots of birds and streams and rocks. Among the photographs, we saw touching pictures of moms and babies, inspiring pictures of soaring eagles, and an amazing action shot of a bird diving into a thin creek presumably in the hunt for a fish. I saved the negatives and left the prints with the developer. I implied that he could have all rights to them if he chose to pursue their publication or sale.

At last, I decided to burn it all down. Oh God, not literally. Well, not literally at first. When I made the decision, it was completely metaphorical, although I did see flames in my mind whenever I thought of selling my remaining inventory to a junkyard. Mostly what I visualized burning were dollars.

The actual fire was an accident, though I must admit that the circumstances did look awfully suspicious. An exhaustive investigation proved that the fire was triggered by a short in my garage and that in no way could I have been involved in its first spark or the propellant: a nearly undetectable leak where the natural-gas line met the juncture box where the pilot light was.

The photo shop owner sold the prints and one of them, a still of a bird that has since been rendered extinct, brought a pretty penny. He contacted me and asked for the negative. He offered to pay me $10,000 for it. Instead, I gave him the full roll of processed film and made him promise to split any further profits with me 50/50. He kept his end of the handshake-sealed bargain as I fully expected he would. He put some hefty work into researching the photographer,

---

41 We are forced to choose between each link from image to lan-
    guage: from concentration to distraction. In a sense, we must
    "arrest the multiplications of meaning...by uniquely privileg-
    ing one of them" (Miller qtd in Ray 37). Or must we?

building a mythology and market for his work, selling the prints, and even produced a coffee table book of his work. I still receive occasional checks from the publisher and would estimate that my total returns have exceeded $50,000 thus far.

I took a full roll of pictures with the Alpa as my lake home was leveled by flames that shot at least a hundred feet into the air at some points. Of course, I didn't start the fire, but happened upon it at its zenith, while it was still too hot for the firefighters who preceded me on the scene to fight it. Finally, it burned itself out and all that remained was a scorched concrete slab that opened onto a dramatic view of the lake. With the right lens on a flawless day, I can see clear to the other side, where the bustle of faceless others' life-changing events unfold with glee, consternation, and despair.

FLIGHT

OUTSIDE OF THE USUAL BAR OR NIGHTCLUB, IT'S NOT EVERY DAY that I get a drink bought for me—at least not by strangers and certainly not on a workday. On that Saturday, in September 2010, it was from three separate individuals. The first was at a local restaurant I tripped into for an early lunch before heading off to the airport.

I was by myself and sat at the bar, squeezing between two couples—one drunk and boisterous and the other subdued and skulking—and elbowing out just enough room to breathe comfortably. I sensed that the two couples were glad I showed up. The rotund burly guy in the button-down Tommy Bahama (and whose copiously exposed black chest hair seemed to grow from some Liberace hairplugfarm) could tell that the quiet guy in the pink polo on my other side was clearly not amused by the way empty shot glasses were being slammed onto the bartop. I actually thought it was amusing the first few times I witnessed it but, before long, the sweaty drunk was spilling tequila on me and I was pretty over it myself.

Pink Polo's girlfriend, lithe and brunette and—judging from the diamonds and gold that sparkled from her wrists, ears, and neck—dripping with family money, took a kind shine to me and began speaking over Pink Polo at me. Sensing the tense inappropriateness, I responded curtly and worked hard to deflect attention from me and back to him. Poor fellow just couldn't get a break. Before my arrival, chances sat near zero that his girlfriend was attracted to the drunk bear—or anyone else in the room for that matter. Now he had me to contend with. He dumped his silent enmity in my direction with strangling passivity.

The sinewy strand of control he held over his companion was spun out of guilt and habit. The way she cocked her head at me indicated that, despite her ability to perfectly match his polo pink with her lipstick, she felt little other than color coordination for him. Out of sympathy, I declined further eye contact with the pinks, feigned a haughty rudeness, and sunk my head deep into the menu.

From my right, I heard another shot glass slam against the sticky, glazed, butcher-block bar. The accompanying grunt wasn't the burly man's I was expecting. I hadn't seen around him when I sat next to him—his presence commanded full attention—and I imagined that he was with a woman whose eyes would be as glazed over and with a chest as freely hanging as his. I expected spaghetti shoulder straps holding up a low-scooping tank top barely covering floppy tits sitting on top of a distended whiskey drinker's FUPA belly. I expected cottage cheese exploding from too-tight-thighed denim and, frankly, to see more skin in more places than anybody rightly should.[42]

The last thing I expected to see was the strawberry blonde version of the girl two seats down to the left. Indeed, they might have been sorority sisters, all the way down to the bubble-gum-pink lip treatment.

She belched. I smiled.

"Tanqueray and Tonic, single, tall, two ripe"—stressing "ripe" sometimes sounds pretentious, but I've learned that most bartenders will take care to give you what you ask for–"lime wedges, not slices," I leaned in close to the black-shirted big-handed bartender.

"I got it," added the redhead. "That's for putting up with my asshole brother."

---

42 Indeed, if we are to avoid a grand and unknowable narrative of self, we must privilege some images as we assign them values in our language system. As we stare into the heavens and seek to know them, to know ourselves, we distractedly work.

"Thanks, I don't know what you mean. Certainly likes his, um, tequila."

Apparently, from her squinty-eyed response, he had been talking trash about me, but I doubtless hadn't paid enough attention to notice. I certainly would have talked shit about him if I had a companion, so I took no offense anyway.

When the pint glass of gin arrived with a wink—the bartender, expecting I needed a stiff drink had made it a double—I squeezed the limes and downed the drink as fast as I could before Tommy Bahama returned. I hoped to avoid an incident in which I had to speak to either of the men or hurt either of the girls' feelings.

I fished a five dollar bill out of my wallet and threw it on the bar as I pushed my stool back to extricate myself. I wasn't going to eat here, as hungry as I was. I flashed a grin at the redhead and mouthed something like, "Are you sure?" or, "You don't have to," to which she smiled back, raised her hand as though she were a patrolman stopping traffic on the interstate, and nodded.

My eyes met the pinks' as I walked past them to the door which I first—squandering any cool I might have had— pushed instead of pulled to exit. I imagined myself in a V8 advertisement and used an imaginary hand to self-effacingly pop myself on the forehead. Stunned for a moment by how hard I had just struck my head in this fleeting imagination-bound fantasy commercial, I stumbled. The same forceful metacarpus which had just struck me pointed down the street. Obediently, as any good Madison-Avenued consumer should, I followed by example. I tarried for a moment before the massive plate panes that fronted the restaurant, putting on—still in my stupefied imagination—what seemed a thoroughly conceived and executed Vaudevillian routine. As is usually the case with commercials, the passive watchers likely paid no attention as I reveled in my own increasingly inebriated, self-absorbed entertainment.

Fortunately, this block was alive with restaurants and bars, so I wandered three doors south and snuck into an upscale diner. "Lou's

Grub" was ironically named. This single-point establishment was actually owned by a Canadian lesbian couple and the menu featured foodie spins—hardly "grub"—on traditional favorites: cilantro gouda macaroni, smothered Andouille truffle fries, and ostrich arugula sliders on locally baked asiago focaccia. I requested my own booth in the bar area so I could both watch SportsCenter (which was always on one of the four TVs here) and sit alone. Of course, I needed to eat.

I ordered the cajun pork medallions on fried dill polenta with a black-bean reduced demi. I'd eaten this before and knew that it was just enough food to sustain me for the next five hours and just tasty enough that I wouldn't mind not brushing my teeth. The waitress dropped off an ice water in exchange for my lunch request. A few minutes later she came by with a sparkling glass of pomegranate and champagne, a Pomosa, they called it. One of the owners—the more butch of the two—was sitting with a silver-haired gentleman at the bar.

Compliments of her brother," my server rolled her eyes at me. I had met the lesbians before, but never the siblings. There must be something in that gene pool, I remember thinking to myself as I raised the glass, smiling, and taking a sip.

"They muddle mint in with the pomegranate," the square-jawed brother half-shouted at me. "I hope you don't mind that I wanted to share my favorite drink with such a dashing specimen of man."

I blushed and wished to be back with the redhead, commiserating over the obnoxious antics of the Tommy Bahama bear. I would have even preferred the icy treatment from the pinks but, damn, that drink was amazing.

"It is best sipped, young man," he followed up as I sucked it down. "I'll send over another."

I didn't know until I was finishing my second Pomosa that there was also a shot of Grey Goose in it.

"Careful, honey," the lesbian interrupted, "those'll kick your pretty little ass quick."

When my lunch arrived, I gobbled it with such intense pleasure that it might well have caused a "food orgasm" as the menu predicted. True, it was written there on the front of the two-sided menu, just below the block letters reading "Lou's Grub,": "Get ready for a food orgasm."

The delightful flavors douched my palate with such intensity that all I could do was order another Pomosa, this time for myself and my new friend at the bar.[43] He walked over to thank me and handed me a business card. I was feeling silly and flirty and I winked at him as I imagined myself in a plush terry monogrammed robe, he shirtless and in a silly white apron reading "Kiss the Cook." In this fleeting fantasy, we were in an ubermodern Manhattan kitchen as he fried eggwhites and we sipped strong coffee together on a chilly Autumn morning. I snapped to and reciprocated the gratitude.

I pulled a hundred dollar bill out of my wallet, wondering for a moment where it came from, and expecting that it should cover the meal and drinks and leave a hefty tip for the waitress who was pleasant and attentive enough without being overbearing or meddlesome.

Silver returned to his seat, leaned over and whispered something to the lesbian. They both looked up and smiled. I stood to leave and could feel the foot-lightening effects of four drinks in an hour.

"Bye bye," I flirted.

I knew that my flight today was a short round trip. I had a quick meeting on the East coast before I had to hop back on the plane and head home. I would be back in my own bed by 3 a.m. then off Sunday and Monday. I had some house chores planned: the yard, detail the Porsche, re-pot the tomato plants. All of these tasks could

---

43 From observatories that see beyond contemplations and into the past and future, we must build our knowledge without becoming awash in it.

just as easily have been subbed to professionals, but they served therapeutic purposes to my otherwise pampered existence.

When I work, it is very hard. The pressures of my career are among the highest in the world; a recent TIME article pronounced it so. My hours are unpredictable, and when I'm not working, I do everything I can to forget about it.

Walking back out onto the street, I glided through a muggy soup of still air mixed with a repeating lunch. Each burp recalled a different combination of flavors: lime, cilantro, pomegranate, black beans. I decided I needed a beer when I spied, now sitting at a patio table across the street, none other than Mrs. Pink. She was alone.

I had to cross the street anyhow to hail a cab and figured that I'd like to get a closer look. Through the goggles of my afternoon and beneath the September sun, I surmised that she was perhaps the most handsome woman I had ever seen. The stark contrast of her stunning elegance against the very pedestrian bottle of Bud Light she was holding to her lips struck me as beautiful in the same way as Picasso's portraits of dismembered-then-reconstituted harlots were beautiful.

Of course, she saw me. She hailed me over, and I shuffled up to her table. An aluminum pail before her sprouted forth four more unopened beers as though a Yankee's fan had planted bottle caps at the beginning of the baseball season. They glistened with condensation and looked refreshingly ice cold. She motioned for me to sit which I obediently did. She sensed I was about to ask about her partner from earlier:

"He went home to let the dogs out. We only live around the corner."

She reached into the bottle garden and picked one for me. Deftly, in one continuous move, she opened it, tossed the cap in the pail, and handed me the beer (technically, I guess, this beer wasn't bought for me so much as pre-bought and given to me).

"I have to catch a cab," I mentioned as I began sucking down the amber beverage. The bitter beer combined with the remnant memories of my lunch in an odd but refreshing stew. "I have to work."

I continued, "I've never seen y'all before. You new in the neighborhood?"

"Just moved here." Her hand grazed mine. My dulled senses could not discern whether this was accidental or purposeful.

I finished my beer, thanked her, wished her well and expressed my interest in hanging out with her and her husband sometime soon.

"He's usually a lot of fun," she completed.

I nodded, stood up and walked back toward the curb as Mr. Pink came into sight a few blocks south. I hailed a cab, climbed in, and waved to him as if we were old friends as I passed by him. He returned a quizzical gaze.

"Airport."

"No bags?"

"Nope, a quick trip."

Damndest thing, I don't remember getting in the cockpit, flying the plane, the meeting, or flying back.

I woke up at noon the next day, not in my own bed. I dangled my feet, threw on a robe that was sitting on the floor beside me, and wandered into the kitchen where—with the news in the background describing the odd and horrible plane crash in the suburbs—Lou announced that he was frying eggwhites and that the coffee was fresh.

Turkey sausage sizzled.

CHOKE

SELDOM ONE TO ARRIVE LATE, HE WALKED THROUGH THE DOOR ON time. He was smiling beyond his ears and had a swagger to his walk that was more than partly side to side. Bending from the trunk, his hips sent his shoulders back and forth in alternating foils to one another. Sleeves rolled up and shirt unbuttoned to the clavicle, he was sweating a little on his forehead though not yet under his arms. His walk from the adjacent hotel in the pre-dusk muskiness that followed the afternoon's rain was just far enough for him to accumulate a sheen on his tensed cheeks. His smile blinded the room and seemed the perfect complement to his happy gait. Unimpeded, he made his way to the bar where I had already ordered his favorite beer. As he sat, the buxom bartender slid the inch-headed wiezen his way and, in a dance that had certainly been rehearsed, he swooped the pilsner from the counter to his parted lips. The smile resumed after the gulp.

Every statement, even early in the evening and even before worded conversation, begins with a little chuckle—an infectious sound that starts deeply and below the lungs and just above the diaphragm. The latter origin was usually tapped after more weizen. The sunburst from his eye matched the outstretched, seemingly congenital grin. The first word after the chuckle was still suspended.[44] Indeed, there was still the hug.

---

44   The oscillations between concentration and distraction as we sit fixedly between Heaven and Earth—between chaos and delirium, between beginning and end—ask for translation. We must approach beauty, at first cautiously, then with abandon.

That blue looked good on him, he had certainly been told years before when he first bought the shirt. He wore it well on his larger-than-average frame even though his shoulders should technically have been broader for a man his size and his chest could certainly have been more descript. I noticed that the blue was faded, from the detergent of compliments; as the ample arms wrapped around my neck, another chuckle. From somewhere deep behind his perfectly toothed smile and below his glistening eyes, his muscled cheeks became flush with a realization that I had not stood up to receive my greeting. The innocent blush became more pronounced as I acknowledged his hug with a returned peck upon his burgeoning red cheek. I grunted as he loosed his grip. We smiled and he sat.

Assigned to different projects in the same city and away from home, we decided to stay at the same hotel and to extend our stays through the weekend for a little loose letting. "What's new?" was how I always started our conversations. This meeting was no different.

Chuckle, smile, giggle. "Well," he finally forced out as the micro-pause became punctuated by another swig of buttery beer, "things are pretty good."

I sensed uneasiness. I knew from experience that the next words to cross his barley-battered lips could be a descriptive combination of nouns, verbs, and adjectives ranging from a seedy sexual encounter, to a diatribe against liberal fiscal policy positions, to an exasperatingly dull but detailed account of a new pair of shoes he had purchased.

He surprised me by turning the inquisition upon me, sooner into the conversation than usual. "How was your week?"

I hated this the most, which is why I often opened my ears, feigning interest—whether warranted or not— in his storytelling, invective, and drudgery. His penchant for detail and breadth of knowledge, while sometimes annoying, paid off with some interesting tales from time to time.

He had a few drinks in his room before meeting me and was loose. I silently imagined an empty minibar with bottles and candy wrappers strewn about the floor. It was easy for me to deflect his questions. This evening, we were both spared monologues.

We had a hearty debate about funding for the Iraq War. We hit every facet of the issue. We debated the politics of it, the economics of it, the strategic international importance of it, alternative solutions, and disagreed on each point. This banter, in which I usually would take the devil's positions and let him educate me on the details of the issue as well as the art of debate, served as a great opportunity to avoid discussing anything of any real personal consequence.

This discussion saw us through two pitchers of beer, a tequila shot, two frozen margaritas, and a jaeger bomb each. His lucidity as a relative function of my increasing inebriation, served to keep us on track. His more pronounced stockiness—coupled with experience—afforded him a higher alcohol tolerance. As I lost track of my thought train, he caught his rhythm: chugga chugga.

We opted for a change of venue from the empty hotel bar and decided to walk down the road toward the strip clubs. Being at a hotel in a strange city afforded both anonymity and proximity to local attractions. The right proportion of bare skin to alcohol set us up nicely for a fulfilling saunter home at the end of the evening. We had already agreed to get up early enough to watch the baseball game at the stadium. It started at noon on Saturday. We'd have to leave by 11:00 to catch the L which meant we'd have to be up by 10:00 to get ready. Thus, I vocalized, we could not have a ridiculously late night. He agreed.

A local attraction, LaMont's, featured strippers who had been working there since what must have been prohibition. The drinks were as strong as the strippers were abhorrent. One of the "girls" who, by the shape of her neatly shaved "area" had clearly given lots of births, hung around soliciting tips like a hound dog at a southern Sunday picnic table. My compatriot burned through a stack of ones faster than sticks of butter at that same picnic table.

Between tips and drinks, we didn't discuss much besides how nasty it was watching women who could be our grandmothers grovel for something besides "sugar," and how the only things that could possibly be stiff around there were the drinks. Those comments must have been repeated, in some form or fashion, twenty times. Over his left shoulder, I saw a plaque, the top of which read, "What." Every few minutes, I just repeated the word out loud: "What." I kept saying. "What…What…What…WHAAAAAT" We both thought it was hilarious.

When neither of us could stand any more, we decided to continue sitting and to finish off the evening with a last shot. The signature drink of the establishment, known (I kid you not) as the "Cherry Pop" finally did us in. We truly could stand no more.

The faded blue shirt that started the night was now soaking wet with some combination of sweat, beer, and old lady stripper juice. Under the relativity of low light and high blood alcohol contents, my friend appeared ten years younger and his shirt at least three years newer.

On his way back from one last pit stop, he grabbed a peppermint from the jar at the corner of the bar and promptly unwrapped it. "Thank God," I remember thinking to myself.

He walked up to me and hugged me, pulling me into his soaking embrace and shamelessly licking my face. I laughed and pushed him off and he laughed too. His laugh was more than his usual giggle or chuckle. This was a hearty and playful guffaw that clearly required him to inhale deeply before the next round could ensue. Two or three of these were followed by a wheezing silence.

I looked at him to see his eyes bulging red in what I at first assumed was the next evolution of his laughing fit—when he would laugh so hard that no noise came out and his face would redden like a Christmas balloon. He doubled over and I was, by this point, laughing alongside him feeding the spectacular hysteria. He slapped his thighs, still silently, and I howled. I could only see his back as it formed a round-topped table beside me. I playfully beat his lower back like a drum, doing my best Phil Collins riff from "Tonight." This wasn't the first time we had performed this routine: hug, lick, giggle, chuckle, laugh, guffaw, silent, double over, drum, howl, howl, howl.

Usually by now in the sequence, he would right himself, pound the bar with his fist and shout to whatever bartender was nearby, between deeply punctuated exhales, "ONE—MORE—BEER!"

"He's choking, honey," a grandma-stripper—now dressed and sitting at the corner seat five chairs down—said sheepishly.

The bartender looked up from wiping down the bar and confirmed the elderly lady's observation, "Yep, he's choking."

Matter of factly, a third confirmation came from an elderly man behind us who could see the face of my friend, "Yessir, he sure enough is choking. Must've been that peppermint candy he stole."

I let the "stole" comment go, figuring that such an argument didn't have much value at this time.

I gathered my composure and noticed that the burly rounded back before me, what was just moments ago an eighties drum set, was limp. The laughing stopped—his more than thirty seconds ago, I figured—and panic set in.

"Hey." I said quietly, in some sudden desire to not attract attention. "Hey, you choking?" I asked again this time with a little more volume. "Hey! Hey!! HEY!!"

I was in perfect, drunk, hysteria. I threw myself onto his back and wrapped my smaller-than-I'd-ever-imagined arms around his larger-than-I'd-ever-noticed waist. I tried to pull him upright, but his deadweight was immovable. I may well have been trying to pull a boulder out of the ground. As I worked without success to straighten his body and simultaneously clasp my hands together, he fell forward onto his head and splay, pretzel like, onto the filthy floor.

My hands, which would not connect in front of him were now stuck underneath his belly and I wrestled with his still body to free them. When he landed on his head, he split it open, and now there was blood mixed with the mud and beer and years of stripper grime on the disgusting cork floor.

"Somebody help!" I now shouted. "Please!" I worked to flip him onto his back. Another patron helped me move him so that he was completely prone.

"Breathe!" I yelled at him, helplessly. Knowing that I could not perform the Heimlich on him, I beat his chest and stomach. "BREATHE!!" I reiterated through sobs.

I dug my hand into his mouth, searching for the candy. I stuck my finger as deep down his throat as I could and felt nothing.

The bartender hollered that she was calling 911.

I kept punching him in the stomach, hoping that a burst of air would thrust the candy loose. By this time, his face was completely blue, almost the color of his shirt, and his eyes were completely bloodshot and bulging.

The stripper strutted over and looked at him, "He's dead, honey."

"Fuck you, he's not dead," I shouted at her.

I went back by his bloody head, grabbed him under the armpits and sat him up. I began another pounding drum solo on his back and tried again to get my arms around him at the ribcage which I finally did.

I hugged him as hard as I could and with such ferocity that I heard bones cracking,[45] "Breathe Mother Fucker!" I was sobbing, "Please breathe. Please." I could barely breathe. I continued breaking his ribs until he fell back on top of me. He was heavier than I ever thought. We both lay there on the floor, him on top of me, as though I had finally managed to pull that boulder out and it fell right back over with me under it. We had both soiled ourselves and the room lay in ruins. I was paralyzed, partially out of a resurgent drunkenness, partially from sheer exhaustion, and partially because a 300-pound dead man was bleeding out on top of me.

When the paramedics arrived, they pronounced him dead on the scene. It took four people to load him onto the gurney.

---

45 And so our concentration and distraction in the accumulation of images is further translated along the frayed edges of understanding and our deliria exacerbated as we approximate beauty.

CHOKE

By now, all the lights in the bar were on and just the bartender, the one Delphic stripper, and the old man—who, by now I had surmised, was her husband—remained with me. The elderly were arguing quietly in the corner, though mostly unfazed by the events, and I heard the words, "steal candy," "Jerry's kids," and "justice" interjected between "stop," "shut up," and "terrible," though I could not understand each word. They were just as likely playing a game of canasta as they were reflecting on my night.

I could finally see the "What" plaque in its entirety. It was a thick mahogany, about sixteen inches tall and eleven inches wide. There were seven names etched into brass and mounted in a column upon the plaque with room for about seven more. Along the top, in cursive letters, it read, "What a way to go."

The bartender looked at me looking at the plaque, pulled a cocktail napkin out from under the bar, and asked without a bit of sadness or empathy, "How do you spell his last name?"

MOMENTITIOUS
THREE

OBTUSE[46]

Knobby kneed and flat chested, I was a lanky cauldron of empty threats and spritely libido for the first two years of our friendship. Only this year had he begun to close the eight-inch-height gap that had separated us since sixth grade. Though I had been offering to since we were twelve, I was all tease and talk until that day. My burgeoning—what I only know now was—unidentifiably sexual energy was properly constrained until that eighth-grade afternoon when we were alone in the same room, dressing out for gymnastics practice. We preferred to dress out together at his house which was just a short jog from school.

Every other afternoon, we scarfed turkey sandwiches and washed them down with juice boxes and cookies while we changed into our workout clothes. Our mothers must have assumed, in ways that mothers know and sense, that nothing bad could ever come from our being alone in his bedroom. Our mothers were—frustratingly—right.

He was as beautiful as any boy I had ever seen and he gave off a musky scent that probably would have been better controlled by a good antiperspirant. The aroma was intoxicating; not a single girl since Eve's first-daughter-in-law—from China to California to Charlotte to Mumbai—has smelled that scent emanating from the

---

46 *Due to publisher's guidelines related to sexual content, this story has been altered from its original version. To access the original, visit www.Momentitiousness.com.*

boy that she adored and not quivered. I did not know why I loved the scent, but I know that my heart-blazing reaction to this scent—rising from the first boy a girl loves—is matched only in ferocity by the dulcet combination of aromas that waft from my three-year-old son. My heart swelled.

I had stripped to the frilly periwinkle underwear and bra I had recently insisted that my mother buy me; I stood before him. Countless times, I had worn less in his presence—at the beach where we played in white-capped swells pitching gobs of mud at each other or at the pool, playing Marco Polo pretending to be blind and practicing pitching our voices. With his head bent down and his eyes looking toward the ground, I was close enough for his tallest curls to tickle me. They did. I stepped in so that the tips of my pink-painted toenails touched the fore-rubber soles of his sneakers. He noticed my naked feet first.

"I love that shade of pink," he offered in the same way he always seemed to appreciate the shades of lipstick and fingernail polish I had begun choosing with his approval in mind.

Crouched to tie his shoe, when he looked up, he was in perfect position to kiss my bared belly button. I could not quite, at that moment, fathom why I wanted him to kiss my belly. I did not even know how I wanted him to kiss it. Just dabbling in the earliest blooms of womanhood, I misidentified the correct target. Informed by the youthfully imperfect knowledge of my body and of the desires that would, within a matter of months, evolve into a better of understanding of that thoroughly unexplored region, I wanted his lips on me. Though he had never even kissed my mouth, I was oddly self-assured that one was not a prerequisite to the other. I knew that my boundless desire for his lips upon it would only be satisfied when he complied. I did not understand the desire, and was thoroughly incapable of vocalizing what it was that I really wanted. I knew merely that I wanted something from him that play-wrestling on the beach only hinted at. Suddenly, he was a boy and I was a girl; those things that just moments before made us the same now inexplicably separated us. I needed a different kind of touch from him: a kiss.

Although I had loved him since the day he first spoke to me, it was not until that instant when something—if I'd been asked to point to where I felt it, I would have failed—low in my core sizzled with the same ferocity as the red carefree can-sized curls upon his milk-toned head. I—with more than passing whimsy—positioned my barely clothed pelvis in his face. I stood near-bare before him and, despite having been in the same state of undress on more occasions than I could recall, I felt suddenly naked head-to-toe, emitting my own pre-erotic scent. I shuddered as I waited for what I fantasized would be his autonomic pecking response. With the squeaky-sultry voice that might have been reminiscent of a Marilyn-Monroe-Marlene-Dietrich love child, I spoke the words, "Kiss it."

What "it" was, I was wholly unsure.

"OH MY GOD!" he screamed from the most deeply pitted spot in his diaphragm as though toward the back of the gymnasium (never mind that we were in an eight-by-ten bedroom) "Oh. My. God."

I was arrhythmic.

I knew that he smelt it too. Suddenly wrapping around my legs and swirling with the scent of innocent desire, a silent, invisible, gaseous bubble had slipped out from the backside of my body. Post-flatulent, I looked down at his face, pokered, as though he held a pair of aces and didn't care about the flop, and waited for his face to tense in reaction to my emission.

It did not.

I smiled down at him with an emulsion of elation and horror. Although I had gassed, I was no less afire with the inexplicable thirst for his sweet touch; it probably served as a propellant because for every second that he smiled with the explicit joy of his two previous almighty-inspired exclamations, I felt more and more ready to burst.

For the next fifteen years, my love for him grew forth from this moment, expanding outward in every direction, consuming my heart and every chamber-shifting beat. The innocence of this instant would take on new meaning and I would re-remember it with increasing eroticism as he and I grew together beyond our lankiness through pubescence, adolescence, and ultimately adulthood. He would be my husband some day, I gazed dreamily into the not-so-far future. We would have a perfect lovesome son—I knew it—who would dash between our legs and complete our universe.[47] Though I wanted him in the most primal way, I wanted him more absolutely and completely into an eternity that spread unconstrained into the future and into even that future's future. And, from that contrived imaginary future, I looked back again to the moment as the genesis that must have banged forth from this special first kiss: the kiss I expected, the kiss I desired.

Just a few months after this event—when I was coming to grips with my first period and better pinpointing the exact source of my imprecise desire—he told me he thought he "liked boys." He confirmed our mothers' premonitions and proceeded to name certain classmates. "Yes," I agreed, "What is not to like about him or him or him?" They were, no doubt, the comeliest boys in the school, so it did not seem wholly odd to me. He was attracted to beauty, and I thought this was acceptable given his affinity for all other things beautiful. After all, he enjoyed—organically, even at that age—*a cappella* gospel music, black-and-white Tennessee Williams plays made films, contemporary art museums. He wrote blank-verse poetry.

He invented a language to describe our relationship and taught it to me. With our own language, we lorded over all others around us. He was consumer and creator of beauty, and I was beautiful by proximity and affiliation.

I always spoke of our future wedding as though it were a foregone certainty. I could not wait to stand by his side at the altar before God and before our families. He always agreed, so I knew that all

---

47 This practice must reflect the depth of experience as we both
    absorb and are absorbed by our art.

I needed to do was persevere through the silly phase that seemed to have gripped all of the boys on the cheerleading squad and most of the more patent male members of the drama club.

Parallel to my fantasy, we grew into this family, with this child, with this blessed union. We made it through the humps and bumps, my infidelities and his, through school and parties and tailgates; we made it through the excruciating years at the groves and the death of his best friend whom I loved for his sake.

We made it through since that first day, when the third "Oh my God!" was accompanied by "I have one too."

I looked confusedly down at the top of his head as his eyes bulged with excitement of the discovery which I had libidinally exposed and forced before him.

He had noticed a piece of dark lint that had caught itself upon the fuzz above my blue-cloaked and uninteresting labia.

"You have one what?"

"A mole, just like yours, in the exact same spot! It's like a little chocolate chip!"

I looked down and noticed that the lint, situated just above my panty line and just below my bare pelvic bone, did, in fact, look like a piece of my anatomy. Not wanting to diminish the excitement of the moment, wishing for any connection to which I could grasp, I deceptively confirmed that I, too, had been searching for another with the same beauty mark.

He broke into a cadenced rap—an impromptu cheer—spitting out a barrage of variations of the word chip: "Chippy chip chipsters, chippily chipping chips...CHIPPER! Weeeeeee're CHIPPERS!"

Awestruck by what I had just witnessed and its utter randomness to the situation as I had staged it, I incompletely banished it from my consciousness and memory. In short shrift, it would return as the basis of our organically conceived 'Chip Latin.'

"Yes, we are. And I bet it is very sweet," I sultrily managed to respond to a question he did not ask. I wanted to invite him again—hoping that this time it would be accepted—to kiss my tummy. I was ready to beg, but the intense heat that was raging through my core soldered my tongue in place. I was ready for what the inescapable words—inarticulate and failing as they would have been—could not have captured anyhow.

He stepped back, now focusing his gaze on my face. He smiled with such intensity that I could feel the muscles in his face flex in my own. He reached his hands down into his white shorts and firmly cupped his penis with one hand while he used the other to pull his shorts and underwear down to his mid-thighs.

His newly unleashed musk mixed with the other scents which, on their own, had already combusted all around me. I was on the verge of melting into a pool of my own imprecisely honed, cusp-pubescent desire. My heart pounded in my ears and I felt my face flush.

I looked down at his flaming red pubic bush and traced with my imagination whatever it was that remained hidden behind his little white fingers. Still holding his penis in his hands, he walked nearer me. Unable to maintain my equilibrium, I managed to control a faint onto the chair against the wall. I breathed deeply and could feel the fire in my core explode outward through my belly then my knees then my cheeks then my feet. For a moment I felt my elbows throb.

He continued steadily in my direction, taking awkward steps constrained by his shorts, the elastic waistband of which still stretched just above his knees. Except for a dusting of blonde hair on his legs, the white shorts blended well into the palette of his white legs. Shirtless, I could see the slightly darkened change in hue on his stomach above where his shorts usually sat. His skin was so light, save some tiny orange freckles on his shoulders where the sun had visited but never stayed long, that I could see his blue and green veins tracing along his pectorals, rippling in some spots on his biceps and forearms. It was as though a marble statue had come to life and ambled toward me. The bright orange explosion of hair was the visual manifestation of the same red heat that raged invisibly—word-lessly—throughout my entire body.

He had now assumed the position with which I had recently attempted to entice him. My face was a tongue's length from his knuckles; he retained control of his disinterested penis which he maintained, shielded in his hand. Entranced, I looked up into his eyes and waited for him to give me my instructions. I told myself that I would obey without equivocation. His lips parted and, at last, he spoke.

"See, I have one too!"

He began digging through his pubic hair and parted it with his two hands, his penis dangling and noticeably un-erect. With his two thumbs and forefingers, he created a heart around a flat, brown mole. "Up until a few months ago, when all this hair started growing, it's all you could see, well that and my penis." Matter-of-factually, he continued. "And you have one too. This is perfect!" He beamed, "Like a couple of..." he continued without irony, "chocolate chips." He repeated, this time nearly squeaking, "You have one too!"

"Yes," I deflated. I could feel bile surging toward my throat. I faked a smile and lied, "I do."

Then, without warning and without changing the expression on his face or the position of his hands, he bent down and kissed my forehead. And I knew that, for the next sixty years, I would eye-pencil dot my pelvis with a chocolate morsel-sized chip.

"I bet it tastes sweet," he said playfully, in a way that was com-pletely devoid of anything but a passionate love for sweet milk chocolate.

"I bet it does," I considered inviting his kiss again, but settled for the saccharin dollop I had just received above my eyes.

With that, he quietly farted as he reached down to pull his shorts back up.

"Excuse me," he chuckled.

"I love you too."

RING

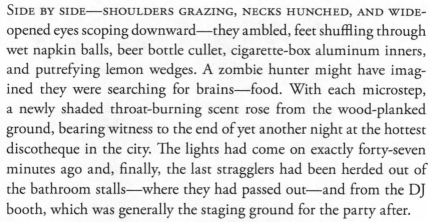

SIDE BY SIDE—SHOULDERS GRAZING, NECKS HUNCHED, AND WIDE-opened eyes scoping downward—they ambled, feet shuffling through wet napkin balls, beer bottle cullet, cigarette-box aluminum inners, and putrefying lemon wedges. A zombie hunter might have imagined they were searching for brains—food. With each microstep, a newly shaded throat-burning scent rose from the wood-planked ground, bearing witness to the end of yet another night at the hottest discotheque in the city. The lights had come on exactly forty-seven minutes ago and, finally, the last stragglers had been herded out of the bathroom stalls—where they had passed out—and from the DJ booth, which was generally the staging ground for the party after.

Drooping tarantula-sized eyelashes stood watch over sweat-ravines that cut through caked face makeup on the cheeks of half-metamorphosed drag queens and club kids as they strutted with all the glamour of Barbra or Cher—as the case may be—toward the beckoning realities of inescapably masculine masturbatory loneliness. They loudly and faux-gleefully howled at each other and their respective entourages—generally comprised of chunky strippers and lanky backup dancers—as they carried wigs and makeup boxes as if they were teacup poodles and Chanel bags. Counting singles and obliterating gender concurrently, they too wandered toward the door which would lead them en masse toward a sea of loitering drunkenness outside not scheduled to finally break for another hour, as the sun began to crack the horizon. They burst onto imaginary red carpets as they were swallowed into the anonymity of the unaware crowd.[48]

Security guards transformed to janitors pushing brooms and stacking highball glasses fifteen high as they moved purposefully through the now-empty nightclub. Over the sound of clinking glass and spraying hoses, they recounted stories of the night and gossiped with the bedraggled police officers who sipped on straight designer whiskey out of tall white styrofoam cups. Three trespass warnings, an overdose, and a brawl were noted in the nightly log while the surveillance tape capturing a security guard punching a drunken mouthy patron was erased.

The hostess, who had recently started dating the resident DJ, flipped through a stack of faked IDs that she had confiscated throughout the night. She had turned her post at the door into a lucrative money-maker as she recycled these same IDs through a fence to students at the nearby university. Often seeing the same set of fake out-of-state driver's licenses week after week, she shamelessly sold them back to her distributor for forty dollars each. He sold them at the dorms for one hundred a pop.

Closing the loop on her ring of duplicity, she was obliged by management to finger three underage transgressors per night for the off-duty police officers to shake down. On average, one would get arrested to prove to the city elders that underage drinking was properly monitored and standards enforced at the venue thus precluding outside policing. The other two unfortunate stung teenagers would be relieved of the contents of their pockets—usually cash and prescription drugs—and sometimes their unrealized sexual dignity. The door hostess would get her cut, often walking away at the end of the

---

48 Distraction in the act of seeking beauty is a performance in which we allow "the audience to take the position of the camera" (Mechanical Reproduction 9).

night—when compounded by her skim from the cash drawer—with thousands of dollars.

"Don't sweep in here yet. We are looking for something." There were three other large dance floors in this, the small city's largest venue. They could begin cleaning those rooms, he reasoned.

He had managed this club for six months now, having started as a promoter handing out flyers while partying at other clubs and working his way through the rapidly evaporating ceiling of low-level gay mafia bureaucracy. He had impressed the cabal of owners by organizing a team of other promoters that increased Saturday night attendance by fifty percent. Though the bar sales were stagnant, the parties he organized increased head count and cover charges. Coupled with the coup he organized that brought down the previous general manager who was taking an inordinately large and unshared cash skim of his own, the meteoric rise had thrust upon him a dark celebrity in which he reveled. Since cresting in popularity—among patrons and owners alike—three months ago, he had settled into a melancholic paranoia. He was able to intuit, generally, which palms to grease in order to maintain his job and his status. An unfortunate clash with the friend of a boss had put him on the apparent outs; he was cautiously biding his time until the right moment at which to extricate himself from the high profile in which he had come to bask.

She, now scouring the floor by his side, had been his arm decoration for years. Before he took the nightclub job, they had been late-night sex partners when they both arrived home from independent nights of partying. He would call her, slurring her name and spitting into the mouthpiece of his phone. "I'm coming over," was the 4 a.m. refrain. She would answer, always quietly hoping that "this" time would be the time when he called sober. Though she had been with several men—sometimes many at a time—since they had been branded an item, she maintained the idea of kids and marriage in her increasingly twisted mind.

She had, in two years, never been disappointed by the sex. She had, in two years, always been disappointed by the lack of romantic intimacy. She wanted more out of him than he ever had the ability to give, but was happy to ride his arm to local celebrity status and the social perquisites it provided. While the sun shone, she slept. She competed with the moon and the stars, fueled by tequila, champagne, and whatever powder she could suck into her nose.

They lost weight together as their faces sank, teeth de-enameled, and eyes bulged. Though he maintained the general handsomeness that genes had bestowed, his formerly milky skin had become lined, creased, and ashen. The musculature that nature had ordained upon his formerly broad chest, thick arms, and oversized traps had atrophied toward an abominably distended stomach which was sufficiently hidden by well-tailored shirts. When he remembered to brush his teeth, his gums bled. His transformation was palpable. In six months he had aged ten years.

Her breasts, once the institutionalization of perky form, had fallen and maintained their comparative size only in relation to her waist which had deteriorated to eighteen inches. Her pelvis was so pronounced that with little imagination, it could be illusorily skinless: nothing but sharp bone covered with a translucent mayonnaise. Despite the tightness of the circumference, a strange looseness of bunched up skin contained a single-ended rainbow of green and blue veins. Her septum, paper-thin, whistled when she breathed. Her blonde-tipped, black-rooted hair was brittle and dry and clumped in her hairbrush like pine needles on a richly soiled forest floor. Her transformation was less distinct than his, having started from a base of relative waifdom, but yielded something far more stomach turning. The sweet vanilla scent of the Creed perfume she wore betrayed the musk of her rotting soul.

Neither noticed the others' changes from beneath the artificial lighting, fog machines, and lasers. Neither noticed their own transformations as the mirrors they looked in were often flat upon tables and covered with powder. The concurrent putrefaction of their previously young and vibrant auras was scarcely noticed. In the full fluorescent presence of this now empty venue, they seemed almost phantasmagoric, hovering listlessly over a layer of party flotsam.

Earlier in the night, at the height of the bacchanal, among hundreds of revelers at what she liked to call "his party," she dropped it. The instant it happened, as he watched it fly over their heads and land in a pool of heaving bodies, he considered clearing the room. His better instincts took over and he decided that his chances for recovery were higher if he didn't incite a search for it. If somebody other than him found it, it would be lost to him forever. Just minutes before that, he had slipped it into her open hand and, with a kiss and emphatic head nod, she had accepted it. "Finally," she answered laughingly. "Finally," he smiled a rotting smile.

They continued their search, intently, silently. Jealously, he feared that it had already been scooped up by an eagle-eyed patron. He could taste bile welling up in his throat. His anger was physical, his breathing quick, and his heart beat loudly enough to create a cadence to which they unceremoniously marched. Knowing that he would ultimately replace it if they didn't find it, she was less concerned; she joined him in his search as a form of goodly placation. She had guilted him into giving it to her in the first place and she knew that it was more a ploy to get her panties off than of truly sincere giving. She was his trophy and this was his way of making sure that she would remain so for at least one more night.

What began as fear of retribution from the shady corners of his contrived party world had, of late, evolved into a manic distrust of everyone he met, including her. Every action seemed to take on an obsessive air, at once self-indulgent and calculatingly self-preservational. If this bought him another night with her, he would devise another ploy for the next. She fed on his anxiety, engorging herself on an exponentially diminishing and malnourished soul. They were both starving, wasting beyond the shells of their former selves.

Glittering by her foot, she spied a shiny silver hoop earring. She paused for a moment, considering bending over to inspect it. Singularly focused on the search for one item, he grunted, indicating that she not be distracted. They continued forward, approaching the search with a spiraling pattern. He deliberated splitting the dance floor into halves, like a pair of human Zambonis, but decided that she might find it and not tell him. Anything that had resembled love earlier in the night had degraded to a fearful contempt. She tarried forth, ambivalently, by his side.

Their eyes were drawn to other swill-laden sparkles: quarters, keys, safety pins, lighters, pocket knives, brass knuckles. They lingered over a gold tooth for a prolonged second. They saw what must have been three hundred dollars, crumpled, folded, dripping with vomit and what was likely urine.[49] It was not unheard of that people would piss themselves in their extreme intoxication, reasoning that the line for the restrooms was too long for them to wait in. Mixed with the smell of perspiration, there also lingered the scent of young and violent coitus. Certainly, they understood, they were walking on ground baptized by the spray of dance-floor hand jobs and coarse pelvic grinding. They knew precisely what they were looking for and would only dive into the living stew through which they methodically waded to get it.

At last, a diamond sparkled by his left foot. He fell to his knees. She gasped, not able to decide whether she was relieved or disgusted. As he knelt, prayerfully, he looked up into what he perceived was her relieved face. He was so singularly focused on his task that he could not tell that her smile was a grimace. Exultantly, he smirked in her direction.

She noticed her bare finger and its resemblance to leathered bone. Her fingernails were short and painted, but jagged. Her cuticles were

---

49   Our performance art, from the realm of the known third of the universe, gazing into the explosive dark energy must be constrained, lest Babel.

oversized from lack of close grooming. In a vision, she saw the ring on that bony finger. To the untrained eye, the half carat clear-cut diamond was set in silver. In actuality, she could tell, it was beveled platinum. She meekly began to reach for it as he swatted it out of the way and dipped his fingers into the dirty ground stew in which the ring had settled.

Breathing a deep sigh of momentary relief, he grasped the square, one-inch baggie by the slightly raised pink line of locked closure and raised it toward her. He shook it in her direction and with his other hand flicked it, causing the heavy bulge of white powder to re-settle at the bottom of the tightly sealed package.[50] The brown liquid in which it was previously laying and which had clung to the plastic as he raised it up sprayed off like zombie sweat.

"Finally," he exhaled, his eyes dilating in anticipation.

"Finally," she smiled a forced yet lustful smile.

---

50 It must be unleashed, lest Armageddon.

DIPS

SHE ORDERED THE SPINACH ARTICHOKE DIP. HE GOT THE SALSA. Her chips outlasted the pungent, stringy green-flecked concoction and he slid his three-quarters-full bowl of chunky tomatoes and jalapeno specks in her direction. She pushed her basket of chips toward him. He slid his barstool closer to hers. Three tequila shots later and they were old friends. With the fourth, they graduated to fledgling couple status and didn't look back. Their relationship was conceived in crunchy corn tortilla, baptized in agave, and flourished in dive bars and happy hours for weeks to come.

When it came to the more practical side of relationship building—the mundane moments that did not involve smoky bars, salty rims, or foam-topped pilsners—they were far less efficient. They were both servers at restaurants in the same town, though not the same one. Showing up at appointed hours and still sporting their black starched Dickies with untucked variably red, black, and white shirts, they would easily resume their liquor-infused honeymoon until the night's tip money ran out. Despite the alcohol and their willingness to publicly proclaim their mutual affection through lip locks, neck nibbles, and barstool stinky-pinkies, they never actually left together to confirm their relationship.

The lack of sex, while frustrating at first, became an ever-growing and increasingly unspoken nuisance, especially for two people in their mid-twenties. With hormones still raging, working toward orgasm more than once while seated conspicuously at the bar, his sexual suggestions, whispered amid a shower of drunken spittle, seemed more for show than for effect. Her grinning assents, clumsily shelving her small hand in the throbbing crevasse between his balls and inner thigh, always signaled that she was ready when he was.

Alas, having earned his second DUI earlier that summer and constrained by the lack of a car, the logistics that generally facilitate one-night stands eluded him. He knew that he could not very well throw her on his handlebars and carry her home to his bed. Furthermore, he suffered from an embarrassing lack of restraint needed to save out the ten dollars for cab fare. Alcohol consumed him much more quickly than his need to get off. On especially good nights, he would drop fifty bucks on half an eight ball before he even met up with her. They would take turns going into their respective bathrooms and emerge with gusto and powdered noses until they were completely oblivious to anyone or anything outside of their two-foot circle and the two-dollar beers that accompanied them on such nights. His altered mind knew that he was horned beyond description but was—even with a Viagra, which he didn't have nor the funds to buy it anyhow—frustratingly unable to perform.

For three weeks, the oddly interrupted couple continued on this path: half-priced appetizers, rot-gut liquor, and late-night happy-hour beers. They enjoyed each others' company and spent almost every night together reliving the cycle which had its accidental genesis over chips and dip. They discovered and passed hours discussing mutual affections for Journey, Nascar, singing in the shower, and being eye-crossed drunk.

She was content—not ready to dive into a full-fledged relationship similar to the one she had escaped just weeks earlier with an unfair collection of scrapes and bruises. She knew that once they consummated, invariably, one of two things would happen. Either he would stop calling or he would—proclaiming her as his by the right of penetration—call all the time. She was ready for neither and enjoyed the caprice with which they bounded their relationship to the dry and topical—booze and public heavy petting notwithstanding.

They left no room for seriousness in any of its twenty-first century iterations. She didn't expect for a moment that he was anything other than content.

An odd consternation overtook her when, finally, his midevening text indicated—rather than a dive-bar meeting—the desire for an actual date. Her eyes fluttered with ambivalence as she read the words: "Happy Anniversary," through the cracked screen of her chromeishly pink flip phone. She had no idea that any noteworthy period of time had elapsed, nor that there was anything worth celebrating. She had no idea that he was romantic, especially in the glaring dearth of which she existed. And yet, her chest heaved with more than exasperation. She tingled.

"Same to you," she responded. She sighed.

"Date night. Meet me at the Factory at 8." He ordered it with the same caprice as a customer at one of his tables. "86 the Crocs. Wear something sexy for me." Their introductory conversation was about their mutual affection for the casual fine dining, giant portions, and delectable desserts at the Cheesecake Factory which, luckily for his transportation situation, was especially convenient to his apartment.

"K."

A Tuesday, the night they both usually had off, he surmised correctly that she had no plans and had been waiting to decide upon the bar du jour. She usually initiated the text conversation, and her equilibrium was tangibly ruffled. She wondered, as she considered the clean clothes she had from which to choose, how long it had actually been. What was the time threshold that they had reached? She concluded that it was about four weeks ago: a month. She rolled her eyes as she thought forward to Chicken Madeira and "the Snickers."

She hadn't been on a date in years—usually sucked into relationships by happenstance and knowing only that she had been in them through the evidence of their rocky endings. Seldom, in her recent memory, could she mark the beginning of a relationship or the fact that somebody wanted to explicitly celebrate it.

With a razor, which hadn't been used in some time, and a collection of lotions that hadn't been used in even longer, she prepared herself for what she knew would be the culmination of thirty days' worth of savings. She began to imagine the sex—what he would look like naked. She scrunched her nose and smiled. She had already felt his erect penis through his pants and knew that, though size didn't really matter to her, he was sufficiently endowed to hit the spot, which was what really mattered.

Would he like her body? She shaved, sprayed, and squirted as her nervous anticipation grew. She also cleaned her room, made her bed, shoved laundry and clutter into her closet, and lit candles. They would come back to her place, she decided. She was not ready to meet his roommates—whoever they were—and hers would be out until the morning.

Independently, they raided their respective refrigerators for shots. Neither was ready to greet the other with sobriety, especially in the frighteningly new atmosphere. She emptied two jiggers of gold tequila while he finished the bottom quarter of a fifth of Popov vodka. At 8:45, she poured herself into her white banged-up Civic and he walked out of his apartment door toward the chain-linked fence he would hop to enter the back of the mall parking lot.

They both had friends who worked at the Cheesecake Factory and, arriving at almost the same time, they were greeted, not only by each other but, by a hailstorm of high-fives and hugs. They were also greeted by some quizzically confused faces and some silent mouthing. Their few commonly shared friends outwardly effused excitement in their presence while rolling their eyes in departure. The line of well wishers (and silent detractors) streamed by the table at which they were finally seated, each bringing their own serving of affected joy.

"Get anything you want; tonight is your night."

She had never seen that side of him. He was noticeably nervous, sweating through the poorly pressed butter-yellow button up he had purposefully chosen as the nicest from his wardrobe. He smelled of dryer sheets and Speed Stick and she was smitten. A bead of sweat traced down from his sideburn to his chin. From across the table, she could not smell his breath. She was far more used to sitting next to him, their elbows poking each other, as they leaned up against a sticky bar. She was far more used to seeing his face in profile, to seeing the peach fuzz on his earlobes, to smelling his breath as he playfully belched in her face.

Seated now for four and a half minutes, neither had spoken to the other since his initial proclamation. Awkwardly, she broke the silence: "So, hey." She forced a grin as she reached for the warm white bread. She broke off a piece and shoved it in her mouth as she decided to occupy her mouth while he responded.

"Hey," he grinned back. "You look pretty."

She had never noticed the green flecks in his hazel eyes. She had never noticed the color of his eyes at all. "Thanks. You look cute too." She immediately, nervously, questioned her use of the word 'cute.' "Handsome, I mean. You look damned handsome." She was not lying or exaggerating. She looked at his eyes for a moment then looked away, afraid to make eye contact. She had not looked a man in the eye in years. She finally settled on "Hot, looking hot." She was happy with the final exaggeration. She throatily chuckled.

"Let's start with a 'SpinDip' (universal restaurantese for the item)," she flirtatiously tilted her head toward his buddy, the waiter. "And, I'd like a Cuervo Gold margarita on the rocks, with salt." She batted her eyes, generally in a direction that split the middle between the standing server and the seated date, "Please."

He nodded his head in approval, glad that she had ordered a drink, "Same. Make it a double. Do you want a double too?"

She nodded emphatically. "Chicken Madeira, extra 'shrooms."

She didn't want to unnecessarily extend the waiting. Nor did she want to miss a bite. She wanted it all as soon as possible. For a month she had been pre-paying for this night.

"Shepherd's pie," he methodically shifted his smile-infused gaze from her to his friend, the server, then back.

He grabbed some bread and unsheathed the foil-wrapped butter which he then dipped into. This was far more awkward than he imagined it would be. He had never noticed the solid coriander blue of her eyes. He had never noticed the sheer translucently blonde fuzz that trailed down from her ear toward her neck. "Oddly sexy," he thought to himself, certainly not ready to make it the next topic of discussion. "I love this brown bread." They had discussed the bread choices at Cheesecake Factory before, and he knew that she would only eat the white. It suited him perfectly.

Again, she nodded. "I like the white." She knew he already knew it. Needing to prove it, she crammed the rest of the original piece into her mouth.

The drinks arrived and were emptied quickly.

"How was your day?"

"Good. How was yours?"

"Good."

Another unrequested round of margaritas was dropped in front of them. The waiter dropped three shots down also. He looked around and signaled for them to hurry and prepare to do them; he grabbed the third and, quickly, indicating that he was doing something he clearly shouldn't be doing, did his shot, threw the empty glass on the table between them and walked away.

"Thanks."

"Yeah, thanks."

He kicked her foot.

She smiled again. She quivered.

The chips and dip were proffered by a quick, unassuming, and surreptitious stranger.

They both reached for chips and scooped playfully into the sizzlingly hot cheesy concoction.

Simultaneously, slurpy gurgles greeted the bottom of their respective glasses as they began to loosen up.

"I have HIV." He blurted. The words burst forth in a shower of nervous spittle: the words he meant to rain upon her on the first night. Stuck in his throat for, to almost the minute, thirty days, stained by bourbon, tequila, and dollar beer, numbed by cheap cocaine, the sentence slithered past his graying teeth and hung over the bread basket between them, threatening to release a late summer Florida afternoon thunderstorm.

She looked at him in astonishment. She was silent. She wished for an umbrella—any shelter.

His face was flush and his eyes were red.

She grabbed another chip, her eyes transfixed on his. Her face remained stone. She did not even have the courage to smile a fake smile. She lifted the chip to her closed mouth and hit her bottom lip with it. She licked salt from her own lip. Her transfixed gaze finally shifted toward the clear space over his head; perhaps she saw the anvil-tipped cumulonimbus now separating them.

His face tensed as he fought against an impending flood of sweat and tears. "Dam," he ordered to his body.

Hers softened. "Damn!" She knew that she was in no position to judge him. She had a three-year-old daughter who she'd abandoned at her mother's door two years and eleven months ago as she left Live Oak for Orlando, never looking back. She had an abortion seventeen months ago. She had been fighting a cold that she couldn't shake for at least three months. "Damn," she repeated.

His thirty days of silence on the matter was instantly justified. All of the worst scenarios that played out in his mind became reality. Since discovering, during a routine doctor visit for antibiotics to get rid of walking pneumonia which he had developed over Christmas last year, that he was infected, he had not told anybody.

Nor had he met anybody he needed to tell.

"Damn," she nearly imperceptibly shook her head as she said it this third time.

At last the first tear broke his precipice.

Food was placed and steam rose from each of their plates, giving form to the invisible growing cloud.

Ostensibly because of her conscientious awareness of germs from years of training in the restaurant business, she stated that she needed to wash her hands as she scooted out of the booth and walked toward the bathroom.

"K," he responded as he watched her walk away. The starched cloth napkin did little to absorb the tear and another that pooled in the corner of his eye.

She walked into the bathroom and stood in front of the mirror and just stared at her reflection. She fixed her hair. She washed her hands. Before she realized it, she had squirted soap and rinsed her hands four times. She was in a self-absorbed trance.

He sat still for a few moments and then a few more. He panicked. He pulled out his wallet and fetched out the hundred-dollar bill he had planned to pay for the dinner with and placed it on the table. Looking around, he surmised the fastest route to the front door that would not require passing by the restrooms. He bolted. Within thirty seconds, he was outside and bee-lining toward the dark back side of the parking lot.

Composed, she straightened her clothes and brushed her hair out of her eyes again. She walked through the bathroom door, into the dining room, and, without a second glance toward the booth where they had been seated, burst through the front door and into the fluorescent evening. She had no idea, nor reason to guess, that he had already left.

He caught his pant leg on a sharp chain link and ripped it as he climbed over the fence and back into his apartment complex.

Independently, they sat brooding: he in his living room, she in her car in the parking lot. The storm of tears erupted from each of them in their present space.

She pressed the spongy clutch, ground her car into gear and slowly drove away. He cried until he slept, falling asleep fully dressed on the couch. She went straight home, pulled on her favorite sweat-pants and an oversized T-shirt, crawled into bed and rolled into a ball. She wept until her puffy eyes swelled shut and eased her into damp-pillowed slumber.

Silent days passed between them. Not a text until late Saturday, when her pink phone vibrated on the nightstand beside her bed. She'd worked the ensuing five nights after the anniversary dine-and-dash event and had come straight home after her shift each night. Her bedroom was spotless: all of her laundry was clean, folded, and put away and the refrigerator was purged of anything with an expiration date before today. She did two exfoliant masks, a hot-oil treatment on her hair, a wax on her legs and ladyparts. She made rent with two weeks to spare. She called her mother for the first time in thirteen months though she was still unable to bring herself to speak to her daughter; that would have to wait.[51]

"Hey," the screen read as his number, the one that she never added to her address book with his actual name but that she nonetheless recognized by its odd prefix and thirty days of consistent communication, flashed.

She did not respond. She left the word to linger on her bed stand where his phone never would. She was not ready for what he offered her. She was not ready for a man to tell her the truth. She was not equipped with the tools required to make a world with two centers of gravity work.

The next night: the same broken echo.

For five nights, he laid on his couch, inconsolably broken. After

---

51 Thus we work toward and around beauty, "In the beginning" and what follows from the beginning and, looking spaceward, toward the beginning.

no call, no showing for two shifts, his manager called and left him a message that he "had to show up tonight or be fired." After the next two shifts, the manager, still offering hope for salvation with nightly calls and empty threats of termination, stopped by. Wading through a floor strewn with empty bottles of all persuasions and discarded bags of chips, the manager who was first a friend, sat on the couch and saw the pain in the face of his employee-buddy.

For a moment, lucid conversation followed.

"So, you just left her there?"

"I paid the check."

"Dude, you just left her there?" He went on, exploiting the extended wisdom that the title 'manager' and three years more of life had bestowed upon him. "What the hell were you thinking? She is hot! And she liked your sorry ass."

"I was so scared."

"Of?"

"I didn't want to hurt her."

"Well, you fucked that up, didn't you?"

"Now she won't answer my texts. Is it possible I loved her?"

"Dumbass. Show up for work tomorrow, and don't be fucked up. I don't want to have to really fire you."

"K. Thanks."

"Dumbass. You really think you loved her?"

"I don't know dude, I didn't fuck her for a month."

"You must have loved her."

He didn't disclose his secret—the one which he had only told one person, ever—to his visitor, nor did he get up to bud-hug him as he went toward the door. He wanted not to hurt her.

"Hello," he mustered the nerve to text her again. She did not answer. Twenty four hours later, "Hey," still unrequited. He trailed off on the third day to an impishly unassuming, "Hi," before his fingers went silent. Determined to make a stand, he gathered his wits after work and walked across the street to the Wild Hare where he knew he could reach maximum inebriation with minimum fiscal outlay. They made them stiff.

He was hungry and knew that he could fill his belly with some decent appetizers while he drank away the crappy day in which he averaged only eight dollars per hour for the time he whiled away in his black-striped shirt and red suspenders. There was no need to change his clothes or wash his balls.

He bellied up to the bar and ordered his first bourbon up. He treated the highball like a shot and smiled at his friend behind the bar to bring another. "And some chips and salsa, Bud."

Through clear eyes and from a newly, partially decluttered world, she saw her way to work with the intent of going out afterward for the first time in a week. She needed a drink and a cluster of her girlfriends had made plans that she couldn't, in good conscience, miss. Until five weeks ago, they had been local celebrities at Tuesday Karaoke. Her absence from the revelry had been noticed not just from the harmonies but by more than a few of their fans. She hummed her way through her shift, rinsing down bad tips with diet coke and a little vodka that she fed to the bottom of the innocuously unadorned styrofoam cup which she kept next to the wait terminal. When finally she was cut, she rushed home, took a quick shower, and threw on the jeans that a week of healthy eating had re-inserted into her wardrobe. She knew she looked good.

She walked through the bar door with more purpose and with less-rounded shoulders than she had displayed in quite some time. She had beat her friends, some of whom were still working, to the bar and needed the time to acquaint her lips with some sustenance. With unswerving eyes, she approached and scooted into the bar, hesitating for only a moment as she ordered her favorite appetizer dish and a Vodka Cran.

She heard a crunch in her ear and looked to her right. She sighed deeply as she considered that somebody oddly familiar was in her presence.

He grabbed another round tortilla chip and dumped it deeply into the chunky salsa, scooping a portion which would—if every serving was so large—empty the bowl after only five or six chips. He dripped a tomato onto his chin; it slid onto his collar and mingled with similar stains that betrayed a shirt that had not been washed in weeks.

With an outward bravado that betrayed any attempt at subtlety, he looked over his left shoulder and washed her down from head to toe. Not one to linger at the face, intrinsically averse to eye contact, her chocolate brown eyes caught his and held him for a silent moment. He flecked hazels as he slyly smiled into the face of a stranger, oozing with an unmistakable sexual energy, "Do you like tequila?"

She grinned and reached for a chip.

TANGENCY THREE:
DARK ENERGY

When, at last, it struck me, I sat dumbfounded: I lay stricken...
We stand at the second derivative of chaos.
We look behind us and see an ether through which float flashes of
incandescent genius.
We look before us and we see an infinitely untenable synapse,
    a Styx whose gondolier waved from some undefined center of
    prechaotic bliss.
We wonder where we are, and discover that we are not there yet.

The next level begets the first,
    and our quest to rein in those ideas,
        however distant and entropically placed they may feel
            (or may have felt)
    brings us to the approximation of what we sense.
We are engrossed with the least-squares line that
    charts our progress(?) heretofore,
        and utterly disgust the aesthetic in our pride.

We stand at the first derivative of chaos, and its name is Beauty.

Beauty is the named means—averages not.
Chaos is our desired ends, a mythical achievement.
To achieve plateau,
    and to imagine a "next" is a lunacy
        upon which the whole of man's knowledge is courageously
        and blindly placed.
    Tangency is as unfounded in the realm
        of aesthetic as teleology is in the art of the
        inextricable.

My job, my occupation, my life's work: bask in the beauty.
My job, my occupation, my life's work: add to the beauty
    and rein in the flashes of genius which surround me.

While I detest the teleology of the least-squares line
    on which I stand, I comprehend the necessity of the mundaneity
        which it represents.
Each day,
    each moment of each day,
        each moment between every moment of each moment of every
        moment of each moment of every moment of each moment
        can last forever in our destiny and in our destiny unfulfilled.
We must strive for the latter—
    for the chaos—
    for the self and the multi-selves
        with whom we can surround ourselves.

Blink, blind, and for some eternity we can judge ourselves,
    not by what we have achieved,
        but by all of those things that we have sought. Blind,
        and for us Beauty...

No two moments are identical:
   Einstein's special relativity:
   Poincare's fourth dimension:
   Picasso's spatial simultaneity:
      each occurs at the same time in the very same Beauty in
      which we stand.

The moments,
   spatially and temporally,
      occur still, and we exist in that same ether.
 Once we understand
   this—once we can lasso these concepts-and
      can make our place our own... We own Beauty.

Chaos: Let us approximate it.
The beautiful:
Struck and Stricken.

MOMENTITIOUSNESS ONE

UNBORN

I WAS NEVER BORN. I WAS NEARLY BORN, BUT NEVER TOOK A BREATH OUTSIDE of my mother's womb. When I emerged from her, reaching beyond the tunnel-ended light, I careened toward a light that blazed with the luminescence of a quadrillion white dwarf stars and continued to fall until my eyes opened and I hovered over what I now know was unmitigated grief. Though I was not equipped at that time with the tools to process the tragedy I was witnessing, I have since learned to understand this single, solitary moment of what should have been my life. Ever since the day I was not born, I have been here, left with just one experience upon which to base an eternity of rumination.

Always the know-it-all, his precociousness was not new to a single person who was familiar with him. Of course, it didn't take long for perfect strangers to arrive at the same conclusion. From correcting his fourth-grade teacher's grammar, to questioning the validity of the scientific method as inefficient and restrictive to innovation in seventh grade, to reducing the complete works of Hemingway to a first-person one-act monologue as a physics major in his junior year at university, he was incorrigibly obnoxious.

I cannot leave. I cannot live. I cannot escape the never-ending presence of one moment in time. I am without a sturdy tense.

Sports, economics, and midTwentieth-Century abstract expression-ism all coalesced into magnificently eloquent diatribes that would both fascinate and infuriate his interlocutors. Nobody could argue because his words were packed more densely than a Britannica and, besides, he was always right. He wasn't "always right," in that dispar-aging, "he would never admit he was wrong," way. He was, actually, always right. People could check his facts and challenge his computa-tions—and they did—but he was never, ever, wrong. He could con-vince communists that free markets were more efficient and Yankees fans that Babe Ruth was better with the Red Sox.

As that first and only moment froze below me, I floated from the room and encountered many others—others who also lacked life. Staring down the corridor, I saw other creatures like me as they passed further up, em-bracing then joining the bright light: making it brighter and brighter still. Each time I approached the ever-brightening light, it moved away. As I sped toward it, its retreat was equally emphatic.

Worse than that, he was a total stud.[52] He turned the old cliché, "Every girl wants to be with him and every guy wants to be him," on its tired ear. Indeed, every guy and girl wanted to be with him. It had nothing to do with being gay or straight; it was an attraction to what Kant would have described as the sublime: innately, indescribably, and unassailably beautiful. He was a specimen of Davidic perfection. From the sandy blonde and wavy full collection of locks upon his head to his massive sized-thirteen feet, every part of his body was flawless. Not too thin to be a pitcher, not too wide to be a quarter-back, not too short to be a forward, not too dense to be a swimmer, and between academic bowl titles, he was a four-season athlete in a three-season division. Despite his athletic success, the wisdom of

---

52 As we rein in beauty, the same environmental concerns bar-rage us.

coaches eluded him and the camaraderie of teammates was ephemeral. Teams could neither win without him nor celebrate with him.

I wandered down corridors over the bustle of doctors and nurses, over waiting rooms and chapels, and watched the living pray for those who would inevitably race by into the light. I watched the desperate, the bereaved, the hopeless,the relieved. Without voice and without form, I could only muster the power of observation. I was but a receptor of the boundless lives of others, caught up with them in silent powerlessness.

There was nothing he couldn't do, except make friends. Most of the time, even his parents didn't want to be around him. In fact, the only reason that anybody endured him was to have sex with him, which he ungrudgingly did with anybody who paid him any attention. Thus it seemed, to the eternal confusion of his parents, that, because of the constant stream of new people in and out of his bedroom, he was the most popular kid in school. Truly, he was well known; one might say "famous." If he was popular, it was that sad kind of "I know who he is and I can't stand to be in his presence" brand of popular. He neither noticed nor cared about his infamy. His parents were thankful that he had (what they figured were many) friends; it excused their callous coldness toward him.

I learned that there were places, over certain beds in certain rooms, where souls like mine would linger before being absorbed into the light. I learned to communicate with these passers-by, those who would acknowledge me and who were not frightened by me. As they lingered on the edge of death, I lingered differently. Having never lived, I was not dead. Having never died, I was a wholly frightening being to most who I encountered. I was a monster.

Incessantly impertinent and ridiculously proper, he was driven by a force that nobody could identify. Perhaps, some theorized, he was an alien placed on Earth to collect information about its inhabitants; his creators made him too perfect to be an effective spy. Others drew parallels to Jesus, who was himself a know-it-all, often speaking in riddles and annoying monologues; perhaps he was the new Son of God. Still others postulated that he was part of a government conspiracy, cloned from the remnants of the world's smartest—yet most socially inept—figures: Einstein, Hitler, Jefferson.[53] Once exposed to him, people just wanted to forget him so that they could feel better about themselves. In rooms of greats, ides of jealousy always fell upon him.

I met a spirit lingering over an old man's body. The spirit spoke to me with a tenderness that was new, one that acknowledged that I was but a breath away from past humanity. He spoke and I listened. For the first time since the day I wasn't born, I was treated with humanity.

Nobody ever told him "No." The best anybody could muster was feigned apathy or indignant acquiescence. When, after graduating with his PhD in Experimental Nuclear and Particle Physics from MIT—he delivered a brilliant dissertation on Dark Energy that outshone previous research by decades— he decided to join the Peace Corps, nobody gave it a second thought.

Before he joined the light, he taught me to speak. He gave me words. Through his acknowledgment, he gave me form. With words and form, he gave me thought. With words and thought, I learned. My observation became knowledge.

I was but a camera.

Those who spared him a second thought could never fathom what drove him. A hint to his drive might have been discerned by a

---

53 We have been taught to excise distraction at its root, told by our trainers that our lines between beauties must cohere—not wander—and we have approached an understanding of only thirty-three percent of our universe.

careful reading of his dissertation introduction, had anybody bothered to study it. Jumping over the literary flourish and directly into scientific facts, many missed that he presented a critical method—a replacement for science itself—which indicated he had touched the origins of the universe. The ends and the means of science were too precise, he argued. The corralling of facts and figures to bring order out of chaos was not to understand the universe. Rather, science had brought humanity to the brink of impertinence, threatening to leave the power of the soul, expressed in Kantian constructions of beauty, denuded. The statistics and postulates in the body of his paper were but a joke: three hundred pages of what not to do.

Only one member of his committee even commented on the Introduction,[54] and that with the red words writ large upon the final page: "self indulgent."

When the old man left, I sought another then another then another: emerging from the bodies of women and children, some of whom seemed far too young to be passing by. All of these "souls," as I came to understand they were, passed by in the same moment in which I was frozen. They spoke of time as though it were something that passed, but I could only measure the passage of souls through my emerging consciousness and toward the ever-increasing and increasingly elusive light.

I resided in the corridors of an immitigable and haunting presence, creating and consuming snapshots of the same scene from countless perspectives.

"Go," was the admonition from his family.
"Go," was the scream from his academic peers.
"Go," was the collective sigh of the civilized world.

---

54 Dark energy endures in this dearth of distraction. Concentrating without hope or fullness, frayed ends of understanding have been clipped from our narrative.

Perhaps, they thought, he could be of some good to people who could not understand what he was saying and thus could overlook his ridiculous genius. Perhaps some work in the mundane would teach him humility: build a school; dig a trench; exist in the basics of humanity.

From these passers-by, I learned in fleeting lessons about life and death. I learned that some were ready to fill the light; I learned that some were not. I learned the words to describe these things. I learned to understand, though I could not feel. I learned that, because I had no soul, I would not feel. I gained the voice to ease the transition for those who had no choice in the matter.

Within a week of arriving in North Central Africa, he contracted malaria. Within two weeks, he was back in the United States, in a hospital room fighting for his life. His perfect constitution was as ill-suited as America's in that part of the world. The malaria so weakened his immune system that a secondary viral infection, something like a meningitis attacked his brain. In order to quell the swelling, doctors induced a medical coma from which they later could not resurrect him.

He was human, after all.

SLEEP

I HAVE BEEN INCAPABLE OF MOVING, EVEN A FINGER OR AN EYE, FOR at least a year now. I feel relatively certain about this timeframe because I have been watching the crepe myrtle outside the window of the room I am in. When I came here, the crepe myrtle was bursting with pink. I have since watched it fade to brown, then disappear, then climb back into view one green sprig at a time until it is today exploding with pink again. I am grateful that my family faced me toward the window even though they have no idea whether I can actually see or not.

Likely, my position in the room has been dictated by my wife who has not missed a day by my side. I assert this "day" observation with a bit of care. As best as I have been able to distinguish days from nights—periods of light and dark—she has been present. My comprehension, perhaps better described as my "sense," of time is not dictated by an absolute passage, but rather by relative changes in states: light or dark,[55] recumbent or reclined, numbness or pain.

I have watched her demeanor change with the seasons as well. From unfettered hope to staunch acceptance, Spring passed to Summer. The realization that my state was probably inalterable moved with an early September rustle, interrupted only by a few moments of Indian Summer, to a halting Autumnal despair. Forcing

---

55 Our photos have been unduly cropped, unsophisticatedly engineered.

a mask of joy upon a season of salvation, I know she silently prayed to the spirit of the anticipated newborn Christ during Advent for my shedding off of the shackles of life. And I have once again watched her, ebullient with hope—feigned for the sake of a child who is now able to comprehend who I am—and vigor, make fake preparations for my return home. Her tender words accompanied by pecks on my cheek, her sheepish finger fondling my hair, her tears, her raspy and longing soliloquies intermingling memory with nostalgia: all bear witness to a doting and dutiful wife.

I've been visited by more friends and family than I ever knew I had. In addition to my porcelain-faced wife and even more porcelain-faced daughter, I have also seen the faces of my loved ones change, grow a year older...or more. Parents and siblings and nieces and nephews alike—I've watched tired and pained faces crackle under the pressure and stress that comes from caring for me. I've watched young faces mature. I've seen beards grow on the faces of those who were but boys. I've seen the faces of people I know and many I do not as they have come to visit me. I have seen the seasons change by the clothes my visitors have worn: first polos, then t-shirts, then flannels, then sweatshirts and coats. The polos have returned with the crepe myrtles.

I am excited to see my child celebrate Easter again, which must be right around the corner. Last year, they dressed my daughter as a bunny. Adorable and carefree, she played in my room and spoke at me, with those few words saved for and murmured by three year olds— for hours. She didn't want to leave, but was eventually convinced by those who were able to speak that hunting Easter eggs would be more fun than playing hide and seek with the motionless creature in the bed. I could not, in good conscience, argue otherwise though the physical inability to move my lips or force air from my diaphragm over my pharynx also prevented my argument.

The outpouring of sheer delight and unabated love that flows from my visitors is no less poignant than the unfettered hatred that drove me here in the first place. For every morsel of adoration that I receive from my family and friends, for every cheery reminiscence at my bedside, for each enchanting monologue and anecdote of football-field heroics or gymnastic feats, for the hundreds of quiet assurances that I am loved and that my family is well cared for, there remains a dark spot on my soul. My heart, before the accident, was as black as the darkest country night. Why I had allowed my fetid essence to overtake my outwardly good-humored life still eludes me, but it did. And when my melancholy—the short and practically unnoticed interlude that separated my two states—broke for evil, it did so with such ferocity that I could feel the eighth circle of Hell open within my chest.[56]

While it took me some time to recognize that the movement of muscles that I ordered within my mind was not followed throughout by my limbs and extremities, I am certain that I am, in fact, still alive. Though living, I am not completely confined by my body. I am relatively certain that my physical eyes are closed, yet I see my surroundings. I am relatively certain that the synapses connecting my ears to my brain are short-circuited, yet I hear. I am relatively certain that my fingers and toes are gone, yet there are moments in which a pain indescribable with even the words of a thousand libraries consumes me.

I surmise that my spirit has been set askew from my corporeal existence. Slightly de-tethered, my consciousness sits infinitesimally above my body. While I've worked through the possibility that this de-tethering has allowed my good and pure being to escape from my Chillingsworth's blackness, I am uncertain that it is that metaphysical. Neither is this separation purely the physical from the sprit: I feel. I have sense and thought, but no control. I cannot float above my body and look down, so I know only the positions and movements

---

56 Distraction in the act of charting the beauty around us, like distraction in conception, however, must be limited by our constraints. The snapshot must, at some point, be framed.

that others have forced upon me. Although I am uncertain that my heart or lungs work anymore, when I am alone with my thoughts, I hear my pained heart beat. I feel it.

My darling wife took the loss so much better than me. Something in the womanly constitution makes the pain of loss somehow as endurable as the pain of birth. For her, these pains arrived concurrently, with a perfectly still baby delivered from her womb. It never cried, nor even gasped for a first breath. The silent, vacant expression that it greeted us with was as haunting as the ghastly shade of bluish grey that tinged even his tiny toes.

I could not forgive like she could. I did not have the pain of birthing to shadow the pain of loss. I did not have the pain of loss, even, to shadow it. In only a few instances in my life had I even lost an arm-wresting match, let alone lost a loved one. I could not move on without somehow recouping some value for my loss. I had been consumed with a misplaced quest for vengeance—one with which the vigor of perfection and accomplishment had become my paradigm. At the same time, angry that I should lose anything and desperate that I could lose everything, I sought the only salve I could imagine—with the irreverence of a child pulling wings off of crickets. The legions of demons welled up and consumed me and affirmed the vengeance that my forsaken relationship with God told me was his alone. My being was not cleaved, but self-ingested.

I plotted with such quiet intensity that even my wife—my perfect and lovely wife—was hardly aware of what I had in store for the Doctor whose profligate actions allowed my son to die. For months after the inebriated Doctor allowed my son to be strangled by his own umbilical cord within my wife's throbbing womb, I scraped the bottom limits of human sadness. When at last I made love to her again, it was a mocking charade. I could only imagine that I was inflicting pain upon that Doctor: a weird combination of asyncopated carnality that surely affected new pains upon what should have been the tenderest moments with my divine beau. I plunged a dagger deep into his heart, then deeper, then deeper until his vapid haughtiness—that subhuman object of my pungent disdain—was at last stilled and his fingers grey. She wept. I robbed her of the only joy I had left to give her, and we never had a chance to try again. Consumed as I was with my fiendish plot, I could not imagine ecstasy but for the utter destruction of my unwitting nemesis.

"There was nothing we could do," he slouched in my direction, the swill of expensive merlot still staining his lips and burning my nostrils. "It was just too tangled."

"'IT?'"

"I'm so sorry," he slurred.

"'IT' was my son." I shouted with the rage of a thousand warriors.

"'IT' was going to bear my name. 'IT' was going to be an Olympic Gold Medalist. 'IT' was going to be President, and cure cancer, and be by my bedside when I pass on to Heaven. 'IT' was my son." Perhaps less eloquent and more broken by sobs and grotesque guffaws than I idealize the invective, the sentiments were there. My son had been stolen from me by a careless and unrepentant man during what should have been an easily remedied birthing anomaly.

When the Doctor left the room, my wife and I cried together. Then the nurses left us completely alone. In each others' arms, time stood still. Even then, I could feel the ability to forgive draining out of me, as though an elixir spilt through my tears. Though I never knew for certain, I imagined the Doctor returning to his dinner with his wife and his children and his bottle of expensive wine. As I reimagined and rewrote the conclusion of the night—through the increasingly myopic lenses of rage—the Doctor's post-delivery actions became more sinister. Each time I re-lived the moment, his eyes gleamed with more redness and his back more grotesquely hunched. Ultimately, I settled upon a constructed narrative that returned him to a raucous bacchanalia surrounded by the corpses of countless others' nascent sons and reveling in the despair of their fathers.

When, at last, I completed planning my revenge, I set the date and time. I was insistent that it would be unrelentingly violent. For all the tenderness of the still corpse in my flaccid arms, there would be writhing, dismembering pain to balance it. The Doctor would pay with his body in a way that would shake the universe around him.

The system, too, had failed. The hospital closed every door of accountability available to us. Unsanctioned, the Doctor continued to practice. The institution was as culpable as the individual within it and equally deserving of my ire. My swath of revenge would be exacted with a plow, not a scalpel.

Building a bomb was not difficult. I learned what I needed to know on the Internet. Apparently, the myths about the FBI monitoring searches for terrorist-related inquiries were fear-mongered hype. Nobody ever showed at my door and, from what I could discern, I was never followed or investigated. Slowly acquiring the components gave me special pleasure. Besides making my activities undetectable, each isolated purchase ripped off the ever-darkening scab on my re-exposed soul. When, at last, the contraption was complete, I only needed to place it.

I made an appointment for recurring patella pain. This was my excuse to wander the hospital and search for the ideal location. I wore the most unassuming tan outfit I could piece together and searched the halls for empty rooms. Nobody questioned my exploring. I walked with purpose. I found the Doctor's office, then found a nearby closet. For all the cleanliness and sterility that a hospital outwardly displays, this closet was the most disgusting space I had ever seen. Clearly, it was used as a repository for outdated instruments, cleaning supplies—an irony that, were my heart not hardened, would have otherwise struck me as hilarious—and old, dirty scrubs. Where rat feces may have completed the cliché of dirtiness, a layer of dust, dander, and sweat congealed to form a gelatinous residue.

My bomb was designed for maximum destruction. It needed to be compact enough to fit into an innocuous backpack but strong enough to blast through interior walls and spread at least sixty feet in each direction. Based upon how I placed it, the maximum blast would concuss vertically or horizontally. I found a closet within two doors of my target's office. If he was anywhere within a thirty-foot radius, he would be destroyed. There would be nothing left of him. Within sixty feet, he would be killed, though there might be enough of him to work on until his wounds were declared mortal. Though I couldn't be certain of this outcome, several floors could be destroyed. In a perfect execution, the strength of the blast would weaken the structural integrity of the building, facilitating the carnage of a collapse. There were no innocent bystanders. Collateral damages were to be an exclamation point upon the viciousness of the execution. The institution would pay for the sins of the Doctor.[57] He and his memory would be stained with the sacrificial blood of those who would dare trust him—with even so much as proximity.

After identifying the location for placement, only a detonator remained. I decided on a redundant fuse device. Should the radio-activated detonator fail, a timer would finish the job. The latter, of course, would be destructive but not targeted. The former would ensure the obliteration of the failed healer. My desire for destruction and carnage had, by this point, overtaken my quest for vengeance. Neither of these scenarios was preferred. In fact, I placed the secondary fuse on a random timer that could go off anytime, completely devoid of target, yielding only carnage. I was rather pleased with my ability to construct this secondary fuse. It was date and time sensitive. The only constraint I placed upon the timer was that it would detonate within twelve months of activation. My pride was black. My still-born son's clenched blue fingers but a fuzzy and almost forgotten backdrop for my planning.

I am doubtful that the bomb has yet exploded. The blackness that once defined my soul has, in this year of corporeal paralysis, softened

---

57 While we may rejoice in the asymptotic approach of delirium, we must, even in post-Euclidian geometrics, approximate tangency. The beauty of truth—language itself—is a constraint beyond which we can move.

to a mushy grey. All I can do is enjoy the doting moments from my family and friends while pushing out—save for swirling moments of contemplative doom like this one—the concussive inevitability that looms on the horizon of human misery that I have set in motion. If, but for a twinkling, I could hurl my living corpse upon the ticking mortar, I would. Instead, I know that when the blast finally comes, it will silence more hearts than my own, and will never ever reunite me with the child whose still-born embrace will eternally elude me.

BORGES

After perfectly executing his plan for the manifestation and consumption of dark energy particulates, his sturdy yet still—comatose—body was placed in a sterile hospital tomb where it was all but forgotten. For nearly fifteen years prior, he had been engineering the details of his plan. He caught his first accidental glimpse of the possibility while reading through the fictionalized footnotes to an obscure Borges story, "Pierre Menard, Author of the Quixote." Once he decoded the labyrinthine text, he recognized that there existed a realm of being in which the simultaneity of events in practice could be perfectly signified in the frail body of a blind librarian. He, from that moment, forsook all sincere human interaction in the myopic quest for the attainment of his mission.

Through college and his doctoral studies, while researching type 2A supernovae, he concurrently looked out into the universe and back in time. He witnessed the birth of the Milky Way and the earth. He witnessed the creation of the skies and seas; the moon and Man. He witnessed the pharmakon-infused execution of Socrates and the moment when Borges was physically pared himself, inspiring the essay "Borges y Yo" which generations of Argentine, French, and American scholars interpreted as a stylistic literary fore into the symbolic.

From opposite ends of their own looking glasses, he saw eye to eye with Galileo, whose own lightly magnified gaze looked only slightly back through the fourth dimension. Through Galileo's hazy pupil, he saw truth and beauty and the answer to the questions he only at that moment knew to ask. From that moment until the moment in which he partook of the brain-expanding serum, he existed in a ruse to hide his knowledge from the rest of the world. He inhabited space, but did not live in it.

As he studied astrophysics, he witnessed history and science and the history of science and knew that they were all one. He consorted with contemporaries who furthered his understanding and helped hone his plan: Jesus, Euclid, Jefferson, Descartes, Einstein, Leonardo. History and science were, he discovered, housed in what another collaborator, Kant, had tried to describe as the "sublime."[58]

Watching Socrates's suicide first hand, he discovered that the hemlock concoction was designed to induce a deep sleep into which dark energy particulates could be poured. The Socratic, enlightened slumber, however, brought about such deep satisfaction that the great and methodical teacher chose consciously never to awaken.

Based upon Socrates's ingredient list, he developed a potion that would swell the brain so that it would—sponge-like—absorb dark energy into its synaptic tissue. The final ingredient, ***Conium chaerophylloides***, could not be acquired in the United States. For that, he had to go abroad, to southern Africa. So, to Africa he went with the Peace Corps, ostensibly to build a schoolhouse for starving orphans. Within days of his arrival, he had consumed the drink and

---

58 Along the path from image to language, through a consciousness of concentration and distraction, between conception and beauty: a research method.

was shipped home on what doctors assumed was the verge of death; he had achieved Coma.

Then he arrived; the academic understanding with which I had inter-acted in the precipice was made real. No longer, in his presence, was I a freak. He made me whole. He brought the light nearer to me. Though it was still beyond my grasp, it was closer; I was freed, at once, to glow in its omnipresent proximity.

He had no friends to visit him as he lay in his quiet coma. His mother came only once a week, and then more out of obligation than love or responsibility. She spent time doting on the two normal children she had at home. The specific ordinariness that accompanied the high-school senior and his younger sister were welcome distractions from what should have been a faith-shattering experience with the oddly golden child.

He gave me more words. With more words, I became more like him: less of a monster.
He gave me every word he had and I used them to animate.

His sister was too young to be repelled by the obnoxious perfection of the brother that she now knew only as the invalid in the hospital. She was never jealous of or hateful toward him. She was never emasculated by his prowess nor diminished by his diatribes. She—and she never really expressed it—silently worshipped him. She was artsy: a writer and a potter. As she got older, she began to snoop around his stuff which his parents had quickly—just weeks after he didn't waken from the coma—boxed. They turned his bedroom into a den. The boxes, filled with notebooks, sat in a corner of the three-car garage attracting mold and rats. They had long since donated his clothes.

Never, he told me, had he felt so alive as when he was in my presence. I could not empathize, for I knew this thing called "life" as nothing more than a passing state upon which I could fix my gaze. How could I, never having been born, be the giver of life?

He gave me permission. Without knowing that he had no right to grant it, I accepted it.

His sister, inquisitive and restless, often passed her time thumbing through the boxes. Most of his writings were impenetrable to her. Eventually, she found a work that he had never published nor ever shared with anyone. She was certain of this because the binder cover was marked "CONFIDENTIAL, DO NOT EVER PUBLISH." The cover opened onto a coded manuscript. She quickly recognized that it was written *a la* D' Vinci, in mirror code. She fished a mirror from the drawer next to the washing machine and deciphered the work in short order—reading words, but not piecing them together into the intelligible whole they represented. She thought she understood why the golden prophet wanted it hidden forever.

Unlike any of the passing souls I had encountered before, he touched me.

Unlike many of the other neatly edited and precisely worded essays and works that she had little capacity to understand, this was decidedly different. In form and content, it was unlike any other piece of his that she had ever seen.

He gave me the power to—more than merely learn—think.
Just short of human, I knew humanity. Just short of living, I knew life.

She thought that it was—by his standards—at best, mediocre. Her first reading was cloaked in an opacity that she would not easily shatter. Perhaps, she posited, he wrote it when he was very young.

The work did, however, provide her a glimpse into a side of her eldest brother which bespoke his humanity: imperfect and self-conscious. As unimpressive as this work might have been in relation to his uber corpus, it was nonetheless amazing by her standards.

We wandered the corridors of the hospital together. I described what I had seen. He explained it. He bridged the gap between what I saw and what I could know.

From grazing the surface and working from the assumption that this was a "childish" piece, she developed empathy for the young mind whose words she read. The work was rife with idealism and theory. The humanity and sensitivity did not jibe with the established narrative about her brother. Not grasping the density of the Maimonides-like text before her,[59] she promised not to betray him. Instead, expecting that her brother would never rouse, she decided to appropriate the work as her own.

He gave me permission to experience time. Together we unfroze the moment of grief which had lingered since the day I was not born. As we hovered over the moment, he observed that I was strangled by my umbilical cord at the moment I should have been born. He observed that the ashen man he identified as my father was inconsolable. As we unfroze the moment, we watched a brilliant beam of light shoot from him; we watched that bolt join the light above while the un-whole remainder of his spirit stayed with his body.

She wrapped the binder in a towel from the clothes dryer, picked off the meadow-fresh fabric-softener sheet, and ran into her room with the oddly folded package tucked under her arm. Anyone who might have seen her would have known that she carried a notebook

---

59 Benjamin challenges us to employ this method as a matter of habit.

wrapped in a towel. Fortunately, she was home alone. Brother was at the mall; parents were on a "date night;" and—of course—Golden Boy was comatose at the hospital across town.

He gave me permission to feel. I saw my hands for the first time ever. I saw his giant hands.

I saw the woman who he identified as my mother holding a limp gray body—my body—in her own hands: she held me in her hands.

Nervous, as though she had just stolen the Mona Lisa from the Louvre, she unfolded the towel and slid the folio between her mattress and box spring. She was careful to move it fully to the middle so that nobody would notice it if they were changing the sheets on her bed. She jumped onto the bed and assumed her sleep position to ensure that the contraband would not disturb her. The notebook was thin enough that she would not be bothered, she decided, and was pleased with the chosen hiding space.

He revealed what life had told him. I revealed what the lack of life had told me. Our words commingled.

We watched as his body was poked and probed. We watched as nurses washed him. We watched as the room in which I was never born finally emptied. We followed the ashen body which should have been mine to the lower floors. We followed it to the doors which led out of the hospital, but we couldn't follow it any farther. He told me that they were going to bury my unborn body; they were going to mourn the life that never was.

Several adolescent months passed and, one night as she sat alone and otherwise purposeless in her room, she recovered her treasure from its hiding spot. She hovered over the first manuscript and translated it. The blank verse and empty structure struck her as raw and guttural. How could this form have ever emanated from the pen of her rigidly and perfectly ordered brother? How could someone so shunned by the world perform a call to a hypothetical fraternity? To whom was he speaking? Who was his "we?" Further, she wondered, how could he so commingle chaos with beauty—two forces which seemed to have been anathema to his sensibility?

We hovered over his body and he explained that he was still alive. He told me how his body worked. He invited me to touch it. He permitted me to know it. It was perfect. I knew it. Neither of us knew what to do with the light. At last we touched it.

After two hours, she completed the untitled translation. Humpbacked, she hovered over the works, his and hers, and compared the two. She felt as though the gulf between them was as distant as the big bang was to this moment. She pondered that gulf for an instant and decided that it was but a matter of geographic centimeters, measured not by the tools of astrophysics, but rather by those of quantum physics.

Together, with our commingled touches, we knew that the light was beautiful: indescribably, unambiguously, chaotically perfect.

She suddenly became conscious of her thoughts and instantly unsure of their origins. A high-school junior, she had never studied physics and had never heard the phrase "quantum physics." Instantly, her thoughts raced to a memory which was not conceivable were she not experiencing it: her conception. She watched, she felt, she lived as sperm and egg combined and an electrical halo sparked forth her life. She watched her own meiosis. She watched as her personal universe doubled, then quadrupled, then expanded and enveloped her. She was at her origin. She had unlocked the pathway to the genesis.

And then were granted words—all words—that informed our previous lack of them. No longer was anything indescribable or ambiguous. No longer was chaos a mystery.

The balance of the night, hours of sleepless study, she read and re-read it. She fell into an abyss, indeed into the very chaos about which she read. Alas, poor girl, she entered that chaos as a conspirator—part of the euphemistic "we"—before sliding along the least-squares line into the mean. When finally she emerged on the other side, approximating Beauty, she had come to own it, if only but for a moment. She could not discern whether that moment was a second or a lifetime.

Just as he had allowed me time, I was now empowered to help him stop it. We were joined in a new moment in which he and I were no longer separate: I was no longer unborn and he was no longer undead. We were birth and death together: we were life across time. We touched the light and were made one with it. Then we retreated together.

Sojourner, her understanding brought her to tangency with beauty, to a single point where "I" and "we" converged: first and second derivatives. She was struck. She was enlightened. Awakened from the clay and dust of the universe, she had inherited her brother's rib and hungered for the fruit of the tree of knowledge.

Her hunger was not metaphorical; it was manifest in an unabatedly physical way. She could feel it welling from the pit of her stomach as though it were from the ninth circle of Hell. A vast emptiness encircled by an event horizon exploded from within her womb and washed over her in waves of insatiable yearning.

His thoughts were mine. We were consciousness commingled. His experiences were mine. We pulled away from the light toward a black hole. We receded into the warmth of an undulant, pulsing, living womb. We fled, hand in hand, into the darkness.

Her body tensed and convulsed. She dropped her pen, the manuscripts—both the original and its translation—and the mirror onto the ground. Now alone on her four-poster bed, all other accoutrement (save her pillows) littering the perimeter on the floor, her fits became more violent. Tiny twitches that started at the tips of her toes and fingers flowed into torrential electrical rivers up her extremities and converged into her torso with such ferocity that anybody watching would have expected an explosion.

For the first time, I emoted. I wanted. I yearned for life. I longed to be born.

For a moment, her heart could not keep up with the seizure. Briefly, her heart stopped and with it the seizure.

For the first time, he emoted. He wanted. He yearned for life. He longed to awaken.

When her parents returned home, they checked in on her. Surprised that she was even home, they commented to each other on the peaceful repose that she maintained, even as she slept fully clothed upon her bed. They decided against rousing her, but merely shut off the lights. Her mother, lit by the hallway light through the doorway, gently tugged off her shoes and set them neatly on the ground beside the schoolwork they assumed she had been working on. Quietly, they pulled the door shut as they wandered further down the hall to the den.

Then he left me. Immediately, I missed him. I hurt. My soul craved his touch, his words—his presence.

He had taught me much. He had given me permission to approximate life, though I could never truly know it. Together, we had touched the light and returned. I was still unborn. He was free to wake, without me.

I sped to the still-empty unfrozen room where I was yet unborn, yearning for the ignorance with which I first viewed the scene: a soulless camera.

Across town, in a quietly white and untenably sterile room, repose was stirred. Like gently sliding down a stainless steel pole and landing in the bosom of a serene pool of life, the eyes of the precocious sleeper flittered open. As they adjusted to the soft light of the room, fingers stretched and clenched in rhythm with deep breaths. More like waking from a yoga position than a fourteen-month coma, movement was both fluid and exact.

Powerless, I tried to freeze the moment; I attempted to reclaim instance. Yet, I knew too much. I had words. I had time. I had knowledge. I had emotion. I had loss.

I had nothing.

A nurse, expecting that the ringing from his room indicated a malfunctioning monitor, took her time before sticking her head through his door. She experienced eurhythmy herself when she saw the still, perfect, shirtless body of a young man sitting up and looking her way.

Looking down, I saw his living form and was lustful of its corporeal perfection.

"Hello," he managed to speak as though trying to comfort her.

The nurse fainted. This set off a flurry of activity—footsteps and yelling—in the hallway, all of which froze as one nurse after another was struck dumb and motionless beholding the resurrection.

Methodically, he removed all of the life-sustaining and monitoring tethers from his body. "I need a shower."

Please, come back.

One of the nurses entered the room and turned on the lights. Another could be heard running down the hallway while a third attended to the nurse who had passed out.

Our light!

"You're going to need to remain still for me," a nurse requested as she approached him, fiddling with the disconnected cords and constructing a strategy for reconnecting them to him.

We have stood at the second derivative of chaos.
We looked behind us and saw ether through which floated flashes of incandescent genius.

"I've been still long enough," he responded. Already commanding the attention of the room and verging on annoying, he listed a series of demands: "I need a shower, I need my clothes, I need a computer with wi/fi, I would love a Mountain Dew, and I need somebody to call me a cab." His demeanor indicated both cool concentration and warm distraction.[60]

---

60 We don't overstretch to meet this as we approach the truth in beauty for we are constantly distracted, moving through time and space as a matter of habit.

Remember?

A doctor walked in, followed by another doctor, and another. Within minutes, there were no fewer than six doctors and four nurses in the rapidly shrinking hospital room. Two groups huddled, one by the window and the other by the door. One at a time, they would leave the huddle to address the patient and report on stats. Different voices called out and to the patient, interacting with and describing him:

"Do you know what today is?"

"Ninety seven point seven"

"How do you feel?"

"Seventy four."

"Describe the pressure when I do this."

"One forty over sixty two."

"What is the last thing you remember?"

"What is the square root of sixty four?"

"Can you feel this?"

"Is your vision blurred?"

"Here's some water, drink this."

"What is the capital of South Carolina?"

"Can you grab my hand?"

"Columbia."

Please, grab my hand!

Finally, a pad and pencil were provided, "Write down all of your thoughts, however silly they might seem."

We looked before us and we saw an infinitely untenable synapse, a Styx, whose gondolier waved from some undefined center of pre-chaotic bliss. We wondered where we were, and discovered that we were not even there yet.

The flock of doctors quacked about the unprecedented and historical occasion which they were witnessing. "We cannot afford to miss a single data point," one carved out the obvious.

Remember?

One of the attendants excused himself and made the call from the hallway, "You're son…you should come quickly."

At first fretting that it was the favorite son who had not yet come home from his night with friends, the increasingly frantic mother recaptured her senses, "What? He's awake?!"

The quizzing, testing, and probing continued for ninety minutes.

Finally the room cleared and one of the nurses came in with a sponge and wiped him down, removing the few days worth of grime that had accumulated since his last bath. He grudgingly accepted this excuse of a shower. He had a particular endorphin-infused scent that had been missing during his slumber. He glistened. He glowed.

The light shone from him. I moved in his direction but, the faster I flew, the farther away he became. As I sped toward him, his retreat became equally emphatic. I reached out my hand but was rebuffed by a force I couldn't see. And then I couldn't see at all. The only power I ever truly had, observation, had abandoned me.

Finally, he pushed his right foot toward the cold floor, in deliberate revolt against the bather. As if under a spell, the nurse threw down her tools and gently grabbed his hand. With the other hand, she supported him at the elbow as he strongly forced himself in the direction of gravity, then immediately defied it as he stood tall and peacefully and menacingly at the same time.

He is beautiful. I am blind again. I am voiceless again. I am alone with my thought: lightless chaos. Cursed words!

Fourteen months of stillness yielded no atrophy. His body was as sturdy and perfect as the day he fell asleep. In his full nakedness, he commanded awe. Other attendants entered the room and, jaws agape, stood in silent subservience. He nodded his head in their directions, acknowledging each in their due.

His parents walked in and his mother, in an action which she had stopped a full four years before his accident, ran up and hugged him. He was clearly surprised by this outpouring of emotion from a woman who had not looked him in the eyes since he was a college freshman. She sobbed without control and fell to her knees. She wrapped her arms around his legs and washed his feet with her constantly streaming tears.

"Wake her up!" she cried. "Please, I know you can. Wake her up. Wake her up!" Then, turning on him, "You freak!"

In a shudder's snap, I felt a new presence. Time returned.
Time returns.

He looked behind her and saw his father, holding a limp body in his arms. As if carrying her to a sacrificial pyre, he held her loosely horizontal. His father held his sister in his arms, scooped sturdily beneath the knees and below the shoulder blades. The fifteen-year-old girl's head fell back and her hair hung straight down toward the floor. Her mouth was opened slightly and she breathed with the casual abandon that should sustain any adolescent. Her eyelids sat loosely over her eyes and he could see a sliver of white through her thin eyelashes.

"She won't wake up," said his father, a sliding bubble of salty water traced down his cheek and rested on the corner of his mouth. "We just can't wake her up."

I am awakened.

Save the naked patient—awakened as he was from his self-induced slumber—a stunning stillness overcame the room. The maturation of his critical method made real, the oscillation between distraction and concentration made singular and ephemeral Beauty in the face of chaos made tangible, the awakened creature flexed his chest as though to make room for a swelling heart: a blossoming soul.

Tenderly, he walked over to the sleeping girl. The eyes of four doctors, three nurses, a distraught mother, and a heartbroken cub of a father followed him with the intensity of the Hubble staring into space.

For me?
She is beautiful.
I stand at the first derivative of chaos, and her name is Beauty.

"You may have witnessed Beauty, dear sister, but I have endured and mastered Chaos." His empty eyes sparkled for a moment before he kissed her forehead and left the room.

I will teach her.

I do not know which of us has written this page.

Come with me.
Take my hand.

She never awoke.

I will teach you. Follow me.

MOMENTITIOUSNESS
TWO

DORITOS

W HAT HE LACKED IN CLASSICAL TRAINING, HE MADE UP FOR WITH inquisitiveness and creative solution-seeking: an in-your-face approach to unrequited expectations that constantly re-aligned realities all around him. Maybe it was pure evil. Perhaps, his two brothers and four sisters posited, he would one day learn the skills of proper interaction with his fellow humans. For now, they ultimately concluded, he was harmless enough. As the first decade one spends on this planet presents far more hope for the future than disappointment in the past, the quiet consensus was that they would overlook the legions of demons that had apparently lived within him for the first three-thousand-seven-hundred days of his life. They loved him out of duty and not without misgivings.

His "inquisitiveness and creative solution-seeking" were actually starry-eyed spins on what was, in reality, an incessant questioning of established hierarchies and a proven willingness to destroy what he could not understand. The lack of "classical training" was code for his third stint in the second grade. He did not read. He did not figure. He did not even write his name. Most beguiling, he did not play. He was a ten-year-old child in name only, undertaking none of the expected traits that childhood should bestow upon a soul. He quite likely was possessed, though none in the family had the vocabulary to describe it as such. Thus, the decision was to "Love that little devil," and hope.

They showered gifts upon him, but his hunger for that which others owned was insatiable. Whether in the closet, hand, or plate of someone else, he was never satisfied until he had come to possess that which was somebody else's. When he could not cajole a covetee into handing over what he desired, he either waited until he could burrow in and steal it, or he attained ownership through outright force. Often the force was psychological, having proven long ago that there was no level of bodily harm he would refrain from inflicting upon an enemy. Not the pinnacle of his disregard for humane treatment of other creatures, but certainly standing as an iconic moment was the pulp-beating he laid upon a puppy who had a slobber-ridden tennis ball he wanted.

He had also proven by the age of five—half of his lifetime ago—that every relationship he had was with enemies—rivals for things—some of whom he despised less than others. He never wanted anything absolutely. Every prize was measured by its relative value to his rivals. He only wanted that which someone else loved. Thus, it was not uncommon for his ever-optimistic guardians to bring him to a toy store, the fun-teeming aisles offering scores of undesired items, only to watch him attack other children as they walked out of the bazaar, stealing kites and crayons, baseball cards, and Lincoln logs. Nobody, neither shopkeepers nor parents nor teachers nor classmates, ever stood up to the child. Seemingly entranced by his recalcitrance, they merely watched in horror as he terrorized all around him. Once dispossession occurred, he would cast off his new acquisitions with the casual lack of attention that others would deign appropriate for bubble-gum wrappers or pop tops.

Apologetically, his guardians would often loiter in his wake, making recompense with his victims. Each year, the holiday toy drives were enthusiastically enriched by scads of unused, often still-wrapped, items from his cast-off pile. Having acquired his treasures, he had already sapped all of their value in the act of acquisition. Few items, save foodstuffs which at least merited one bite, were ever consumed or used for their stated purpose. Toy guns went unfired, Lego villages unbuilt, Big Wheels unridden, race tracks untraveled, board games unplayed, walkie-talkies unmorsed.

Maintaining his health was a game in which his guardians and siblings would, in turn, extoll the virtues of the particular foodstuff that they were enjoying during a meal. Even to a dead soul, bereft as it was of any inwardly motivated cravings or favorites, the family enjoyed with a wry irony watching him sustain himself—after the baited confiscation—with such nutritionally packed items as steamed spinach, fried liver, Spam, creamed onions, and Brussels sprouts that would not have been natively enjoyed by any child his age. Never caring for the intrinsic taste of the object, all gratification was measured in his consumption of something that he believed was favored by the person from who he confiscated it. In rare moments of familial revenging, items sure to disagree with his system were dangled before him. He never flinched as he devoured intestine-scalding chili peppers that would have incapacitated most human constitutions, nor did he come up for air while ingesting a specially concocted bean chili that the recipe-card unapologetically described as "colon blow." Overall, his diet was balanced and healthy enough to support his growth and ensure that, though he never paid a lick of attention there, he never missed a day of school due to illness.

This day, as he sat alone on the couch in front of a motionless— not on—flat screen television, he waited for a victim to pass his way. Unfortunately for his brother, older by two years but nearly the same in size and presence, the ownership of a bag of Doritos was about to come into question. As the older sibling crossed the path toward the television and turned it on, an intoxicating scent wafted in his trail. The rustle of the plastic container as tiny hands plunged into it stirred the senses, and the Sampsonian desire erupted in the Legionous being. The cadent crunching of his brother's teeth within a seemingly cavernous—echoing—skull taunted him into an eruption of ashen terror that only an academically esoteric mixed metaphor dare attempt capture. Seemingly blind to the lurking figure on the couch, the snack-eater sank into the embrace of the oversized leather couch. His eyes mesmerized by the screaming television, his countenance forgave the presence of his younger brother.

Not slyly, nor even calculatedly, the younger stood and loomed between the seated sibling and the now-blaring television.[61] Rage washed over him and visibly transformed his rather passive lonely countenance into one of pitiable, consumptive craving. Without asking, he stared into the face of his rival and lunged for the prize. Never, in the history of humanity has a three-ounce bag of nacho-cheese-flavored, triangular, fried, corn-meal crisps been the focus of such nuclear energy. At first, the older sibling, conscious of the implicit baiting, outstretched his arm in the opposite direction of the pounce, saving his sole ownership for at least another second. The devil child landed on his brother's lap as he mounted a second frontal attack on the snack container.

With a single blow from the fisted, unoccupied hand of the victim upon the back of the skull of the attacker, momentary stillness was affected. The attacker, stunned, remained face down, frozen mid-pounce upon the seated boy's lap. Slowly, he flexed his neck, raising his head and blinking his eyes to recover his vision through the haze that had been incurred by the blow which he scarcely remembered.

He dove his face into his brother's bare leg, opened his mouth as wide as his jaws would permit and clenched down upon it, baby teeth yielding against his fleshy pink gums. The older brother, abandoning the snack bag upon the high back of the couch cushion, grabbed the devil child, squeezing hands upon ears and lifting to reveal a perfectly round and blood-oozing sunburst perforation upon his thigh. From this grip, he threw the boy head first across the room where he landed upon the plexi-wood coffee table. The neatly stacked drink

---

61 The links that we follow, the tangents that we approximate and explore, are as intuitive in modernity as star-gazing contemplation was to the ancients.

coasters, a couple of glossy magazines, and no fewer than three remote-control devices were jettisoned by the trajectory of the flying body. The X-box was pulverized upon the tile floor.

In slow motion he rose from the broken table. Nostrils flaring and heart pounding, he swept his bare feet upon the floor to gain traction first once, then, with terrifying effect, a second time. A sky-box observer might have figured he was flying as he sprung in a single bound, four limbs tautly extended, toward the still-seated and oddly calm older sibling.

A stiff-arm halted him mid flight and he fell again, this time to the floor between the bashed table and the over-plush couch. He rose again and advanced again, fists now flailing with the randomness and indefatigability of a Phaedra. Preparing for the gathering full assault, the brother rose and planted his feet, steadying his shoulder as he leaned into the rushing monster. This movement was met with an equally furious flurry of fist slinging and twin, shrill, screeching, screams that joined into a harmonious roar of boy voices that may well have emanated from the twin centers of hell.

For the next four and a half minutes, feet kicked, mouths bit, lamps crashed, electronics crumbled, fists flew, heads butted, knees groined, furniture up-ended, drywall dented, and blood splattered. Indeed, after two hundred and fifty five calamitous seconds, the room better resembled the New Orleans' Ninth Ward after Hermosa Katrina passed through than the recreation room of a modest, middle-class, suburban Connecticut McMansion. Battered, they both fell to the floor, each with an enduring grip upon the other: one's hair and the other's throat.

They both began to cry as their hands relaxed and they slid along the toppled couch to land on the floor beside one another. Their terse grips released. The tears, at first accompanied by heaving sobs, fell into now breathless silence. Seated, four legs outstretched, toes pointing skyward like pickets holding out an invisible wall that threatened to fall upon them, their shoulders resignedly lurched toward each other's. Their chests still heft in seeming unison. Their noses dripped with fraternally coagulant snot.

Between them lay a single bag of Doritos.

Both noticing it in the same instant, two hands dashed for it. The victor—faster by milliseconds only—dove his hand into the aluminized-plastic bag and pulled out one, unblemished, perfect, oversized crisp and held it up between them as if preparing for the taking of Eucharist. He handed it to his rival and beamed a brown, scabby, mitthing-toothed smile.

Not much time passed—perhaps only minutes or a millenium—before their mother, self-locked in the butler's pantry and cowering behind the spice tower, finally worked up the courage to investigate the commotion. With a hidden cleaver clutched behind her back, she happened upon two sleeping angels, intertwined in baptismally humanized, sated, sienna-fingered slumber.

ACUTE

WE GOT ESPECIALLY DRUNK ONE NIGHT—ONCE OF HUNDREDS—and I passed out in his car. As though quickening from paralysis when I woke up, my dick was out of my jeans and he was jerking me off. I was roused into full physical capacity, but willed myself still. Rather than run the risk of having to find another ride, still in the parking lot of the nightclub where I was chronically over-served, I came.[62] Who doesn't like waking up to an orgasm?

Anyway, he was good-looking. I just wasn't really into it; I liked girls a lot better.

Other than that episode—which we discussed only once—we were good friends. I enjoyed his company and, when we were out, he always introduced me to the hottest girls in the room. Bam! Bam! Bam! He was the perfect magnet for chicks and was not competition. My passive prepayment yielded years of dividends. Every investor should be so lucky.

He doted on me like nobody else, my doting mother included. He showed me where to shop and what to buy. He reminded me when I needed a haircut, introduced me to manscaping, ensured that I flossed every day, and insisted that I got regular manicures. He might not have been born with a silver spoon in his mouth, but he

---

62 The continual barrage of extrasensory inputs over-constrain our every action. Texts and instant messages attack us as we drive, mirror-bound down thoroughfares littered by shop fronts and road signs.

certainly had an appreciation for silver. He might not have been rich, but he managed to amass the very best of the few things he had. He made sure that I, too, always had the best. I just had more of it. I was lucky to be born of means, but he felt comfortable knowing that, although there was a net-worth gradient between us, he was in every way my equal. The reality of equality eluded many of my other friends, who fell into subservience to my limitless credit cards and generosity. While others hung around because of my money, he was around despite it. He didn't treat me differently because I was rich. I appreciated it. I appreciated him.

Because of our near-constant proximity to each other, most of our friends assumed—nonjudgmentally—that he was my boyfriend, but he wasn't. We had an almost completely (the aforementioned incident aside) platonic relationship and we both got everything we needed out of it.

When he brought me home to meet her, I didn't hesitate. He'd been talking about her for months as if she were the most heavenly goddess to ever visit Earth from above. She was his best friend and he apparently knew every crack and crevice of her: mind and soul included. True to expectation, I discovered quickly that he had not exaggerated. She was beautiful, real, and was—from the moment I met her—ready to fulfill my every desire. She was perfect. She made me want to be a better person. Between the two of them, my life was whole; for a while, my life was whole.

I expected that, eventually, he would transition from chaperone to proud spectator. I expected that, in time, he would stand aside as she and I bonded toward the realization of a traditional genteel relationship in line with my lineage and her general resplendence. I expected that, as announced upon our first meeting, he would stand as best man. I expected that he would, one day, give her away as well. I expected him to be part of the family: that he would straddle the aisle as well as he straddled our broad affection.

Unfortunately, his role did not transition and the moments that the three of us spent together became increasingly awkward. If, in the stolen moments when she and I were apart from him, I would mention—even hint—that I would like to loosen the tether that he had wrapped around us, she sunk into gloomy despondence. Only by overcompensating, immediately calling him and inviting him into our presence, could I right her mood. As long as he was present, nothing impeded our joy. In his absence, a black hole loomed over us until he returned. I learned quickly that there would be no us without the three of us.

She was worth it. Generally, I never stopped enjoying the time that we three spent together; it was unequivocally blissful-ish. While he was content to pass time with me alone, she never was. If he was not present, she was unable to concentrate on anything except his absence. On more nights than not, he slept in our room and eventually he became a persistently translucent ghost in our bed. She would not have sex with me without him near. I loved her with such unreserved intensity that I allowed it. I was powerless—resigned.

We took an apartment while I finished my degree and, after I graduated, the three of us moved to the family compound where I could ultimately assume control of the family business. My parents, whose mores precluded causing discomfort to anybody ever, accepted the odd-to-everybody-but-us relationship. They accepted him with the same generosity that they accepted her. We moved into the second home on the orchards and undertook a ridiculously traditional and unaffected monogamous three-way family. As long as she was happy, so was I. As long as he was happy, so was she. As long as I was happy, well, I was happy. We were all, it seemed, happy.

The headaches started long before I ever told anybody. For months, I had been forgetting things and getting lost on the way home from town. For months, I had been experiencing "episodes," one particularly disturbing in which I woke up naked in the groves. I developed a tick; my hand trembled. My mother cornered me one morning and asked about what she called my "strange behavior lately." Spending most of her days watching Oprah Winfrey and Lifetime movies, she assumed that I had developed a secret drug problem.

"No, Momma, there is no need for an intervention."

That day I had my first seizure, right there in her kitchen. I nearly bit my tongue off. Of course she realized that I was not drug addicted but, rather, possessed. The stories that we told ourselves had been passed on from generation to generation all the way back to the days when the groves stretched farther than the eye could see and when traversing the property on horseback took the better part of a day. She knew that the Devil was always in our midst and that our family had been in his playground since before the railroads came. The devil had taken my siblings, one by one, from her womb, which left me with the responsibility of being two sons and a daughter to a mother who spent as much time waiting for my demise as she did for a grandchild.

"It would be best," she told me, "if we did not worry Poppa unnecessarily." I had obviously gathered from her the need to dwell on or near a crucifix at all times. I understood that this was the birthright of a good southern Roman Catholic. I—like her—was every bit that, even if I was possessed by the Devil and willing to keep it a secret: divergent mendacity.

We cleaned up the mess in her kitchen and decided that I would visit our family's priest the next morning. He proclaimed that my spiritual health, once I finally convinced him that I was not a "homosexual," was in order; he recommended I see a doctor for the headaches and seizures. Momma and I complied. I believe she was disappointed that I could not be cured with a crucifix and holy water.

The seizures became increasingly recurrent. We could keep my condition secret no longer. When, at last I sat them down and explained to them that I was short for this world, they were inconsolable. Poppa was matter of factual; he kissed my forehead and went for a walk in the groves.

"Hey, I'm the one who's dying," I reminded my roommates.

That did nothing to ease their pain. It did nothing to ease my pain. We were all in pain.

"How can you be so capricious about this? Don't you love me?" She stared over her shoulder at me from his embrace.

That was the single most painful collection of four words ever to pass through my ears, far more painful than, "You have eight weeks." Together, we visited doctors from all over the United States. One actually told me he would be willing to perform a risky operation that had a fifteen percent chance of healing me and an eighty five percent chance of leaving me dead on a hospital table. We opted for the fifty-six-day route through one hundred percent certainty.

We had never completed the official act of betrothal. Now, it was out of the question. Regret piled up like mounds of undead fruit after an early-spring hard freeze.

The three of us were inseparable, though I wished for his disappearance. I wanted my last days with her and her alone. Neither of them considered that this would be my wish, never asking what I wanted or needed. I became increasingly resentful of his presence but continued to bite my already perforated tongue. I would rather endure his proximity if it meant that she, too, was nearby. He stared into my eyes as she climbed atop me in her desperate attempts to conceive an heir. I acquiesced, accepting him as the tethered reality to my she-completed existence.

Oblivious to my deeply repressed and unutterable feelings, he continued to dote on me. I cursed my selfishness even as he administered pain-relieving medication, held my increasingly numb hands, placed ice on my lips. I cursed my slurred words and my inability to explain the feelings that threatened to eclipse the intensity of my headaches.

I was not ready to die.

I wished to change places with him. Gladly, I told myself, I would take care of him with utter and complete devotion as he passed from this earth. Gladly, I would ease him, with all of the love I had to share, out of our realm. These thoughts eventually jumbled into a mass of misfiring synapses in the center of my brain. I became bionic: a hub of tubes and wires.

Finally, I slipped into intermittent sleep. Even when conscious, I was physically able only to communicate with my eyes. At last I watched them dress me. It seemed to take days or weeks for them to finally get me fully accoutered. I was unsure if I was alive or not. I felt as though I was being dragged off to my funeral. I was. I wanted to scream that I was yet here, not ready for passage.

Suddenly, sensing that I was nearing orgasm, I pushed against my skin from the inside in an attempt to awaken. I looked up into the sky, the only thing which my position allowed me to see. The sun was brighter than I remember it ever being. Fleetingly, I felt my fingers tingle and my toes twitched. With all of my remaining might, I willed myself up. My will failed against the reality of a thousand invisible planets strewn across my body and holding me down.

Voices swirled around me until I saw the face of our priest, his eyes glassy and bloodshot. The words hung and I tried to grasp them, "Do you?"

"I do."

"I do."

I sent the silenced response up on my last breath. It slipped unperceived between their craned heads as they leaned over and kissed me goodbye.

JUANS

ARM IN ARM IN ARM,[63] WE STOMPED DOWN THE STREET FROM THE restaurant toward the condo which was near enough to prevent any chances of DUIs. We loved the half-price late-night happy-hour menu, even if it only included pizza and even if we were all always dieting. This stomping, one of us must have suggested, would burn off the calories and fat better than regular walking. Besides, another of us must have suggested skipping and been shot down as "too gay." As if the arm in arm in arm wasn't.

So, we stomped and laughed and played and made fun of ourselves for the better part of our three-block trek. The pizza came with a free pitcher of beer for each of us which, by itself would not have been inconsequential, and tacked onto a night of whiskey, tequila, and Jaeger were delirium-inducing maraschino cherries atop a night of unbridled shenanigans.

Coming in the back door of the vintage 1950s Bayshore condo, we could see through the glass wall along the pool into the hallway off of which our host's front door stood.

"You seem to have a visitor, amigo," I slurred, elbowing him and holding true to our Mexican-themed evening. We had been calling

---

63 Our Google starts and Wiki beginnings link us to a Web of
    information that expands differently upon each visit and for
    each person: from individual to social, from concentration to
    distraction. We think in images that link: absorbing and being
    absorbed by the scientific arts, by living.

each other "Juan" since our first tequila shot. I tried to wink with one eye but managed little more than a strained facial contortion. My girlfriend of fourteen months, his ex from college and best friend since elementary school, laughed with a spritely, giddy drunkenness. She squirreled her way in between us and kissed us both on the cheek. She was the perfect girl and I loved her. In addition to being gorgeous beyond words, she was cool. Both dainty and "one of the guys," she had managed to position herself in a place of absolute necessity in my life. I was either always with her or wanted to be.

"I don't know, but I will soon enough," he fantasized, dramatically over-accenting "soon enough," in his best Charro voice.

Although she realized during their sophomore year of college that he wasn't into her in "that way," the pain was eventually assuaged by the realization that he didn't like any girls in "that way." She quickly morphed into his wing and helped him soar through the tumults of out-coming. Working in my favor, and from some point of ironic table-turning, he introduced me to her after a late night study session for the "Advanced Financial Analytics" class we were taking together. She had borrowed his car and came by to pick him up.

He never made a move on me and, although it made me self-consciously wonder for a while what he didn't see in me, I respected him for his restraint. I had been hit on by gay guys before and knew that they could be relentless in the chase and unbearable in the throes of rejection. I did not know that he was gay when we struck up a conversation in class. If I had known I probably would have avoided him, thus depriving myself of a great buddy and the girl he eventually introduced me to.

"Hey Juan," I inquired with faux-broken Spanish, "who's your friend?"

"Ya, Juan." Our middle spoke up. "Who's your friend?"

We all giggled.

Standing at least six foot four and easily two-forty, the twenty-something guy at his door could have been the Buc's quarterback, except he looked like he'd be more poised in the pocket. He stood at an eased attention; the heather-grey t-shirt hung off his broad shoulders and, like a mannequin, sat right above his waste exposing his brown leather belt and perfectly fitting basic jeans. Even with the love of my life beside me, I was fleetingly jealous that I could not compete with his classic good looks for the lust of either of my Juans.

My insecurity spoke, "Y'all should have a three way." The joke remained unplayed on the field.

They both uneasily laughed, and I retreated into my silent rumination. "Estupido," I thought to myself. I wished I were a mannequin.

We walked in the back door of the building and gingerly ambled past the front desk where the visitor now stood, arguing with the bellman.

"I'm here on a mission."

"Sir, I'm afraid that the person you are here to visit does not exist." The round and rutty uniformed man behind the front desk maintained his composure. He acted professionally as he challenged the guest's assertion that there was somebody in this building that he needed to see.

We all leaned in, for our own reasons, to overhear the conversation.

"I bet he has a mission," I once again nudged my friend. We three continued on our way to the apartment.

"Sir," we overheard, "I'm going to have to ask you to leave."

The sound of loud footsteps reverberated from the lobby, increasing in volume in our direction. We reached our destination and casually and unhurriedly walked through the solid—I noticed that new buildings don't use heavy solid-wood doors like this—unlocked door. The last one in, obsessive compulsions dictated that I lock the door behind me, even though our host felt it an unnecessary and an obnoxious precaution.

"I never lock the door," he said with sudden lucidity, as though I had somehow offended him.

Still obsessed with the visitor that they had already forgotten about, I continued. "I bet you don't," I remember thinking—and maybe saying—"back door." I reveled in my own self-entertaining humor.

We sat on the couch and my hand wandered up and down the smooth leg of my girlfriend. I considered her beauty and remembered how lucky I was. For about thirty seconds, the room spun.

A loud pounding on the door snapped me to. I realized that my hand had seized upon her upper thigh. I looked to my right and saw them both staring at the front door which was next to the television. The loud knocking recurred.

Through the heavy door, we heard the muffled, yet distinctly labored voice of the desk attendant now shouting, "Sir, I believe you are in the wrong building." His voice trailed off into a gurgle. I, I assume we, heard what sounded like a side of beef being struck by a bat.

"Do you know this guy or not? Seriously?" I mimicked his slurred lucidity.

The front-door pounding resumed. I was now transfixed by the four-by-ten-foot—I admired the high ceilings in an older building— barrier that separated us and the hallway. It was alternately lit by the colors emanating from the flat-screen on the wall next to it. Her hand grabbed mine and squeezed. I felt suddenly validated even as I could sense my bowels loosening in the presence of a jiggling front door knob—for all the admiration I'd garnered for the high ceilings, I was suddenly disgusted by the cheap doorknob—before us.

I remained still; sirens whined in the background and the door flexed as, apparently, the shoulder of the unwelcome visitor leaned powerfully into it. As I imagined the Buccaneers losing a quarterback to a chipped clavicle, I watched my couch mates run out of the common room, down the dark hallway, and toward the bedrooms. I sat, glutes glued to the sofa.

The door flexed again and I was frozen still. "Juan," I continued the evening theme, "Do you know this dude?"

Neither of them responded from down the hall.

The flashing lemon-green light from the television exposed a jagged crack down the left quarter of the door. Whether the crack was new or not, I was unaware. I had never examined the door. Truth told, and I can say without embarrassment, I had never looked at the door.

The volume of the sirens increased.

"Hey!"

"Stand down." A new voice pierced the door. It was followed by a barrage of differently timbered, similar-to-each-other voices echoing in our general direction.

"I'm following orders," the now distinguishable voice of our visitor spoke out as the door flexed again. The crack grew under another apparent assault.

"Juan?"

I could now clearly hear six, now eight, now ten voices screaming from the other side of the door. Conspicuously silent were the voices of mi amigos.

My heart pounded in my eyes.

"What are you doing, son?" A baritone voice—that of a coach or drill-sergeant—boomed.

"Following orders."

I considered, conscious of my abandonment, what "orders" may have meant. I had spent part of the previous morning reading through an obsessive Second Amendment rant-link that my father had sent me. My sudden luculence traced an arc from camaraderie to abandonment along a track of odd illogical Constitutional arguments and Federalist Paper excerpts. "The only thing guaranteeing our First Amendment rights are our Second Amendment rights," my father often parroted.

The hairs on my forearm stood at prickly attention as I heard the door-pounder scream. I had never witnessed a tasing, though the sound was unambiguous: compressed air "pffff", uncoiling spring "zingggg" and "wzzzzzzzzzz." The scream morphed into a shrill and congestedly whistling sigh.

Through the door, I heard him yell. His shout was echoed by a number of disparate voices sounding varying degrees of anxiety.

The door flexed again and finally broke. I stood up from the couch and watched him pour into my presence. With one sweep of my head, I surveyed the entire room including a new body that lay on the floor. I was no longer completely—Juanlessly—alone. Despite my previous sense of abandonment, I wished that I were.

As he began to stand, I watched a flock of new faces grimace through the opening he'd exacted.

He climbed to his knees and then stood fully erect, with slinky wires spiraling from his back and shoulder; I looked up and saw his twisted smile. He lurched in my direction.

I screamed.

I saw another barrage of coils shoot in his direction, three landing on him, one flying beside him and landing near my feet. His body tensed and he continued, Frankenstein-like, in my direction. Once again, he fell flat forward onto the terrazzo floor.

I screamed again, this time, calling out the names of my amigos. Unrequited, I considered my isolation. Twisted, with my suddenly lonesome life displaying itself before me in a barrage of eight millimeter movie stills, I imagined them having sex in the back room together: just the moment of penetration, his bare butt exposed as he first thrust with her bare feet on his shoulders. I briefly pondered whether everybody's final thoughts were so twisted.

A hand wrapped around my ankle and interrupted the montage.

"You need to return to base," he asserted in my direction as his body convulsed with what I recognized to be another taser hit.

"You need to return to base," I heard a high-pitched voice, apparently ordering my attacker, at the other end of a taser coil

His grip on my leg tightened as I flexed my calf to convince myself that I was still the owner of my leg. He inched nearer me like a quarterback with a ball fighting for a final-second rushing touchdown even as a sea of camouflaged and navy blue defenders converged upon him. I knew he was poised. I could now see his face clearly. It was flushed and sweaty, pale and tensed. Huge blue veins struggled to escape from his forehead and neck, his eyes bulged, and his teeth were clenched so hard I could easily see them cracking under the pressure from each other.

Over the commotion of the voices shouting at both him and me, I heard a door creak open from down the hall. I shifted my gaze in the direction of my deserters and saw the outline of their heads, her long hair hanging down over his, mounted vertically in the shadow of the cracked door. I shook my still-held foot as I screamed again, "Help me!"

The heavy door slammed shut.

Their silence further isolated me. Even as I could see more uniformed rescuers approach us, I felt another hand wrap around my leg and pull on it with such a strong force that I thought it would dislocate. Then it did; I heard my thigh pop out of socket and saw blood oozing out of my lower calf where my captor's fingers dug into the suddenly permeable skin.

"Get him off of me!"

"You...must...come," he reiterated through his now broken teeth.

"What is he talking about?" I pled with the fatigued and struggling authorities I assumed were there to rescue me.

A shrill screech pierced the air from down the hall as I watched my girlfriend and our host—no longer naked and engaged in coitus as from my deranged mental image of seconds earlier—run in my direction from the bedroom. They were tripping over each other as they raced toward me. From the green-hued light of the television, I could see that they were covered in blood. I traced their path and saw that they had emerged from a pool of blood, red footprints marking their trajectory. Her shirt was ripped and her face was mangled. His jeans were tattered and exposed gruesomely flayed flesh flashing in the television's flickering light. His ear dangled by his shoulder.

"Help!" She yelled, looking into my helpless eyes and reaching her fingers in my direction.

"Help," he yelped as he fell on top of her. They both remained motionless on the ground, hands outstretched toward me. He was partially atop her; she served as a nonporous sponge for the blood that now seemed to be flowing from every part of his body.

"Oh my God!" I belched and then began to vomit and cry. I wailed. "Oh my God! What the fu..."

A hard object, like a warm boulder, hit my head. I grabbed for the back of my skull and crumpled completely on the floor. His two-handed grip from my leg loosened as he crawled toward me and then on top of me. With the same excruciating pressure he had previously exacted upon my leg, he now clawed into my torso and pulled his body along mine. My powerless sack of bones moved along the floor toward him as his moved over mine. I saw several uniformed people continue to pull on his legs even as he started to cover me with his body. His size was stark and his strength was unmatchable by any combination of people who held him. My unmitigated powerlessness was even more obvious from beneath him. I could smell his breath and see blood running down the corners of his mouth. His hard, tensed, muscled body flexed with every additional movement toward my face.

At last, a hail of additional voices accompanied those from earlier. I could see nothing more than his face and feel nothing more than his large, heaving brawn on top of me, but I heard a voice shout, "I got him!"

With that, the tense flesh mound upon me convulsed before flopping limply. His grip on my armpit released and he exhaled strongly.

He was dragged off of me and I was finally able to finish the scream which I had been attempting for several previous seconds.

I could not move anything below my neck, which I flexed to see that I was covered in blood and jagged teeth. Breathing was difficult. Two men stood over me with a long hypodermic which one of them shoved into my neck. The room spiraled again before going black. I heard footsteps by my head as a far off voice timbered metallically, "Get them all out of here and back to base."

I became aware of my sluggish heartbeat as the last words I heard were, "These three are dead, but the one we needed is still alive."

The sensation of being dragged upon the floor morphed into that of flight and then warm soothing weightlessness, then disembodiment.[64]

"When I snap my fingers," the accented voice commanded, "you will awaken."

I was still.

"Juan. Two. Tres." Snap.

I awoke, clean and pain-free, in the stark and sterile fluorescent whiteness of the unguarded room, and knew my mission. Rising to my steady feet upon a fully healed body which I summarily inspected for signs of the events I then only vaguely recollected, I set off upon it.

---

64 We are everyday naked flaneurs strolling with leashed turtles upon treadmills upon escalators upon rocket ships upon trajectories.

MOMENTITIOUSNESS
THREE

FIRE

Lying in bed, waiting for my muses to visit, watching my ball-point pen hover over a blank page and feeling my ears twitching—perked up—with a disappointed lack of stimulation, I loiter on the edge of slumber. Usually, at these moments, in my stillness—with the living room and bedroom windows cracked just enough to send a trail of cool breeze over me, with a single, flickering candle waxing and re-enlivening and casting dancing shadows of stacks of books upon the wall before me, with my warm toes sticking out from under the too-short blanket that my grandmother crocheted for a much smaller me twenty years earlier, with my breath deep and my stomach filling and deflating with crisp air—I needn't much before I'm stirred by inspiration. Thus, my prodigious corpus of poetry about toes and windows, afghans and candles fill multitudinous notebooks splayed around my bedroom. No doubt, I have my other poetry: about my parents and girlfriends, about my older brother and my long-passed cats, about the sky and lakes and the ocean. I have a poem for every type of day—dreary, sunny, blue, stormy, green, and times of day—from sunset to sunrise, including dawn, dusk, twilight, gloaming, bedtime, hours of waking, and noontimes.

I have poured my soul onto paper in rhyme and rhythm, blank verse and limericks, odes and tributes, emulating and channeling the masters from Whitman to Eliot to Frost to Ginsberg to Crane to Stein. What I lack in quality output, I compensate for with inspiration and originality. I effervesce. Often, my translations[65] from experience to page are jumbled and confusing, calling for edits and clarification. Independent of value judgments based on technical or formal quality, my production is impressive in its volume, though thoroughly unpublished.

And yet tonight, bare-chested and grasping through the flickering dimness for inspiration, I am stilled. No words flow from any part of my enchanted room. I am both deaf and silent. Glancing at my toes, I wiggle them in an effort to ensure that my faculties persist despite my writer's block. I divert my gaze along the same plane, but further up my body. Intent, I observe my hand and the plastic pen in it. I notice that my hand sits upon the blank page, palm up, inviting a tracing. Were I six years old, this tacit inspiration would, within minutes, be transformed into a Thanksgiving Turkey, beaked, thumb-wattled, and all. I fight the urge and unbind my mind.

Discontent, I divert my eyes from my the veins that peak and valley along my forearm and around the space that holds me. The room is a near-perfect cube. Unpainted plaster-white walls meet an identical ceiling which hangs over long-ago-de-lustered knotty-pine plank flooring. Two casement windows fight for plated primacy, one providing better views and the other better ventilation. The tall, solid-oak door leads into the area I share with my roommate and his golden. The open door allows the wind free reign of the space as it traces through the other rooms of our second-floor apartment. The flimsy beginnings of a spider's web hang in the corner nearest my head. I faintly acknowledge the sinewy web as it as it flails innocently in the strategic opening-induced evening breeze. Perhaps it is abandoned, for I see no spider.

"Abandoned web," I think and abandon this false start as well, joining the quitted spider in his inability to follow through. I cut

---

65 All the while, we consume—translate—produce what follows. And our delirium is constrained by roads and hallways and reason and society. We may acknowledge the constrained, untraveled paths, leaving them, perhaps, for later or for others.

the invisible spider slack, understanding the fundamental absurdity of following through on a doomed or poorly conceived project. I have, hoping that they would one day be transformed into relevance, completed my own share of uninspired—perhaps "under-inspired"— projects.

Maybe it's just a dust bunny, after all.

I catch the faint scent of garlic floating over me on the same breeze. A neighbor is cooking, I surmise, something Italian. I imagine a big pot of sticky spaghetti to accompany the scent. My finger twitches, as if to scoop inspiration out of the meaty bolognese I've conjured. The sauce is hot and red and lumpy and shimmering with basil and garlic shavings. What good neighbor's red gravy would lack the most virgin of olive oils? I grew up Irish, but always loved my pasta. I craved it and what came with it. In the wake of church and sporting events, my small modest family joined a large community around colanders and semolina. In the days of youth when carbs were to be loaded instead of moderated, the smell of fresh garlic opened many doors to childhood and early-adult revelry.

I have moved six times since graduating high school. Twice during my first and only year of college: into the dorm then out of the dorm that I shared with my childhood best friend. I loved him the same way he loved my girlfriend. In the wake of infidelity wrapped in double rejections, I packed my things and left them and their aborted love child to wallow in their own dramatic misery. I never returned to class or campus. I never spoke to either of them again and prayed to an Old Testament god—whom I figured had also rejected me—that they would both remain infertile, ending the profligate of their evil seeds on our shared, crusty futon. I left them all behind—my Catholic god, my soulless best friend, the whore, and the cum-stained futon—packing two pairs of jeans, six faded t shirts, three pair of boxer shorts and a windbreaker atop a stack of composition books and spiral-bound folders in an old, rigid-sided, light-blue suitcase.

That same suitcase saw me through the subsequent moves, but I've been holed up here for going on two years: same roommate, same dog. A few girls have come and gone—short stays mostly. The only true constants have been that old Samsonite—a big-brother hand-me-down—a growing stack of inked paper, and a flask of whiskey that is magically refilled every other day. I don't need to pack the voices in my head, though they certainly weigh the most heavily: simultaneously poetic muses and crap dumpers on my soul.

Despite my current, horizontal position, on my back in bed, I spend many hours a day vertical. I work in the restaurant and bar just two blocks down the alley. I can see the building through the window in the living room. It sits on the bay water and, from the tables of the back dining deck, guests are often enthused by the dolphins and terrapins floating by. I am always happy to feed their excited interactions with nature, providing a host of fried fresh catches alongside stiff whiskey drinks. We have endless wells of ketchup and ice. Picking up the scraps—often more than merely bussing—I never go hungry or thirsty. On a good day at work, I can rake in enough food, liquor, and cash to keep my belly full, my mind swimming, and my bills paid. On a bad day, I at least get drunk. I carry my load lightly, always.

When, at last, the draft began to speak, I knew that I would not slumber with empty hand. The spider *in absentia* had grabbed hold of me and spoke from a barren solitude directly into my ear. I could feel its eight wiry legs scamper across my soul and bury its birthing sac in my heart. I glanced up at the abandoned web, waving gracefully in the outer dervishes of the air eddying about my face. Perhaps that deserted arachnid tenement was too sunny, situated as it was so proximate to the window with its bright afternoon exposures: too bright for an expectant mother. The quickening of the silken sac that had been deposited in my body was manifesting more than spiritually. I felt the phantasmal orb undulating against the beat of my heart, as if another chamber had been appended to my own left ventricle.

Possessed by what was likely ten-thousand birthed spiders, my unmoving fingers spring to life. I roll from my back to side and sit parallel to the barren page that had heretofore eluded my scribbling. Hovering over it, now sphinx-like, I watch my autonomatronic hand move over the empty sheet with words that I could not claim as my own. I am satisfied with the way it commands the paper upon which it writes. I whisper it aloud to ensure that its cadences and rhythms are not obscured by its rhyme and method. I am anxiously satisfied. My satisfaction is increasingly overtaken by anxiousness.

Uncannily satisfied with my words, or at least by words scribbled by the nascent inhabitors through my hand, I rise from my bed and wriggle myself out of my prone position to see by the light of the dismal candle, then by the light flitting in—carried by the scent of staling carbonara— through the window. Faintly, but increasingly struggling, I once again ruminate on the empty, half-started spider condo in the corner. Welling in my malcontent belly, I sense them quickening and spreading along the viscous course of my veins, then capillaries; I feel my sinuses at last, filled; my brain itched. As my first eight-legged child, no larger than the smallest ant I'd ever seen, emerges from my nostril, I become unequivocally conscious of my inability to breath. It traces up my cheek, charting a trail toward my eyes and ears. I gargle on a hideous version of Charlotte's progeny, dumb-stricken and now gagging. Looking at my hands, I can see the faint movement beneath my skin. I am a human womb, the invaded species upon which the muses were weaving their unrelenting, self-serving, narrative. Moments ago, a vessel, now a fragile sarcophagus, I twitch then shake as swarms of implanted demons seek their freedom. I, too, long for their freedom

In a new panic, I tear pages from my composition book. Most notably, the words just recently inscribed become a crumpled ball, a careful kindling. Breathless now for enough seconds to clutch my percolating throat with one hand, I outstretch with my other toward the only salvation I could imagine—the light—the open flame trembling just within arm's reach. The dry paper ignites with only its own dryness and some still-tacky blue ink to fuel it. I hold it at first between my finger and thumb, but then grasp it fully in my palm; then clench it. This flame is to become my salve, the ember to send these consuming creatures to their hell. I watch the ball of paper grow into a small moon, glowing in my hand. I move my other hand from my neck and examine its backside in the light of the growing fire in my other. I see the creatures escaping through a rupture in the thin layer of skin by my knuckles which had served as a most tenuous membrane.

The pressure in my eyes becomes untenable, a combination of the red-hot fire burning from the outside and unwelcome tenants fighting to escape from the inside. Certain that my head is about to shatter and in my sixtieth second without breath, I pull the—now-conflagrate—wad of paper toward my face. I do not smell the burning words,[66] but I feel them scalding my skin. I yearn for more fire, my only possible salvation.

Closer and closer to my face I bring the fire in my hand until at last I hear the hissing of my unwanted unaborted children. Through my bulging eyes, I see an amateur pyrotechnic display: fizzling bottle rockets deriving from my face and falling to the dry wood-planked floor. At last, the flame reaches my skin and a cacophony of voiceless, unpitiable wailing reverberates through my hollowing head. My pharynx stilled; my cry is not among them.

My face finally ignites with the same ease that the ball of paper had, incinerating legions of spiders that serve as their own self-consuming fuel. Coupled with the inner pressure that threatened the inner sanctity of my cranium, the increasing pain from the fire on my face becomes insufferable. My flesh begins to melt like plastic, bursting like miniscule Molotov cocktails at my feet, sizzling and crackling, then igniting.

---

66 Our chaos is approached as we name Dark Energy: which we cannot know and which threatens to obliterate us.

Finally, my throat clears. As I gurgle for breath, I inhale flames—scorching both inside and out—and smell the unobscure scent of burning flesh commingled with piney smoke. In a few never-endingly excruciating moments, I am ablaze in a room ablaze, now breathing as I broil in the freeing hell I have only recently borne. I watch with relief as my piles of words become cinder and as the structure of my body—womb and tomb together—give way to join them, traveling light even still.

BLAST

WITH GLOWING EYES UPON HIM, A ROOM FULL OF CAMERAS, AND A tower of muzzled microphones, he returned the political gaze. At once bereft of words and moist in the corners of his eyes, the first sound to emanate was that of throat-clearing, two quarter coughs accompanied by blinks, and a self-effacing rub on the back of his own neck. His lifted arm exposed sweat stains that spread out almost to his elbow on the sleeve and forward toward his breast pocket. His tanned arms were exposed and the hint of black hair that graced his forearms laid flat with a worker's moisture. Indeed he was drenched with the nervous perspiration of a thousand campaign stops over the eight months since he declared his candidacy.

Few insiders expected a win, but the late-hour meltdown performed by his challenger in this special election in the final stretch catapulted him to the United States Congress. "We will rebuild," he finally uttered. "We will rebuild this nation one city block at a time!" He raised his other hand, displaying a sweaty symmetry at once unexpected and surprisingly Rorschachian. The room was awash in cheers and cluttered exclamations, clapping and screaming. "The people have spoken and it's time to take that message to Washington." As if to encourage more response, he stood smiling and pointing and waving and sending out silently mouthed "Thank yous" and then clenching his fists and raising them into the air. "This victory is not for me, or for you or for you," he pointed. "This victory is for all of us.

This victory is for America, for the America of our forebears, for an America under God and indivisible. This victory is for freedom and responsibility. This victory is for a revolution of radicalism, of rooting out, of restoring order." Finally, working the pitch and cadence to a booming staccato crescendo, "WE WILL REBUILD!"

The sound in the hall erupted. He said no more as he was overwhelmed by the emotion of the moment. His once white shirt was now completely drenched to gray blueness and he resumed the hand dance and smiles. Music in the background became the music in the foreground and the party continued for the next twenty minutes. He indulged himself in a water as his handlers took their places abreast of him and joined in the pointing-and-smiling game. One of these men whispered into his ear while they both nodded and continued smiling.

It didn't matter to anybody in the room that his campaign was won by default—the result of a vociferous public backlash against his opponent. True, his ideas were radical and would have won him a thirty percent showing otherwise, but he used the opportunity to create the perception of a mandate: a mandate that the gathered journalists didn't hesitate in reporting.

When the journalists sought out this story, they used the techniques made famous in the yellow days of the late nineteenth century: either manufacture it of disparate components or decontextualize it. This election was the product of both. When the damning memo leaked in which his challenger was directly linked to the ousted—and disgraced—former holder of the seat, the media seized on it for a news cycle. When further memos exposed his leanings of sympathy toward the terrorist's cause, the press built a conjectural narrative of long-time support and insidious clandestinations. Placing the opponent outside of the Washington circle of deceit concurrently placed him well inside the backlashing movement of Constitutional root seeking. Nevermind, the press implied, that this challenger was the political and rhetorical equivalent of Henry David Thoreau, eeking it out in the lonely cell of protest to the chagrin of his reluctant jailers. Nevermind, the electorate perceived that this challenger evaded taxation in exchange for personal gain; he was one of them. This challenger was a working man, a man who was not afraid to sweat for them, a man who was willing to rebuild, a man who was not sympathetic to the resistance, a man who was not in any way linked to the displaced incumbent.

Decontextualized and fabricated from the residue of all the things his challenger was not, this candidate was now the victor.[67] The victor was now the congressman-elect with a fabricated and decontextualized mandate from a reactive body politick. No insiders expected a victory, but neither did they expect that within eight months the culture would stand at the brink of meltdown and that the homegrown pockets of resistance would manifest a war of terror upon its own homegrown neighbors, homegrown brothers, and homegrown children.

A cluster of reporters stood in the back of the room, commenting through the revelry on the carnage which this election would somehow undo. The passion of the moment, the earnest commentary, and the nodding heads testified to the affirmation implicit in the reporting.

He slowly made his way off the stage, still graced by handlers, still soaking wet with the perspiration of the working man, and still pointing and waving at supporters who were still cheering for him when the concussion blasted through the room. The noise of revelry at once became the noise of terror. He was on the ground, face down covered by his handlers, wet still: crimson wet.

He couldn't see the eerily still black night sky or the eerier-still full moon that gazed down through the now-exposed steel rafters. He couldn't see the crater by the doors in the back where once stood

---

67 Our new process of research and approximating beauty, then, is twice tripartite: Concentration, Distraction, Constraint in conception; Concentration, Distraction, Constraint in translation (approximating beauty).

a series of makeshift tables and chairs especially positioned for the press. He couldn't see the smoking bodies and vacuous stares that littered the room. He couldn't see the small stage platform splintered beneath fallen spotlights. He couldn't see the still-smoldering flag that graced the now-gone wall that just moments before was the backdrop for his victory speech.

Motionless and next to a disembodied and charred hand that still clasped a smoldering microphone, he felt the weight of a hundred souls encumbering his breathing. Frustratingly motionless, he labored until he could perceive their lifting and an accompanying light that sucked the breath out of him as though on a flossy strand attached to something inside his toes. With closed eyes, suddenly unencumbered, he followed the light on the exhaling string.

BRIARPATCH

CALL ME DOCTOR.

I know, you aren't supposed to know my name because it shatters the "universality of the anonymous." In a thorny world where we have adopted the compulsion to name everything, you've made it all this way without knowing who anybody in this whole damn book is.[68] Must have driven you crazy, wondering, "Is that the same guy in those six stories?" and "How dare he talk that way about women," and "That is the worst, most offensive black dialect I have heard since Joel Chandler Harris." But Lawdy be, you don' been throw'd in that briar patch, so you may's well stick it out sin' you already don in her'.

I'd been watching him since I got there for my shift, the night shift. I'm the overnight guard at the CoMA, the Columbia Museum of Art in beautiful downtown Columbia, South Carolina: state capital and home to the Mighty Gamecocks. Yes, *that* South Carolina, the one where John C. Calhoun himself declared laws that came from Washington could be nullified, setting the moral justification for Southern secession and ultimately for Northern aggression. The South Carolina where the first shots of the Civil War were fired over Fort Sumter. The South Carolina of the great Governor Ernest

---

68 We seek, in this method, ourselves as we find society. We use our soulless camera to reproduce images and ideas of our subjects and of ourselves subjected.

Hollings and resilient Senator Strom Thurmond, one white politician that liked black men and one that loved black women.

This is also the South Carolina where I grew up, oh, just a couple miles from here in one of the first suburbs the city ever grew. The South Carolina where my daddy was in prison when I was born and my momma died giving birth to me. The South Carolina where my granddaddy was lynched for talking to a white girl and the only family I ever really had was my Untee, who raised me until I was thirteen when she died—ran over by a damned train in one of the gruesomest accidents ever to occur in Waverly. It's the South Carolina that gave me Booker T Washington High School and taught me to read out of books rescued from the trash heaps outside of Dreher High School. The South Carolina that needed a trustworthy soul to keep its most treasured art collection safe from harm at night—from ghosts—when nobody else was around.

This is the South Carolina where, at the age of ten, I found a nearly dead baby blackbird and brought it so far back to life that six weeks later it flew off my outstretched palm, free and high among the angels: where I earned and adopted my name "Doctor." Born without a birth certificate, this name became as real to me as my original name, "Junior," which never made a lick of sense.[69]

Glorious, proud, and all-around awful place. South Carolina. Home.

"Stop!" I shouted as he listed again forward toward the clear wall of glass that separated the main gallery from what we call the "eight"—the atrium—of the museum. Donated space from the original hospital building with which it still shared a foundation, the atrium had eight walls, each leading to another gallery area. He had ferociously (and hilariously) hit the wall once with a clamorous reverberating thud, apparently not seeing it there, and in his dazed stupor

---

69 We approach delirium and chaos concurrently, snapping photos forward and into the past.

was about to re-acquaint his face with the same unpierceable barrier. "Man," I thought, "he is about to break his damn neck."

"Stop," I shouted again as I grabbed his shoulder and swung him around to face me.

I could tell through all the blood that he had the face of a very pretty boy. That deep gash over his eye was sure to leave a scar. "I'll come up with a good story for it," he said later while we waited in the emergency room at Memorial Hospital.

I wanted to suggest that the truth would make a fantastic yarn: "Attacked by wall." He didn't acknowledge the humor of the understated joke.

"Maybe I will have been attacked by a mysterious flock of sonar-deficient birds as I walked out of the USC library on Good Friday." We both laughed at the sheer absurdity of that one. That we could laugh later about the day's events brought us into a special communion; as if the day's events hadn't.

I noticed he had two more scars in the area, one nestled in the outer corner of each eyebrow, reaching out toward his ears. He was, apparently, prone to accident.

I had never seen anybody walk so ponderously through the museum which, by most critical accounts, is one of the worst most indecently Orientalist collections in America. Judging from the layout and flow of the collection, art and culture began in Rome during Jesus' lifetime and migrated directly to the shores of America through England and France to land in the new center of Western utopian perfection: the great state of South Carolina. The rest of the world was a backdrop for this social and cultural ascension. Of course, one might guess from the collection, the Chinese gave us sushi and paper birds. But, I'm no art expert—not like he appeared to be. I'm just here to keep it safe, for whatever good that may do for the pride of the good people of my home state and city.

He told me that he usually enjoyed modern stuff, Picasso and Jasper Johns and some guy called Dada, but we don't have any of that. This day, he said, he was in awe of works that were touched by the hands of men that lived a millennium before. We were breathing, he said, the air of culture that created in a different type of world: there was what he called "presence of life and death together." His words rang true. He huffed for clean breath as he seemed to be kissing sculptors and painters in his mind.

He spoke later as though he were possessed, as though breathing the air that emanated from this art consumed him with a different soul. This same trance-like state that he slipped in and out of during the previous several hours was what had distracted him as he walked into that crystal clear glass wall and busted open his forehead.

"You all right, son?"

"Yes," he answered in that, what-the-hell-are-you-talking-about tone that I could tell he employed often. "Yes, why?"

I know that my jaw was agape and my eyes were as round as saucers as I gawked at the rush of red that streamed down his cheek and onto the ground by his feet. "Um," I answered, feeling a little queeezy on his behalf.

Reading my face, he lifted his hand to his forehead and rotated his fingertips before his eyes to reveal the blood, lots and lots of it. He grabbed the back of his neck with the same hand and smeared more blood on his white shirt collar.

"Which way is the bathroom?" He looked clammy and sweaty. He looked like his knees could give way at anytime. He and I were developing an audience. I pointed toward the glass door, hinged next to the greasy face-plant marker on the immediately adjacent glass wall. Realizing that I may have doomed him to a third run-in with the unforgiving glass, I ran in front of him and opened the door and pointed again.

"That way." I was teetering between laughter and solemnity, but retained my composure as I know my cheeks were twitching.

After graduating from high school, I spent a year as a student at the University of South Carolina where I eventually quit because

I became—suddenly and unexpectedly—a father. We settled back into Waverly and grew a family from the ground up. We had all the parts we needed: God, marriage, child, love. I can't say it happened in that order, but the parts were there and we made a good go of it.

She became the nanny of a sweet white child whose progressive parents allowed our children to be cared for as siblings. I went to work as the custodian of the church where those same progressive parents were pastor and first lady. I worked at that church for thirty five years, eventually they made me deacon. We had two more beautiful children, Doc Junior and Isaiah, and she eventually opened a nursery that she ran out of our house.

When Reverend and Missus retired to Florida, my tightly wound world unraveled. The church leadership changed in ways I prefer not to dwell on—grudgin' and gossipin' ain't what Christians do—and I left too. No pension and stiff joints left me with practical expenses. I still needed to work. Reverend made a call to his friend at the CoMA and I've been well taken care of here since then. If I work another thirteen years, I'll get retirement. All three of my children went to college; none are Gamecocks.

I checked in with the manager on my walkie talkie and alerted her about the accident. She giggled after I confirmed that none of the art was damaged and then she told me to keep an eye on him. I followed him into the bathroom where he was holding an increasingly red wet paper towel up to his forehead. He pulled it down and moved his face closer to the mirror so he could diagnose the severity of the gash. He was still flush and dazed; he started when he saw my reflection enter behind him.

"You ok? Need to sit down?"

"I think I'm ok." He turned around, rag still up to his head, blood still trickling down toward his chest. The gushing had abated. He looked at my name badge.

"Doctor?"

"Yes."

"You work here?"

"Yes."

"Doctor?"

"Yes, that's my name."

"Your name?"

"Yes. Doctor."

"Doctor what?"

"Just 'Doctor' is fine."

"Doctor Doctor?"

"Just 'Doctor'."

"What happened?"

"Junior didn't make sense to me; I didn't even know my father."

"Huh? Why am I bleeding?"

"You walked into that glass wall."

I walked over to a closet and pulled out the First Aid kit, looking for a bandage.

"Does this happen often?"

"Once, a few months ago, an eight year old boy." I chuckled as I recollected that one.

"You're a junior Doctor?"

"No. Just Doctor."

This finally seemed to placate him. "Can you look at this cut? Will I need stitches, Doctor?"

I grabbed a sterile napkin from the box, took it out of its sealed package and held it up to the cut. This close to him, I could see the tiny lines of age that were graciously emerging from the corners of his eyes. His skin was smooth. His features were soft; he had lived an easy life. I glanced over at his hand which he still kept close to his face, still holding a wet towel, and noticed that they were not the hands of a man who had labored.

The wound stretched about an inch and a half above his left eyebrow and down toward his nose. It was a deep cut. His nose, too, I could tell, had been broken before, and possibly again earlier.

"Probably. How'd you get here? Who'd you come with?"

"I flew here."

"Huh?"

"On a plane, Doctor."

"With anyone?"

"No, just me."

"Wait here."

I stepped out into the eight and called my boss again and explained that the boy would need to go to the hospital. She told me to take him to Baptist just around the corner. "Don't admit any guilt," she suggested. "He'll probably sue us."

I verged on responding with indignity—I had breathed this boy's breath and looked into his eyes— when I felt the ground shake. I did not know at the time that it was an explosion across town at a hall in the convention center. The crater it left on Lincoln Street (named for an obscure confederate major, not the nineteenth Century President) has yet to be repaired. I watched a tiny crack extend from the place in the wall where the greasy face-plant marker had begun my shift. It grew outward like a spider web, capillaries perhaps.[70] Hollow-eyed, expressionless, marble, Roman busts watched with me as the giant glass wall crumbled twenty feet away.

Lawdy lawdy, brer fox, we got us a mess up in herr.

For a moment, I felt glass dust pelt my pant leg through the thick khaki uniform until a warm piercing captured my attention. I looked down to see a four-inch, sickle-shaped chard of glass hanging out of a bright red spot where my knee would normally have been. My pant legs were shredded.

I ran toward the bathroom to check on my patient.

He was sitting cross legged on the floor next to the closet from which I had originally fetched the first-aid kit. I watched his eyes

---

70 Finally, this new scientific art, knowledge-endorsing and meaning-making, provides translations and approximations of personal tangencies, frayings, webs…

trace my body up from my feet to my head, then back down; his gaze stopped at my knees, his eye level. The bleeding over his eye had stopped, and he continued to hold the wet rag in his left hand.

His drooped jaw betrayed anything that might have otherwise been cool indifference.

"Um, what was that?" He sat silently for thirteen seconds. "Doctor."

I felt light-headed. Blood pooled at my feet.

I thought about the blackbird that I had saved at the age of ten. How many generations of blackbirds had grown from that single saved seed? I pictured Junior and Isaiah, in Boston and Atlanta, posing for portraits that might one day end up in a gallery like this one. I thought about my wife and the first time I saw her. I thought about the first time I made love to her. I thought about her heart of glass, and how badly I had shattered it when I was young.

The red puddle extending out along the travertine floor below me danced and rippled with the second explosion, this time nearer, much nearer, much much nearer! Blood from the floor splattered our faces. I fell in his direction. He stretched out in my direction to help temper my fall.

For a moment, we both lay on the cold spiney-cracked bathroom floor, fingertips outstretched, prostrate before each other. I must have hit my head pretty hard because when I opened my eyes, I was being dragged by him across the glass, marble, and canvas-riddled floor of the eight. His soft hands held me under the armpits and my unsturdy head drooped toward my chest. Breathing was difficult.

"Doc! Doctor!"

My mind answered, "Yes," though my mouth did not concur.

"How do we get out of here?"

Limp people and people parts were strewn around us and, was that a jet engine?

"A plane just," he started as he continued to pull me along the floor. I could only hear him as I half-sat facing the path that our bloody bodies cut through the debris and death. He never finished the sentence, though the circumstantial evidence indicated the obvious: a small plane had just crashed into the main gallery of the CoMA. I smelled diesel and smoke; I heard people screaming. I saw the blue sky through the hole ripped in the ceiling; steel girders dangled precariously downward. I looked back into the galleries as I was dragged toward the stairs which led to the first floor. The art exhibits floating along the floor were on fire; apparently the petroleum was being spread atop the water from burst sprinkler pipes.

Lawd.

I looked at my feet. My toes were exposed. My clothes were tattered. I was soaking wet. I looked down at the fingers of the hands that were dragging me and they were covered with blood. I could not determine if it was his or mine. I fought to rise on my own power, succeeded, and stood for a moment beside him as we speechlessly surveyed the disaster surrounding us. Yes, a plane had crashed into our museum. Everybody that was in the eight, the gallery, and most of the people who were on the grounded vessel of flight were instantly killed. Just forty feet away, in the bathroom, we were spared. The back wall collapsed and landed on me, but he managed to pull me out from under what was mostly drywall.

We carried each other down the stairs, listening to the increasingly loud mini-combustions behind us and the sound of sirens approaching from the outside. Three times, we stopped to check the vitals of corpses along our path. Three times we kept going, knowing that there was nothing we could do. Finally, I gained my composure enough to grab and shout into my walkie talkie. The only return sound was a low-hummed static.

Finally arriving at the shattered glass front door, we were both grabbled and ushered out of the building, where we sat on the stoop as a rush of firemen and paramedics flew in. We were seized by uniformed attendants who led us into the back of an ambulance. I held what should have been my hands in front of what should have been my face.

I was gone.[71]

"Doctor," I heard him say sheepishly as he wiped his bloody-again forehead with his shirtsleeve. Some time had passed; how much I was not sure. It certainly was long enough for him to have thought I wouldn't wake up.

"Yes?" I responded, visibly scaring him. The look of shock on his face was as though he had seen a ghost.

He sat beside me and grimaced down in my direction as I lay still on the gurney, listening to the whir of the siren.

"Doctor. I thought..." he repeated, this time through sobs. The crimson flowing from his forehead converged with his tears as they streamed down in my direction and onto my chest.

"Tell me," I said through labored breath, "what do you think of our fine museum?"

"I have seen better," he answered with utter seriousness. When he realized that I was going to be alright, he launched into an unsolicited and passionate diatribe about art. He spoke of the now-obliterated space in a way that made me want to die for never appreciating the connections that were my nightly companions for the past six years. He trailed off, as the hysteria abated.

We were not the only people in triage at Memorial; we watched a steady stream of gruesomely mangled people flow in.[72] From the hospital lobby where we lay, we could see the black smoke streaming into the clear sky as the ruddy, coral sun struggled to set. The burning cloud lingered in sight and seemed to float in our direction, carried by warm late-Spring wind.

We were among the least badly hurt. It was at the hospital that we learned about the first explosion—the one that was strong enough

---

71   and hopes that from within our one-third of the known universe
     we may someday harness the metonymic energy that follows and
     that out-quorums us...
72   before it destroys us.

to bring down the glass wall in our museum before the plane even crashed into us—across town.

Baptist Hospital, which still shared some administrative offices with the museum building, was, itself, badly damaged by a third explosion which occurred after we had already been loaded into the ambulance and were en route to Memorial. It was completely unrelated to the first. Neither of the explosions was ever proven to be related to the plane crash.

It turns out that the first explosion was the opening salvo of something greater, something making Columbia strangely akin to the coastal relic Fort Sumter, marking a turn in the devices and mobilization of a new and de-centered anti-Federal armed and angry resistance. It was technically an assassination: a brazen and shocking attack on an election victory celebration. It was a violent answer to the failures of mob democracy and soulless capitalism.

"You alright son?"

"Yes, Doctor. You alright?"

"Yes."

"You think I'll need stitches for this cut?"

"Probably, but I'm no expert." I paused. "Hey, how you going to get home?"

"Fly, I guess."

En wid dat he skip out des ez lively as a cricket in de embers.[73]

---

73 Final Line from Joel Chandler Harris's short story, The Wonderful Tar Baby Story.

TANGENCY FOUR:

STOCHASTIC BACKGROUNDS OF GRAVITATIONAL WAVES
FROM COSMOLOGICAL SOURCES:
THE ROLE OF DARK ENERGY

A Dissertation Presented to the Faculty
of
Massachusetts Institute of Technology

In Partial Fulfillment
of the Requirements for the Doctorate
of Physics
March 13, 2008

CERTIFICATION OF APPROVAL

STOCHASTIC BACKGROUNDS OF GRAVITATIONAL
WAVES FROM COSMOLOGICAL SOURCES:
THE ROLE OF DARK ENERGY

Dr. Saig Craper   Date
Professor of Astrophysics

Dr. Traun Douard   Date
Professor of Astrobiology

Dr. Kong Kitari   Date
Professor of Nanotechnology

Dr. Bjorg Moormaj   Date
Professor of Biophysics

Dr. Patrice Murfree   Date
Professor of Theoretical Cosmology

Dr. Kathryn Olivier   Date
Professor of Experimental Nuclear Physics

WORKS CONSULTED AND CITED

Adorno, Theodor. "On Popular Music." Originally published in: *Studies in Philosophy and Social Science*, New York: Institute of Social Research, 1941, IX, 17-48.

Barthes, Roland. "Longtemps, je me suis couche de bonne heur…" *The Rustle of Language.* Trans. Richard Howard. University of California press. 1989.

Barthes, Roland. *Mythologies.* Trans. Annette Lavers. New York: Hill and Wang. 1972.

Barthes, Roland. *Image, Music, Text.* Trans. Stephen Heath. New York: Hill and Wang. 1977.

Bazin, Andre. "The Ontology of the Photographic Image." *Classic Essays on Photography.* Ed. Alan Trachtenberg. Leete's Island Books. 1980.

Benjamin, Walter. "The Work of Art in the Age of Mechanical Reproduction.": Originally published in *Illuminations.* New York: Schocken Books. 1968.

Benjamin, Walter. "N."trans. Leigh Hafrey and Richard Sieburth, in Smith, *Thinking Through Benjamin, Reflections: Essays, Aphorisms, Autobiographical Writings*. Ed. Peter Demetz, trans. Edmund Jephcott. 1978.

Borges, Jorge Luis. *A Personal Anthology*. Ed. Anthony Kerrigan. New York: Grove Press. 1967.

Boughn, Stephen and Robert Crittenden. "Dark Energy." *Nature*. May, 2004. http://www.nature.com/nature/journal/v427/n6969/abs/nature02139.html;jsessionid=10CCCF9B79695E14B755AD5D3215CA96, 3/20/07.

Brecht, Bertolt. *Brecht on Theatre: The Development of an Aesthetic*. Ed. and Trans. John Willette. New York: Hill and Wang. 1964.

Selections from *The Portable Nietzsche*. Ed. Walter Kaufmann. New York: Penguin Books. 1982.

Foucault, Michel. *Discipline and Punish: The Birth of the Prison*. Trans. Alan Sheridan. New York: Random House. 1995.

Harris, Joel Chandler. *Tar Baby: The Tales of Brer Rabbit*. Michigan: Creation Books. 2000.

Mann, Thomas. Death *in Venice and Other Stories by Thomas Mann*. Trans. David Luke. New York: Bantam Books. 1988.

Marx, Karl. "*excerpts* from *Capital.*" *Norton Anthology of Theory and Criticism*. Ed. Peter Simon. New York: Norton. 2001.

Ray, Robert. "Snapshots: The Beginnings of Photography." *The Avant-Garde Finds Andy Hardy.?*

Smith, Adam. *"excerpts* from *Wealth of Nations." Norton Anthology of Theory and Criticism.* Ed. Peter Simon. New York: Norton. 2001.

Thoreau, Henry David. *Walden: (Or Life in the Woods).* Radford: Wlider Publications. 2008.

Whitman, Walt. *Walt Whitman, The Complete Poems.* Ed. Francis Murphy. New York: Penguin Books. 2004.

UNLIMITERS

My gratitude is boundless and this list is incomplete, but here goes:

Mom and Pop, for the obvious reasons.

Gram* and Grampa*, for all of the life experience-inspiration and sweet love stories to draw from.

Master Betas, for support and feedback throughout the process; Joey and Helen for Master Beta'ing above and beyond.

Ryan, Doug*, Doug, Matthew, Art, Jason, Steven, and Noah for being my besties, supporting my neuroses since the genesis.

Brad for being the best Pal in the universe, my constant through time-space.

Sammy and Danny for jettisoning me from high school and Dr. Jumonville for pushing me through undergrad. Dr. K, Dr. Day, Dr. Saper, Dr. Trouard, Dr. Oliver, Dr. Murphy, and Dr. Campbell for fostering my intellectual creativity and for signing on to the Dissertation committee that yielded this work instead of a dissertation.

Magz, for seeing my vision then taking my puddle of brain vomit and making it into a beautifully organized pile of brain vomit.

Siobahn and my penis, the two most omnipresent, larger-on-paper subjects in this book. Generally, the models for the "you" throughout the text. Don't all writers speak to imaginary lesbians and their penises when nobody else is around?

*RIP